FAIRIE TALES: VOLUME I

NEW MANAGEMENT

FIRST DAY

TRANSFER STUDENT

Don't miss the other books

in the Rise of Fall Series

DECHARLATHAN
PUBLISHING

Fairie Tales: Volume I

ISBN: 978-1-954298-10-1

Cover design by Chiara N. Monaco

Special thanks to:

Teresa Wheeler – Lead Editor

Charlotte Graves – Alpha Reading

Nicole Young – Developmental Editing

Catherine Graves – Line Editing

Lacey C – Beta reading & Development

Gabe Wheeler – Beta Reading

Jess Loftus – Beta Reading

First Printing Edition, 2021

Join us on the web site to browse upcoming volumes and enjoy full color maps at:

www.decharlathan.com

For Teri,

Thanks for helping me look like my grasp of the English language is so much better than it actually is.

Note to the Reader,

All of the short stories in the Rise of Fall series are ordered to follow the novel of the same number. While effort is put into allowing the novels to stand alone, the shorter stories allow me to introduce more world building and give a deeper back story into the characters. Reading each in order will provide a better experience.

Book 1.5, *New Management*, takes place about nine months after the end of Autumn's Outcast.

Book 2.5, *First Day*, follows the events of Winter's Challenge by a few months.

Book 3.5, *Transfer Student*, takes place both during and just after Spring's Contest.

I truly hope you enjoy reading this volume.

-Jeremy Graves

NEW MANAGEMENT

The Rise of Fall – Book 1.5

WRITTEN BY

Jeremy Graves

CHAPTER 1

Disaster can come in many forms. A threat doesn't need to hate you to be deadly. It doesn't need to stab with a blade or tear with tooth and claw. In all the worlds the greatest risk is indirect. By the time you realize it's there, it's already too late.

Autumn is a kingdom of agriculture. Only nine months ago a new queen was crowned, and with her came new ideas and changes. The people still planted seeds and reaped harvests. While most planters were human, a few brownies and one very industrious clan of pixies also maintained farm plots throughout the kingdom.

The best fields had nothing to do with the quality of the soil. That could be altered; fertilizers would build it up over time. No, the best plots were those that ran along the southern border of Autumn, the area just across from the border of Summer. The warmer air and direct sun were fuel for the best crop yields.

It was here that the young man worked his plow. The ox slowly plodded along, pulling the wide bronze blade through dark soil. The land belonged to his father before him, his before him, and so on for as long as the oral history could reach back. The sun worked its way up over the horizon of the distant mountains to the east.

The bright rays of light began to bring a sheen of sweat to his dark brown skin. He mopped up the moisture with a square of white cloth that had yellowed with use and age. He'd been plowing his rows north to south, and then back.

It was essential to get as much of the morning sun on the shorter plants as possible. He stopped and turned the plow to start another row. He glanced up at the Summer side of the Shinez River. This rapidly flowing waterway separated the two kingdoms.

The dark sky before him seemed to indicate a rather intense storm rolling in from a distance. He started to pack up his plow and loosen the straps on the ox's harness. A sound interrupted him; the faint hum reminded him of the times he would visit his beekeeping brother, north of Grimfield. The hives were safe enough to walk near if the insects weren't upset, but the noise was off-putting.

He finished unhooking the plow and started walking to the barn, ox plodding along behind him. The animal seemed on edge and soon passed him, trying to get inside the structure.

The man started to feel the unease too as the hum grew louder in his ears. He made it to the barn and set the plow safely down. He looked at the clouds once more and began to shut the large door. His dark eyes grew wide as he could finally see: this was no storm. His barley crop on the far end of his property was already covered by some sort of foreign mass.

It wasn't a cloud; he was certain of that. He took a few slow steps toward his precious plants, his livelihood sitting under a blanket of writhing buzzing creatures. He was only a few paces away from the barn door when something the size of a large potato landed on his arm, the weight causing the limb to dip slightly as he looked down. It was a bug.

It had four grasping legs, with two larger ones in the back. The body of the thing was coated with a hard shell and on its broad head were a set of thick black pinchers. The color was the same as the things on his barley fields, but up close, there was a distinct pattern.

The thing bit down on his arm, sending a pain so immense he almost passed out. It was as if the arm was broken and set on fire all at once. He screamed loud and long; pain and confusion rang out from his lungs. He swatted the thing down hard and looked up to realize his cry had gained the attention of many more of the creatures.

He ran back into the barn, pulling the thick door closed behind him. The swarm reached the building with an unbearable hum. Terrified, his ox and the sheep bleated and paced up and down the stalls. Panic gripped him harder as he remembered the livestock door.

The farmer sprinted to the other side of the structure and slammed the door into place just before the central mass of the swarm reached it. A few got in, and he went for a long-handled manure spade. He brought it down on one. A wet crunch told him it was dead.

He turned and swung hard, catching another in the air and sending it bouncing off a wall. Horrible pain in his leg forced him to drop the tool and swat a third of the terrible things off him. He stomped at it with his heavy work boot.

After two attempts, he heard the wet crunch of its demise. The one that bounced off the far wall crawled slowly toward him. A series of clicks sounded from those pinching jaws. He picked up the spade and finished his grisly task.

It was two long hours before the creatures left the roof and walls of the barn. He once asked his father why they'd put so much effort into building such a sturdy structure for tools and animals. His father insisted it should last lifetimes. Now he was glad for the thick walls. He waited longer than was probably necessary, but finally, he cracked open the door.

There was no hum, no sign of the terrible things which had both his arm and leg raw and swollen. In a pen next to the barn, he found the two sheep that hadn't gotten inside. The remains turned his stomach. There was virtually no flesh left on the skeletons of the two animals.

In the distance he could see that the barley crop was gone, the stalks of the plants eaten down level with the soil. He moved to check the vegetables, and they too were almost gone. Only the potatoes and carrots were still present, and then only the parts that were underground.

He looked to the west and could see the dark haze of the pests moving to the next farm. The man shook his head slowly. He would survive; he was still single and had some savings. Others would starve if this happened to them. He looked at the remains of the sheep and moved to hitch his wagon. He needed to get to the Blood Keep.

Someone needed to warn the queen.

***

The area outside the home of the ancient child, known to most of Autumn as the Oracle of Wreaths, was just close enough to Winter to make for chill days and freezing nights. To the tall, dark man sitting at her kitchen table, she was Issabol. He saw her as a wise and aged scholar who seemed to be able to make anything if given both materials and time.

The lean boy next to him, comically, had taken to calling her 'Aunty Issabol.' Jack had a bit more bravery than sense in Gray's estimation. Still, the boy had earned a bit of respect, considering Gray had seen him fight like a demon.

He heard that nickname was making its way through the other kingdoms. It was likely, since when the boy of fourteen autumns got angry, he tended to catch fire. It was a peculiar habit, and the sight of a lean young man who appeared to be a walking matchstick tended to spark stories.

The trip to Issabol's wasn't about either Gray or the Demon Prince. This was about a silly hound who was currently curled up on the floor under the table. She would lay perfectly still right up until someone dropped any sort of food.

The creature wasn't made of flesh and bone but instead was formed of clay and rock. Yet she would dart to the food, chew it up, and then leave the mangled mess sitting on the floor.

Maeve, the pupper Claire had Named, was a curiosity. Gray had been begging the prince to allow him to perform an experiment of sorts.

The question was simple. How big can Maeve get? He'd seen her go from a little brown dog appearing to be maybe sixty pounds, to the size of Claire's death dragon. She seemed to just be whatever size she thought was needed, and never worried about the power required. The question had eaten at the big nerd's curiosity for the past several months, until one day the prince had agreed to test it out.

Today they would be taking a short trip to the northwest. There on the edge of the Forbidden Sea lay a range of mountains and a place devoid of people. It would be private and open, allowing them to let the strange hound get as big as possible.

Since they were heading this way and would need to pass through Issabol's home, it was a great excuse to get breakfast with an old friend. The kitchen was bright and cheerful. There was a low hum of purring coming from the windowsill; a large yellow cat with a tuft of lavender fur was soaking up the rays.

Gray took a big bite of bread and jam as he listened to the boy and his many greats aunt taunt one another.

"My dear boy, you can spout off all you like, but I have socks older than your grandparents. You might want to grow more than wispy stubble before you tell me what I should and shouldn't do."

Jack nodded with wide eyes. "Fair enough, I can smell those old socks from here."

The ancient girl's face reddened. Only this fearless boy would speak to her so.

"You want to talk to me about smells? When's the last time you changed your tunic? It has the same stain on the back as the last time I saw you three days ago!"

Jack shrugged. "That's mustard... I think. I'm saving it."

The boy made a point of reaching around and putting his tongue to the stain. By the look on his face, it wasn't mustard. The girl who looked younger than the boy, though was in fact older than most dragons, shook her head in disgust.

Gray noticed she clearly fought a smile. Whatever either of the two said, they'd gotten close over the past few months. The verbal duel was halted as a clear bell of a voice chimed through the cozy room.

"Are you two at it again? I swear you're so alike you would think you were siblings."

Jack rolled his eyes. "That makes no sense. I'm nothing like my sibling."

Joobel's forehead wrinkled. "You're right. I'm nothing like my brothers, either."

Gray was happy enough to listen to the fourteen-year-old boy try his wits against the three-thousand-year-old girl when he had a full plate, but his was two bites from empty. He was ready to see Maeve grow to her limits. He spoke through the final mouthful.

"We best get moving. It will take some time to get to the border, and I don't want to be rushed."

The gnome huffed. "Silly man, I've been ready. It's you boys who decided to eat our dear lady's cupboards bare."

Joobel had found out about the little experiment and insisted on coming too. Not that he minded. The gnome was impossible to dislike, though her appearance had become distracting since she'd grown from the spirit Name Claire had given her.

Once Joobel was a cute little pal sitting on your shoulder and jabbering in your ear. Now she was probably the most beautiful creature he'd ever seen. He didn't have those kinds of feelings for the woman, but she tended to draw the gaze of any man in range. She seemed to know this fact and enjoyed making them uncomfortable.

It wouldn't matter, regardless. She was completely smitten with the odd boy. Jack was now stuffing all the food left on the table into his face as fast as he could.

"Eh erm redder."

"Jack dear, please don't try to talk with a mouth you can't even close," the gnome chided. She pecked a kiss where his dimple would be if his cheeks weren't inflated with four biscuits.

Gray moved to grab his pack. It contained some paper for notes as well as some measuring tools to gauge the size and depth of footprints. He shouldered the bag and thanked Issabol for the meal and entertainment.

Jack hopped up and gave the ancient girl a hug and a kiss that left breadcrumbs on the poor girl's cheek as he ran out the door. The little hound bounded right behind him. Joobel wiped their host's face with a napkin and handed it to her when she saw she was just smearing jam around.

"Sorry, you know how he gets when he's focused."

Issabol just nodded, still trying to hide a smile.

Once he walked outside, Gray could see that Maeve had already become the size of a large horse. A makeshift saddle and grip were shaped into the stone of her back. The prince was already mounted. He'd also finished most of his chewing when he shouted to his gnomish girlfriend.

"Would you like to sit with me, or are you going to ride the sky?"

Joobel seldom declined an opportunity to sit near her young man, but Gray had once ridden Maeve. He'd gotten blisters in places he didn't care to share. The gnome flitted her wings and, with a loud hum, rose above the boy and his mount.

"I haven't gotten to stretch out for a bit. I will fly up here with Gray."

Jack looked to the taller man and smiled as he nodded to the other spot on his hound.

Gray shook his head. "I'd rather challenge Harvest to a duel."

The prince laughed, then with a tap against Maeve's side was moving like an arrow across the grasses of the Twilight Vale. Joobel shook her head and rose another dozen paces straight up, waiting on Gray to pull his construct for flying together. He focused his spirit of air; long hours of practice had helped him with his form.

A bit of experimentation improved the platform he stood on, adding small wings and a kind of rudder. Finally, he pulled a blast of air, both under and behind his construct. With a smooth motion, he moved up and away from the little hut.

***

Queen Clarissa Ashotok had learned several things in her last few months as the highest authority in the land. First among them was that ruling was often a thankless job. She had such vision for her kingdom, lofty goals to work toward, and a stack of ideas to discuss with her advisors.

Only recently she'd helped ensure that the kingdom smelled much better. Gray introduced her to the concept of a flush toilet. Many of the guy's ideas seemed strange; he made claims that seemed impossible. This one sold her immediately.

Now the Blood Keep, the guard's quarters, and all the new constructions included facilities that had no need for chamber pots. The tall man called his new creation 'portal potties.'

When flushed, the waste was sent through a small portal that emptied to deep pits west of the bogs. The waste would eventually be treated and used for fertilizer. Things smelled better already. If she never saw another chamber pot, well, she could live with that.

It was good to see real progress. Yet the queen spent the vast majority of her time playing referee to the varied races and factions of her kingdom. She spent so much time putting out fires that would smolder and reignite the second her back was turned. Ruling was easy. Ruling well was hard.

Currently, the issue before her was the builder's guild. Her first order of business upon reclaiming her throne had been the urchins. Oh, how she hated that word. Like children were somehow less because they hadn't been born wealthy. The orphans of the kingdom, the entire kingdom, had been gathered up and given homes.

Some lived in the guest quarters of the Blood Keep; others lived in spare bunks of the empty guard dorms; more yet were now in tents and camps just outside the walls. Her decree guaranteed food and housing to every child under the age of seventeen in the kingdom. She didn't for a moment regret her decision, but the consequences had become somewhat overwhelming.

On top of all that, in addition to all her other headaches and challenges, Gray had convinced her to build a structure for no other purpose than teaching. Just a giant building that would stand there and have thousands of kids show up and have adults tell them things. He called it a school.

The infuriating man worked her over with his blasted logic and long rants. About how children were a resource that shouldn't be wasted. It seemed like a beautiful idea when she agreed to it. Now she needed to actually deliver.

Gorsh was a dependable sort. He was the kind who rose early, got a full day's worth of work done, and then ate breakfast. As the leader of the Shaper's Guild he, like most of his workers, was of the earth aspect.

Many earth spirits are born in Autumn, but he was one of few who were gifted enough to shape stone. If you need a small house or a barn, you can use some of the wood that gets harvested in the south. Anything of greater size really needed to be made of stone.

Her mind drifted to a story Gray had once told her about pigs building things and then having to pay taxes to a wolf or some such. If the man was talking, it was either pure genius or complete gibberish, and never anything in between. She sincerely hoped this school idea wasn't the latter as she faced down the old builder before her.

"Please, I know your people are stretched thin. I have thousands of children stacked like firewood in every building in or near this city. I need to have more housing soon."

The man wasn't the sort to question her decisions. Sadly, he was also not the sort to tell her what she wanted to hear and then make it real somehow.

"I understand, and honestly, I think it's the right thing you're doing, but I have stone shapers working every waking hour of the day. I'd love to work faster, but I either need more strong earth spirits or shorter buildings. I want to make this work; I just have nothing left to offer."

The quill tapped against her pale lips as she considered his words, 'more earth spirits.' She already had refugees trickling in from as far away as Spring.

Summer had most of the powerful earth spirits. The southern kingdom wasn't a great place to live if you were not wealthy and connected. The rich wouldn't do honest work anyway.

She began to smile as she rang a small bell on her desk. The guard moved over to stand just inside the meeting room. Once, she'd held court from the broad red stone of the throne.

Claire only sat on the thing for half a morning when it became clear that giant ornate chairs are a stupid way to conduct business. The meeting room sat to one side and contained a massive desk with maps, books, and her ever-present writing tools.

She looked up to the guard. "Do we still have the representative of the forest sprites from the south here?"

"Yes, your grace. She's staying in one of the guest suites downstairs."

The queen grinned. "Please fetch her. I have an idea."

The man was swiftly walking, not waiting to be dismissed. Most of the guards had picked up on her informal manner and tried to be productive instead of subservient. She turned back to the man across from her.

"The project budget... would it be affected if we added to the number assisting you in the construction?"

Gorsh thought for a long moment, then shook his head.

"We have a backlog of projects; more workers would move us through the list, but the cost wouldn't change much, assuming they're skilled and willing to work for a fair wage."

Claire made a note and looked up to see that the sprite had flown ahead of the guard. The little woman landed on the high platform she'd set out to address the smaller races.

"I normally would greet you by sitting low...." Claire said.

The squeaking voice chuckled. "Think nothing of it. I hope you have news of work for our Moiety?"

The forest sprites of the north and south contained a single tribe. Yet the interests of each were separate, and each of the Moiety often worked apart. The north was plenty busy with the berry harvests, but the south wouldn't have much work till the next barley crop.

"Yes, little one, I need you to spread a rumor."

Both the little sprite and the older man looked confused. Claire took a deep breath and explained.

"With the refugees coming from Summer, we know that homes are being abandoned. When empty houses and huts sit around, it pushes the prices of new builds down, and so the builders have less work to go around. Each will lower the price of their labor to keep busy. Soon they will start to suffer from the lower wages and will grow discontent."

The old man smiled as he finished her thought, seeing the logic come to its conclusion.

"You want to poach the builders from Summer... while avoiding sending out a decree. You want them to choose to come so you don't appear to be working against the southern kingdom."

Claire nodded. "They choose to treat their citizens poorly; I won't lose sleep over making skilled workers a fair offer. Gorsh, please let our sprite know what you can propose to these workers, and she will make sure the rumors reach the forests of Summer."

Then the queen looked to the sprite. "I will see that your efforts are compensated. Hopefully, the labor will get your Moiety to the next harvest, and we can go from there."

The queen thanked both her guests and moved to grab her notes. She liked to meet with Joobel and Norim at midmorning to take a break and discuss her decisions. The naiad who'd helped raise her had experience and could see the consequences of decisions. The gnome had boundless compassion and a knack for getting people to agree to terms.

Claire was moving to the door when the same guard from before stepped in her path. He seemed nervous to speak to her when he knew she would be taking leave.

"Queen Claire, there is a new arrival. I'm... well, I know you normally—"

The queen rubbed one temple. "I'm tired, Jasper. Just say it."

"Your grace, I think you should hear him out now. Something isn't right."

She looked at the concern in the young man's eyes. He was good at his job and had helpful advice when she chose to ask for it. The queen nodded and stood back by her chair to greet the new arrival. The man who entered hadn't taken the time to dress for this petition.

Claire was accustomed to people petitioning her wearing worn suits or out of date attire, but this young man was wearing dirty work clothes with much of the work still on them. His sleeve was torn, and a considerable welt had formed on his right arm just above the elbow.

He had a severe limp, and the leg on the same side was swollen and stretching against the fabric of his trousers. The whole of him was covered in dirt and a bit of blood. The man looked worried.

"Please sit down! Do you need a healer? By the spirits, man! What happened to you?"

She listened to the young man tell his story, about working his fields, the swarm, the bites, the sheep, and the complete destruction of his crops. Claire listened as the man told her what he believed had come to Autumn. She was a bit skeptical, until he pulled open a satchel and pulled out a dead insect the size of a large potato.

She looked at his swollen arm and leg, then considered his story. Considered what this would mean for Autumn. Suddenly the queen wished her biggest problem was a lack of builders.

***

The far western border of Autumn had sandy beaches to the south that ran along the Forbidden Sea. As you moved north, the sand gave way to jagged rocks, then stone hills and finally tall mountains lining the high cliffs. It was here that the experiment would take place, in the northwest corner of the Vale just out from the mountain ridge overlooking the deep waters of the sea below.

Jack gave his little hound the hand sign he used to have her grow. He spent no small amount of his time training the creature. It was clear to him that she might be needed for more than fetching and snapping up scraps. Even Autumn's death dragon had a healthy respect for the strange construct that often sat on the prince.

As she saw his gesture, Maeve wagged and began to draw soil and rock from the ground at her feet. As she reached a size akin to the black dragon, she paused and looked at her boy.

Joobel landed on the ground near the prince. She only had one job in this whole endeavor. It was her job to make sure that the hound didn't sit on her master while too large for the prince to survive the encounter.

The gnome stayed a couple of steps back as Jack gave the hound the same sign again. Maeve once again pulled the surrounding dirt and stone into her form. She was now the size of Depth, the most enormous dragon any of them had ever seen. Jack looked up to Gray; the tall man sat on a dense layer of air hovering high above the ground.

He was scribbling furiously in a notebook and making notes in his ledger. He looked down and nodded. Jack gave the signal three more times. Now his hound was just slightly larger than the Blood Keep.

The same being that would jump out of a five-story window to chase a bird, the little hound that would slide into walls inside the Keep because the smooth stone floors gave little traction, was now the size of the red castle sitting in the center of the capital.

More than a few biscuits had been lost to the sharp jaws that would destroy food and then leave it for someone to clean up. Jack looked up to the man sitting in the sky, Maeve could almost tap Gray with her nose. He looked down and nodded again.

Jack held up his hands as the gnome lifted him with a loud hum. Once all three were on the floating platform, the prince spoke as he tried to suppress a smile.

"I think we should see how she moves while this size."

Gray cocked an eyebrow and looked around on the ground. The taller man had a slight sheen of sweat from holding all three so high in the air. He spotted a fallen tree a hundred paces away.

"We can send her after the tree. I can throw it if you can give me a boost."

The prince's eyes flared as he set the palm of his hand against the back of his friend's neck. The platform grew denser, and the wind picked up speed. Gray lashed out a hand and, with a strong gust, launched the entire trunk toward the mountains on the Autumn border. Jack's word echoed after it.

"Fetch!"

There's a tendency for things to move slower as they get bigger. It's hard not to hurt yourself when you're both large and moving fast. None of this had been explained to the little hound, who often seemed to forget what size she chose.

The trunk was already a good deal away from them and moving at increasing speed when Jack gave the command. Maeve shot from her standing position and launched at the tree. She was just short of her goal when there was a noisy rumbling sound.

They hadn't yet checked the limits of the hound's size, but they had discovered the limits of what the ground could support. As the vast paws lunged forward, the ground beneath caved in.

Perhaps a sinkhole or an underground cavern had buckled under the immense weight of such a creature dashing about. Whatever the cause, while running at full speed, the hound tripped and stumbled into a mountain. One of those overlooking the Forbidden Sea.

The insanely heavy hound went headfirst into the mass of stone reaching into the sky. There was a distant rumble and a series of sharp distant cracks before one of Autumn's mountains slid into the waters of the sea below. The splash shot up into high into the air. All were careful to avoid getting hit with the caustic water.

Maeve shook her head, healed the broken leg, picked up the tree that looked like a toothpick in her mouth, and brought it back to the prince who was standing on the platform of air high in the sky. It was the gnome who spoke first.

"Um... I think maybe we should just say this is as big as Maeve can get."

Gray slowly shook his head. "Yes... I think Maeve is much safer in a smaller form."

Jack smiled for a moment, then paused and looked worried.

"Claire can never know I broke one of her mountains. This never happened. We were never here."

The trio all nodded as Jack gave Maeve another sign. To the sheer terror of all, the creature began to shake.

CHAPTER 2

Claire had arranged to connect her entire kingdom with portals. A large building called 'The Hub' was on the list of tasks she'd set for the builder's guild. A few portals were operational and allowed travel from some of the distant villages. Truly a fortunate circumstance since it was the only way she'd gotten advance news of the swarm.

The young farmer had come straight to her even before seeking medical attention. Even in his current battered state, he didn't ask for help. He simply said that she needed to know and then took his leave. He'd made no request for aid and was only concerned for those with fewer resources.

She hoped Autumn had a good deal of people like him; it would seem she would need them. The queen sent him to the healers anyway. If there were long term effects to the bites, she needed to know.

Claire could've taken a portal to his farm, but she wanted more information than the aftermath would give her. She didn't need proof that the young man had lost crops; she didn't doubt him and he had no reason to lie. The queen needed to see her enemy and learn what to do to stop them.

If she'd estimated the direction of the swarm correctly, she knew she could arrive ahead of them. But she realized that she would be hard-pressed to learn of an enemy while they were trying to eat her. Claire sent guards to all the farms and villages in the path of the threat. Each carried warnings for people to get themselves and their animals inside. She chose another mode of transportation for herself.

Harvest had grown in the months since she got home. Not as much or as quickly as before, but he was still gaining size as time passed. He was genuinely breathtaking as he greeted her just outside the courtyard of her home. She could call him from miles away but hadn't needed to do so. The drake hadn't yet left for patrols, and she was in the air only minutes after sending out her warnings to the people.

Few things could travel as fast as a dragon. The ebony drake covered the substantial distance with the rhythmic beats of his vast wings. They set a course southwest from the Keep.

The swarm seemed to move quickly before stopping to feed. If Harvest could get ahead of them, they could catch them in the air. She knew they were brutal little creatures, but dragons didn't lose often. Much of her food crops were grown to the south. The loss of so much of what her people needed to survive could spell disaster.

It was hours in the air before Harvest pointed out that they'd misjudged the course. Down below was a communal farmstead, where five families worked together to manage several large plots of wheat and beans. As of today, they managed nothing but bare brown soil.

Nothing was left of the vegetation. Only the livestock they'd rushed into the overnight pens and the people who'd gone into the cellars still lived. She landed her dragon a few dozen paces away and spoke dragon-speak through him to put the people at ease.

"Peace to you, farmers of Autumn. I come to offer aid and gather information. Fear not the dragon who watches over us all."

A short man with thinning hair and a straw hat in hand approached her. A boy of maybe twelve ran over to look at the dragon. Neither she nor the farmer stopped him. The shock of the loss of crops weighed heavy on both. Claire nodded to the man, who seemed to want to bow and scrape; she waved a hand and put him at further ease.

"Let's do away with the formalities. Just speak as you would to a friend and tell me what happened."

"Yes, your...," the man paused with a nod. "Well, we got the warning from a mounted guard only half an hour before we heard what he was talking about. We got the animals inside and the children safe and then grabbed what crops we could before we got scared and went inside."

The young queen listened as the older man shared his tale. It was as she expected; any animals or crops that were not protected were ravaged by the invaders. She held her panic inside, not letting on how much his words bothered her.

Farmers as a group weren't prone to embellishment, and she wanted as many details as she could get. As he finished his story, he added one thing she hadn't expected. It sent chills up her spine despite the warmer southern air.

"... then meh boy walked out and said that a dark cloud was headed off to the west... and another was heading north."

The queen's eyes went wide. "Wait, the swarm split? So, half moved one way and the other half took a different path?"

The man waved her over. Thousands of split open husks lay scattered on the ground. They were smaller than the creature the other farmer had shown her. Her eyes went wide as she realized that these were shed skins.

The light grey shapes were like thin parchment. A bit like the skin her own dragon still had to peel off, though not as often now.

They were evidence of the growing menace. She turned to the man who seemed crestfallen at the bare soil of his fields.

"Thank you for your help. I will do everything I can to halt this threat. Send someone to the capital to request whatever aid you need to get started again. Please ask for no more than the minimum. This will affect many, I fear."

She remounted and was off. The voice of her dragon spoke in her mind as they lifted off the barren land.

"The threat grows, then?"

Claire had kept her calm as she spoke to her citizens; she was collected and gave sound advice with no hint of panic. Now she was alone with the being who was closer to her than any other. She wept openly, the tears chill against her cheeks as they moved swiftly through the sky.

"Harvest, the adoption of the children was going to nearly deplete our food stores. This is going to be a famine. People will starve. They will look to me, and I'll have nothing to give them. What am I going to do?"

"My queen, I'm a protector and a soldier. I'm going to fill my role, and I am going to kill this threat; you're going to lead and think your way around this challenge. You might well be the most powerful queen to ever rule in this world; three strong spirits wrap around your core. Yet the people have begun to love you because you're clever and caring. I have faith in you."

She listened to his words, to his attempt to encourage her. It just made her feel more inadequate. She chose to follow the swarm to the north.

They needed to learn how to fight these things.

***

Gray looked over his notes. The whole experiment had been both disaster and success. All agreed Claire probably wouldn't miss the mountain, and no one felt it really that important to bring up.

Maeve was perhaps the creature best suited to have the power she possessed. The hound had simple desires and only used her power to protect the people she cared about. It wasn't like she was going to decide she needed to conquer the world or anything.

Still, it was a frightening thing to behold. He couldn't get the vision out of his mind, of the wiggling hound changing the northern skyline because she tripped and fell. Perhaps they should keep the whole thing low key.

Power tended to attract attention, and Autumn was still getting things in order. He'd moved with the others to Issabol's. Through her home they strolled across half a kingdom to the Blood Keep in a moment.

Gray had a room of his own in the east tower next to Jack's. Joobel had moved in as well and shared the central apartment with her adopted sister, the Queen of Autumn. He thought this might have as much to do with Claire keeping the gnome from temptation as much as fondness.

On some occasions, he'd dine with Claire. She allowed it only occasionally, to his dismay. Most nights, he ate dinner down with the guards, or sometimes with Jack or at Issabol's. Tonight, he had decided to let the prince and his gnomish company have some time alone, and he moved to eat dinner at the guards' mess hall.

He grabbed a tray and was held up by Jasper, the man who attended the queen during her version of holding court. The guard seemed worried and pulled the taller man aside. He spoke quickly and didn't mince words, yet kept his tone low.

"Our queen flew south to investigate a danger to the kingdom."

Gray's eyes narrowed. "Alone? Why did no one go with her?"

Jasper shrugged. "Well... she did take the dragon. Have you ever tried to argue with our queen?"

Gray had done so daily for months. He'd won out a few times, but it was neither a fast nor straightforward process. He nodded to the guard, who gave him a brief rundown of the threat. The guard finished with the description of the creature the farmer had brought with him.

The taller man's eyes grew wide as he started to realize the impact of such a creature. He clapped the man on the shoulder and thanked him for confiding in him. Gray decided to miss dinner.

He found Joobel and Jack eating from a tray the cooks had sent up to Claire's sitting room. The room opened into the two bedrooms for Claire and the gnome, and included an office complete with a large desk covered with stacks of parchment. Two large walls were shelved with hundreds of books he'd been working his way through.

The gnome was destroying a plate of fruit. The prince was nodding at her story while chewing a mouthful of roasted animal.

Gray plopped down next to them and began to explain the situation. It took only a few minutes to give the two an idea of the threat. He helped them clean the tray while he spoke. He'd missed dinner, after all.

"If it's that small, what real harm could it do? A single farmer killed three of them with a shovel," Jack said around an oversized bite.

Joobel frowned. "Silly prince, it's not the size of the enemy, but the number of them. If they're eating crops, then we won't have enough food."

Jack's eyes went wide. "We have to stop these things!"

Gray nodded in agreement. In the country of his birth, he'd learned of the swarms of locusts and how they could destroy a year's harvest in just a few days. If this was a similar threat, then they could all be in trouble.

There were plans for public food stores, but they were months from being built and would take no short amount of time to fill. Food was scarce enough with the Keep buying it up to feed those who had none. He thought of how his queen would be feeling right now.

"We need to have some suggestions for her when she returns. We need to decide how to get rid of the creatures and make up the shortfall of food. Claire will be fretting right now; she needs our help. We're all sworn to serve."

Gray laid out his plan to help, and the roles they would all play in it. Joobel had several suggestions to add. By the time the tray was empty, they each had a task to complete.

The tall man had the honor of speaking to the oldest child in the world.

***

Issabol stood trembling as she heard the description of events at the kingdom's southern border. She had Gray's full attention as she spoke.

"The last arrival was almost two thousand years ago. Our queen called them the Dark Host. They wiped out everything that wasn't protected by thick walls. It was a difficult time for Autumn."

Gray looked up from his notes. "How did you defeat them?"

Issabol shook her head slowly, her small face holding a deep frown. Her words frightened him more than the guard who had first told him of the invasion.

"We didn't. The horrible things starved off in the end. Once they'd eaten everything in the whole of the kingdom, they wasted away and eventually died."

"How did you eat? What did the queen do?" Gray asked, his brow furrowed.

"Most didn't. The queen made a deal with Summer for a small amount of food, and in the end, we were in debt to the southern kingdom for almost two centuries."

"How many died?"

The ancient girl's face went dark, her features sad and distant. Issabol paused to take a sip of her tea. He could see her knuckles whiten as she set it down.

"About two out of every three people died over the following weeks. The queen could only afford to buy so much, and Summer's prices were high. In the end, she had to choose who would live...." she paused, wiping one eye.

"...and who would die." Gray finished.

The tall man's eyes narrowed as he realized how bad this was. His jaw clenched as he imagined Claire making those decisions. He wasn't resigned to a repeat of history, and again looked down at his list.

"What kills them? Will Harvest's miasma work?"

Issabol nodded. "If they're the same creatures, they hold a weak earth spirit. Miasma worked, though if they got close, dragons were swarmed like everything else. The creatures went for their eyes; two of our dragons were blinded, another suffocated."

Another tear ran down her pale cheek, the girl wiping it away with disgust.

"There were eight death drakes before the arrival of the Dark Host; in the end, we had four. Those blinded were eaten along with the one who was killed. The scales protected it from being stripped down. Dragons consume a good deal of food, and we couldn't waste the meat."

Gray shuddered at the truth that stood before them, but continued his list.

"Fire? Can we burn them? Also, can we eat them?"

Issabol nodded. "Fire will work, but the amount you would need is quite large. Even Jack could be overwhelmed, I think. Many tried to eat them. They're venomous though, and those who tried ended up with such stomach cramps and illness that they were worse off than the hungry."

Gray scribbled her words, looking up once again. "Could I hurt them with air? Other abilities? Was anything effective?"

Issabol sighed, then shook her head. "We had no air users of note. Those of certain earth abilities held up well, especially those who could armor themselves against the pinchers. There were a handful of water spirits that hurt them. In the end, a club was quite effective, but you could only kill a couple before you'd be overwhelmed."

Areena walked in. Upon seeing her lady in such a state, she moved to sit next to her, taking Issabol's hand in her own. Gray wished she were holding his; there had been no good news here.

The man looked down; the options were much worse than he'd feared. Yet he wasn't ready to give up. They had resources those in the past did not. One of them was his own mind.

He began to draw some designs.

***

Many people walked the shores of the Loch. Some had even tamed wargs or hunting hounds. None of them walked around in nothing but a sleeveless stained tunic and a pair of short trousers. The young man would've stood out if he hadn't been so far from the fishing villages.

Usually, when Jack came to visit his friend, he would have Claire or Joobel with him. Both spoke the language of dragons and could call out to the leviathan he wished to summon.

He had no such skill and opted for another technique to get Depth's attention. The Demon Prince of Autumn pulled a substantial amount of power into a tight ball, building the pressure higher and higher until it was the size of a small pumpkin. Then he slung the bomb into the still waters.

The explosion launched a spout of water ten paces in the air. Bubbles and dead fish began to rise to the dark foaming surface. Maeve shook off the cold water that rained on her. Jack just stood as the liquid hissed and steamed off him until both he and his clothes dried. The prince didn't get cold.

It was several minutes before a vast head started to rise from the surface. A long thick neck lifted it at least as high as the water had spouted. He looked at Jack, then down to the fish. Then he rumbled his words into the mind of the boy.

"Hello, morsel. Do you know how loud that was for those underwater?"

Large triangle teeth lowered down menacingly as Depth loomed over the boy. Jack only tapped his lip in a decent impression of his sister.

"About one-twentieth as loud as I could have made it, I should think."

The rumbling chuckle boomed as the sea dragon scooped every fish up, swallowing them with a single gulp. The fish weren't to blame for the blast, but they wouldn't be wasted.

The dragon had tried many times to intimidate the strange boy who'd shown up near his home in a dead world. He'd met few he couldn't scare, but the boy seemed to either think he was invincible, or that fear would do him no good. It was a game they both enjoyed.

"Have you come to play with me again? I seem to recall you losing rather badly the last time we tried Ganteque."

The prince shook his head. "I'm pretty sure you cheated, but no. I have other concerns."

Jack summed up the situation with the pest in the south in fewer words than his sister would use to wish someone a good afternoon. The sea dragon had grown used to reading between the sparse lines of his little friend's speech and nodded as he listened.

The prince asked him about the things Gray had discussed, at least most of them. The paper was a bit wet for some reason, and the ink had run. The sea dragon smiled his wide grin, his triangle teeth looking terrifying as he agreed to meet both tasks for the kingdom.

The prince stayed to talk for a bit. He knew that the mighty Depth was still lonely at times. Soon enough, they would all be busy.

At least if they remained alive.

***

The Blood Stone mountains had been among the first places to get a direct portal. This was justified by several reasons. The gnomes were craftsmen, and transporting goods from the remote location would've cut into profits. They held a good deal of sway with the queen as they contributed significantly to the new economy. This is the reason written in the ledgers of the Keep.

In truth, it was mostly because Joobel asked Issabol really nicely. The ancient child agreed as long as the gnome promised to help prank her, many greats, nephew. In the end, it really is all about who you know.

Joobel liked to visit the home of her sept at least once a week or so. Normally she would fly over with Bloom and take Jack with her. She was loved among her people and was a legend in her own right.

Jack was the subject of many songs and stories, to his dismay, and the green dragon had been adopted by the sept when Joobel declared the huge green drake her sister. The sister of a gnome is a gnome. Claire was also a declared sister, but had to decline membership due to the politics involved.

Ghamep was the leader of the Sept of Fallen Leaves. He was old, even for one of the smaller folk, and had gained a size a head taller than most of his kin. This made him almost four apples tall. Assuming they weren't large apples.

Honestly, it's best not to use fruit as an accurate tool of measurement. Gray had estimated the average gnome to be nine to ten inches tall and the leader was a solid twelve.

Despite the difference in size between the sept leader and his much taller granddaughter, he still thought of her as his special lil snuggle punkin. More than one negotiation between the man and the emissary was settled by pouting. She was using no short amount of it today.

"Papa, I know we need to hold our secrets, but people could die!"

She puckered perfectly as the old man slowly shook his head.

"I know ye think it dearie, but meh first duty be to the sept, and the Blushing Maiden protects us."

Both of them moved through a large underground cavern. This one was excavated even before the time the gnome race spent in the dark dream, a time that most only remembered vaguely. A time that ended when the prince freed them of the curse. Most of Jack's songs centered on this fact.

Joobel was enamored of her boy's actions that day, but she mostly loved him for a different reason altogether. Her loyalties had grown past the sept to the entire kingdom. While she'd die protecting the gnomes, she understood that they could never stand alone.

They strode through the pathways surrounded by a thin layer of soil. Tiny sprouts of red and white were poking up in neat rows. The smell that rose up was like rosewater. Joobel looked around as she waved her hands.

"We're part of something bigger now!" She looked down as the old man seemed to take offense. She rolled her eyes and added, "Silly Papa, you know what I mean. These traditions of holding back, they bring harm. You know the queen has called in the children?"

Ghamep nodded. "Oh aye, it's well and good. There be none of our folk needin that sorta help though."

Joobel leaned down, hand on hips. "We both know that had they needed it, she would've done the same for them. There are more than a few brownies and pixies who are getting meals and a warm bed. We cannot treat her as we have the queens of the past. She isn't Wenette!"

Ghamep's face grew dark. It was a sore spot, and they both knew it. Only the dragons had suffered more than the gnomes at the hands of the mad queen. Even now, they had numerous members of the sept who'd never been found. Decades had been lost to an existence of rage and fear.

It was a calculated risk and likely anyone but she would've been exiled for the words. Joobel loved to speak, but she knew when silence served her better. Finally, the old man deflated, eyes misty with the pain of memories.

"No. I suppose this queen is a might bit better than that. What do ye propose to do with our little Maidens?"

For the first time since Joobel entered the mines, her pout shifted to a bright, enchanting smile.

***

The black drake gained altitude as he approached the rear of the terrible swarm. They'd heard the earsplitting hum only a few seconds after the dragon's keen eyes spotted the dark cloud.

Claire wanted to get the drop on them, and the dragon moved to where they could get a position of advantage. It's always easier for a dragon to breathe down than up. As they got closer, the queen spoke through her mind.

"By the spirits... there must be millions of them."

Harvest was afraid, though not of the swarm. He feared little that might hurt him. But he didn't want to engage so many with his bond-mate on his back. If they all rushed the pair, there would be little he could do to protect her.

"I think I should drop you off. I can swing around and see if I can thin them out some."

"There isn't time. It's been less than a day, and they've wiped out a third of our crops. We have to try and stop them!"

"My queen, I cannot risk—"

Claire clenched her jaw. "It's an order, Harvest."

She hated the words. The bond he shared with the realm put him in service to the queen. Her hatching him required even more loyalty. Yet only the Naming required total obedience. He couldn't refuse a direct order.

"I don't have to be happy about this."

"No, but we need to help my children. Who else could hope to fight this battle?" Claire conceded.

They moved closer. The swarm was packed tightly. She was hopeful that the dragon could hit them with miasma and take out the bulk of their number. As he hovered only a wingspan above the cloud, her words came.

"Don't hold back! Hit them hard!"

The last death drake let loose a massive wave of his miasma. The death mist rolled through the swarm like fog on a twilight moor. Vast numbers of the hideous creatures faded from the plane of the living, and the ground below received a downpour of strange dead husks.

Claire whooped for joy. It was the first small victory she'd had all day. The breath of her mighty dragon was quite effective. They had a chance now. They could....

The swarm folded in on itself as the creatures engulfed the black drake. From all sides and all over his ebony scales, the thick pincers attacked him. His scales were robust, armored against the teeth and claws of his own kind, and no mere bug could pierce them.

He was Named and stronger than any other death drake Autumn had seen. Yet they seemed to understand that he had two points of weakness and the creatures honed in on each.

A mass of the creatures went for his yellow eyes. With his growth, they were the size of wagon wheels, and instantly he was forced to close them against the onslaught of the caustic venom. Then he heard the screams.

His other weak point: the woman he loved more than anything, his bond-mate, the Seer who Named him, his sworn queen and family.

Harvest could feel the swarm gathering at his back, at the point where his body merged into his long serpentine neck and the same place where his saddle carried his queen. He tried to speak to her through the bond.

"Claire! Claire, are you ok? Can you defend yourself?"

He heard the screams through his ears and his mind. The woman's pain was such that she couldn't speak; they were tearing her apart. He whipped his head around and bit down hard on the strap that held her saddle in place, ripping the thick leather and releasing the harness that held her to him. Then he rolled swiftly to the left.

He'd once seen a creature save two people from a horde of stone hounds by holding them in her mouth. Her armored jaws saved them from the teeth of her foes. Maeve had saved the lives of both Jack and Joobel that day. Harvest only hoped he would be as lucky. As he rolled, the saddle was slung hard from his back. The queen was screaming so hard he doubted she would even notice the fall.

He estimated the distance in his mind and dove after her. His eyes were still closed, but he couldn't make the bite blind. As he approached his bond-mate, he opened his left eye just enough to see and focused on his target.

Harvest caught a glimpse of her, and pulled the queen into his great maw. A thick tongue pushed her form to the roof of his mouth as he bit down, blocking the things from getting to her.

He couldn't get his eye to close completely. Dozens of the creatures had injected venom, and the swelling was both awkward and painful. He didn't care. His words went through the bond again.

"Claire, can you kill the ones on you? Use Entropy! Transmute them, just get them off—"

The Banshee Wail ripped through his teeth. In her terror, the queen reverted to the defense of her childhood. She hadn't screamed in an arc; there was no focus or aim to the attack. She let the wave of power go in all directions.

The creatures biting his tongue and eye fell away, the squirming movements in his mouth halted, and a wide sphere of the creatures around him dropped from the sky.

Her power was strong, yet the Banshee Wail was weaker against those of change. No creature of change was more powerful than a dragon. He was unaffected.

Harvest sent his next words through his dragon-speak, not to the queen who was fading to unconsciousness, but to his sister Bloom, Autumn's other dragon. He needed a healer, and none were better than the strange green drake.

"Sister, are you near?"

He waited long seconds, the swarm chasing him through the skies. He'd taken hundreds of bites, probably thousands, though most were harmless on his scales. He could feel the venom inside him, making him groggy and sleepy. He wouldn't fade; if he passed out, his queen would die. The response finally came.

"Hello brother, I just finished my work in Grimfield. What's wrong?"

There was a good chance Bloom had some of the empathy the charming gnome seemed to possess. She always knew his mood.

"We've been attacked; Claire is hurt badly. I need your skills. Head straight toward me."

Then he pushed the bond, not with words but the with pulse that would carry his unspoken message. Depth had taught them how to use the dragon's voice to overwhelm minds, to talk over vast distances, and to locate other dragons.

It also worked on bonded humans. He unapologetically tracked Claire and Joobel all the time. He was a protector, after all.

He received Bloom's pulse back in moments, and they used the skill to move directly toward one another. It would have taken close to an hour to reach Bloom. Since they were moving toward one another, the distance was half, and both were motivated by fear.

He spotted his sister in just under twenty minutes. All that time, he hadn't been able to get a response from Claire. She was alive; he would know if she passed, but he feared they might be too late.

Harvest landed on tilled ground. The farm they met at had already been hit by the swarm. Bloom wasn't aware of the threat and had many questions.

Later that evening, the Blood Keep received a notice that two farmers had witnessed a strange event. A giant black dragon with one eye puked up a woman. Then a giant green one began blowing glowing smoke all over her.

The queen's sense of humor was such that she later framed the report and hung it above her desk.

CHAPTER 3

Gray made it to Claire's sitting room to find that both the prince and the gnome finished their meetings before him. He had notes of his conversation with Issabol and some new ideas on how to fight off the threat. None of the news was encouraging, but the tall man had already started working on a plan.

He looked to the window; Claire's apartment was on the fifth floor of the east tower. The sun had just begun to set far in the west, and Claire still wasn't back at the Keep. He was anxious, but worrying wouldn't solve anything. When she did return, he wanted to have accomplished something. It was time to get started.

"Ok, well, I have little in the way of good news. Our wise benefactor basically summed up our problem as the worst possible scenario. Last time they came around, the queen had to beg Summer for help, and then only was able to save a third of the people. Claire won't deal with that well."

Joobel's eyes went wide. Jack could be pretty callous, but even he balked at over half his people dying. The gnome was having none of it. Her livid voice made it clear that it was unacceptable.

"That's NOT going to happen. There's not a chance we'll allow anyone to die, much less—"

The door to the room swung open, and the Necromancer of Blood Keep stormed inside. The woman was covered in something sticky, her clothes were torn in dozens of places, and there was a multitude of grass, dirt, and what seemed to be large insect parts stuck all over her.

The guard closed the door behind her, terrified but still somehow managing to assure her they'd be close by if she needed anything. Eyes the color of maple leaves glanced at the small group assembled in her personal quarters. Maeve was already wiggling against her leg.

Gray jumped up and moved to her, but the woman held up a hand to stop him. Her words were even and her tone commanding. Yet all there knew her well enough to see the fear in her eyes and the quiver on her lips.

"We're facing a danger not yet seen in this kingdom. If we don't act soon, our people will starve or be eaten alive. I don't... I don't know...."

The queen began to break down as Gray pushed her hand away and moved to sit her down. Joobel was instantly sitting by her. The taller man could see that the day had taken its toll on the queen.

"Claire, you've been gone all day. We've been doing what we could. This isn't the first time these things have attacked this kingdom. The last time was over two thousand years ago. I've spoken to Issabol, and we have a plan to halt the advance. It will take all of us."

Joobel hugged her arm. "The gnomes have agreed to share a secret weapon. Let me introduce you to the Blushing Maiden."

The gnome reached in her bag and pulled out a large mushroom cap. The whole of it resembled a happy face with bright red cheeks. She pulled off a small piece and handed each of the people present a bite as she continued.

"It doesn't have a lot of taste on its own, but properly cooked and spiced, it's quite good. You all ate some when you dined with us before we left to find the Oracle. It will grow in dirt mixed in any sort of plant or animal matter. It also absorbs and neutralizes poisons. I think it smells nice."

Jack finished chewing and stood. "Depth has agreed to deliver some large fish of the Loch to the southern shore, as well as to help in any way he can to stop the threat. He's been speaking to some of Winter's drakes and has arranged for them to deliver big game from the Wyld until our crops are ready again. Apparently, they like him."

Gray was glad to have the sea dragon's help. As the prince finished his report, he looked at Claire and gave his own update.

"Right now, Issabol is arranging to set up portals to let us stay ahead of the swarms. As of earlier, one swarm looks ready to split while the other is much smaller for some reason. I've set up a plan for three different teams to each take one on. It will be a close thing, but I believe it will work. It's imperative...."

His voice trailed off. The queen began weeping, her tears running freely down her face. Great wracking sobs shook her form. The gnome hugged her close, and all were silent as she released the anger, terror, and frustration of the day. Finally, she wiped her eyes and turned to the others.

"I felt so alone.... Harvest and I tried to stop the things, but it was too much. The whole time I was thinking I was going to fail... you were all working to make sure I didn't...."

Claire wiped her eyes again, and Gray handed her a kerchief. She wiped and dabbed as she finished her words.

"Thank you all. I may never be a great queen, but Autumn might live through this yet."

Jack shook his head. "You are a great queen; that's why we all want you to succeed. Your only mistake was in thinking this was all up to you. We all live or die together."

It was a good deal of words for the prince, who usually went out of his way to make her life harder. Joobel held her close and then stood, lifting her off the floor.

"Gentleman, you know your business. This lady needs a bath something terrible." The gnome paused and turned to Claire. "I swear if I didn't know any better, I'd think a dragon puked you up."

As Jack and Gray headed out of the room, a guard brought a report. Gray set the envelope on Claire's desk before the two men left to prepare for the battle to come at first light. The women would learn of their roles after Claire collected herself and smelled better.

It would be a long night.

***

Joobel hovered in the air just outside the large farm. The gnome had been waiting since before first light. Various vegetables dotted the landscape below. Just south of the town of Grimfield, it was one of the few farms that hadn't yet been hit by the swarms.

To the north lie the many orchards and vineyards that could thrive in the colder temperatures of northern Autumn. Claire made it clear that while a barley crop could be replanted and harvested in months, the loss of the orchards would take decades to recover. The swarm couldn't reach the north.

Joobel was part of the first team to battle one of the groups of the Dark Host, as Gray said they were called. Her team was made up of her and two others, one of whom was far away in her workshop. Issabol looked on through a portal just below the clouds. From her home she made sure all was under control and ready for her part in the battle.

The farms and villages to the south had evacuated through portals as best they were able. Livestock had been moved indoors or evacuated as well. The few ripe crops were harvested with every available townsperson's help right before they left.

This farm was left untouched. They wanted this location to have something to steal. Joobel had only one job here. She was bait.

Joobel often liked to play the maiden in distress. At heart, she was a romantic, and the thought of her brave Jack coming to rescue her was a favorite daydream. The reality was that she was physically stronger than any human in Fairie.

She was fast, could fly, and had yet to lose at arm wrestling with the boy she loved. Or anyone else. Strength wouldn't serve her here; Claire was clear that even Harvest was overwhelmed and had to rely on a swift retreat. The queen was holding back some details, but the gnome decided to let the woman have her secrets.

The wait was longer than she expected. The people who lived here were evacuated in the middle of the night. Now she hovered and waited with no one to talk to and nothing to do. She decided to practice her flying maneuvers to pass the time.

It was only another half an hour before the black cloud came into view, a swarm of hundreds of thousands of strange creatures. The reverberating hum followed only a few seconds later.

She waited until the crops on the far end began to get hit by the things and took a deep breath. Autumn's largest gnome screamed. Unlike her queen, her scream could kill nothing other than silence and eardrums.

Just the same, as soon as it ended, Joobel screamed again. Accounts revealed that the things were attracted to loud noises, and few were as loud as the sound she was making. Already many were heading her way, yet she wasn't satisfied with some. Joobel wanted all of them.

Gray's description of two-thirds of the kingdom starving mortified her. Only two creatures of renewal lived in Autumn. Joobel and Bloom. Their spirit revered life above all else.

These terrible beings consumed all and left nothing for life to continue. Their very existence was the opposite of her nature. She hated the idea of killing, but wouldn't weep for these creatures.

It was with the fourth scream that she gained the full attention of the entire mass of swarming creatures. She waited until they were close enough to see clearly. She wasn't afraid of the things. Of course, if they caught her, they could probably strip her to the bone in minutes.

If, that is, they could catch her. She was quite fast in flight, swifter than most pixies and any sprite. That was before she'd been Named and her power multiplied. If motivated, a drake might keep up.

Nothing else could come close.

***

The swarm that had kept heading west looked to be the largest. Gray estimated it would reach the area east of the bogs by midmorning. The Demon Prince was bored and fidgety, waiting for the fight that he seemed to be looking forward to. The taller man shook his head as he looked over at the prince and spoke.

"You know, some would say the period before a battle is a time for introspection."

Jack stopped juggling the balls of energy and turned to look at the taller man, his face a mask of innocence. He shrugged and smiled.

"How often does a man get to fight a million enemies at once?"

Gray rolled his eyes. When Jack put it like that, well, he felt terrified now. Yet if he had to fight such an enemy, he wanted the kid who gave the bad guys nightmares at his back.

It would be just the two of them. Neither could do this alone. The only way he could break up those powerful enough to fight three different swarms was to have the prince and himself carrying this burden together.

Gray tried to share his comrade's calm demeanor, but his voice still squeaked a bit. He had one more secret weapon to reveal.

"So... care to make a wager?"

The prince cocked an eyebrow. His half-smile slid toward the dimple on one side. Man, the kid could be creepy.

"What are the terms?"

Gray was a nerd. He'd long stopped caring how people felt about that. As he sat waiting for the confrontation, he thought of the legendary rivalry between elf and dwarf. He never thought he would be in a position to act out such a scene. He was definitely a Gimli.

"Oh, I was thinking... most bugs squashed watches the other clean your Aunty's kitchen."

Gray could have said 'drink the Loch through a straw' and the boy would have still said yes. Wagers were bargains, and bargains meant something in this world. Jack paused, his smile widening. Finally, the prince nodded.

"Done. May the best man win."

Gray gave him an evil grin. "I intend to."

Jack was beaming now. Gray was going to go to Issabol's and install some upgrades anyhow, and didn't mind cleaning. There was little chance he could win, but a motivated Jack greatly increased his own chances of living through this.

It was only moments after they shook on the wager that the hum could be heard. They'd been entirely focused on the bet. The black cloud to the east and the sound that came with it almost caught them off guard.

They too, stood on a farm with crops remaining on the ground. They also waited until the swarm reached the edge of the property. Gray wasn't going to have much of a scream, his deep voice long past being able to hit a note that high. The tall man wasn't so brave as to ask the prince to do so; the objective here was to survive after all.

He concentrated as the shape of a cone of dense air formed in his hand. The end on the narrow side had a small opening and he placed a thin reed over the hole so it could vibrate. This wasn't the original reason he'd come up with this contraption, but it worked quite well.

Gray held up his horn and forced a thin stream of air through at high speed. The sound was plenty loud enough; he wished he could free a hand to cover his ears. The Dark Host responded instantly.

They didn't need to gather the whole swarm at once and so could allow some to linger. The bulk of the creatures rose to the sky and swept down on the two men like a tidal wave of humming wings and snapping pincers.

Jack was all smiles.

***

In the middle of a small field of black beans, a little brown hound was chasing the fluttering dragonflies that hunted the insects among the short stalks. She'd been given the command to stay in this area until the big bugs arrived.

Maeve had a simple mind. Nothing like the cunning of Her Boy's first girl, who smelled of parchment and ink. Or even Her Boy's second girl, who smelled of strawberries and lavender. Maeve liked long runs, fun play, and a warm spot to curl up near her family.

She'd been bored by the idea of bugs. The hound tried eating them many times. None seemed worth the effort. Yet Her Boy's first girl had shown her an image that made Maeve very upset. A picture of big bugs biting Her Boy. That was never going to happen.

Her instructions had been sent into the hound's mind many times until she seemed to understand her role in this third group of exterminators. So it was that as the sun rose and almost two hours passed chasing little bugs, floppy brown ears began to hear something very strange.

The hound looked into the distance and could see the storm rolling in. A storm that was no storm. A low growl rolled from a mouth that began to grow. Large portions of the bean rows started to fall in on themselves as the soil underneath was pulled into the swelling lupine form.

Maeve was just short of Harvest's girth when she decided she was big enough to face the threat before her. The swarm was on the far end of the bean field when she began the first howl. A long, baleful sound that was just high enough in pitch to attract vast numbers of large pinchers that sought a target.

When it was clear she had their attention, the hound began barking in fury and excitement. Then she was covered in fluttering wings, grasping claws, and long black pinchers.

***

The gnome shot straight up into the air, a whirling mass following close behind her. She made one wide circle, picking up the attention of the few who hadn't already focused on the screaming gnome. Now her wings were making a good deal of noise as well.

Between that and the continued screams, she had the full attention of the host behind her. She continued flying and made a complete circle as she headed toward the barn.

Joobel aimed for the side of the building and flew at full force. While reviewing the plan, Gray asked her if she could, in fact, hit the broad side of a barn. Silly man, she could hit a flea mid-jump.

Just before she hit the old wooden structure, a portal opened up. It was much larger than she would've needed, but she hugged one corner. Joobel screamed all the way as she took a hard right just past the edge of the doorway through space.

She looked down onto the still dark waters of Loch Mozeg. As she cleared the gap, a massive dark head rose to fill the opening she'd passed through. The gnome didn't stop moving, flying as far from the dark shape and what was coming as her wings could carry her.

Depth had been happy to share his flavor of spirit. He was, of course, of the water aspect. His ability, the magic that hatched him so long ago, was called Pressure. Those of his kind could stun the largest of sharks or crush ships with the wave of force they could breathe.

He hadn't used his in centuries. With his size and strength had come the inability to give a half measure. When Depth blew out his power, nothing survived. Joobel had wondered why she wouldn't be safe to stop just behind the mighty sea dragon. That is, until she felt the wave of force throw her forward hard. It was all she could do to stay in the air and not drop into the cold water below.

The sound was overwhelming. She had to hold her hands over the side of her head, and even then, Bloom would need to fix her eardrums. A trickle of blood ran from each of her ears, and she was left dizzy by the experience. As the wave of pressure ended, she swung around to look back through the portal.

The house and barn were rubble. All the crops near the doorway looked as if someone had hit them with a hammer until they were paste. She couldn't hear the hum anymore. Joobel couldn't hear anything.

The land was littered with tiny pieces of the enemy, none more significant than the tip of her little finger. She looked to the enormous face that smiled with huge triangle teeth. The words he spoke were still quite loud in her mind.

"That felt good. Did I miss any?"

Joobel shook her head, using dragon speak to answer.

"Silly dragon, there isn't enough left to even know what you squished."

***

The largest of the swarms had found the two young men. The smaller walked out fearlessly, still juggling balls of energy. As they got close, he absorbed all of them and then pulled up a curved wall of flame that covered the side of his enemies' approach. Gray let the horn dissolve into a wisp of air as he pulled together his construct.

Building elemental constructs is problematic. The tall man had flown mostly out of desperation the first time. That attempt was one platform and the frantic power behind it. His newer versions were more intricate. They took more effort to build and maintain, but the energy needed to fuel his elevation and movement was reduced.

Air seems like it would be weak at stopping things, but was unexpectedly good at making shields. They weren't as good as solid earth, or water if the user could freeze it. Still, unlike fire that had to pull energy into a physical form, the air was already there. You just made it dense and gave it a shape.

A wall could be thick or oddly shaped and still serve its purpose. The shield he pulled into place was well made, three inches of dense air that formed a dome around him. The addition he'd practiced was a variation of the blade he liked to wield.

The three-bladed fan spun in a menacing circle. Gray thought it looked like the kind his mother warned him would cut his fingers off as a kid. This one would cut off much more.

Building constructs is complicated, but building them with moving parts takes a tremendous amount of concentration. Each of the blades was connected at a center point on top of the dome. Each was slightly tilted in the same direction. Gray could have powered the spin with his will, but he had something else in mind.

The cyclone of power and wind formed just above him funneled down to the top of the creation that looked much like a propeller beanie from old comic books. The dome protected him from the enemy, and the funnel pulled them down on top of him.

As the first of the fiends came down on the spinning blade, a smile crossed his dark features.

***

Jack hadn't had a good battle in months. Despite the threat these pests posed to his home, he felt there was little reason not to enjoy his work. As the bulk of the swarm descended, he raised a wall of flame.

Fire was the worst aspect for constructs. Making the essence of flame into something solid was both draining and difficult. He could do it, but it was tedious. This wall wasn't solid, only very hot. As the enemy began to push through, they found that their thin wings no longer held them up.

Many rained down like little meteors of burning ichor. Others only lost wings and took bad burns. All were blinded as they passed through the sheet of hot flame.

The prince was nearly giggling as he moved like a cat, using a staff of fire to crush and bat away the enemy. He was enjoying the exercise and was near to wading in the gore of his enemies when one managed to hop onto his leg.

The bite was like the burn of his own flames. He stumbled down and others came at him from all sides. He felt another shock of pain from one arm, then the other. He felt tiny legs moving in his hair as pinchers appeared just above his eyes.

The prince's head ignited into a ball of orange flame. Crushing these things was fun, but those bites hurt. A wave of heat rippled out from him. The moisture in the large bugs caused several to pop, the steam cooking them from the inside out. Another wave of heat, then another. With the juices cooked away, the dry husks began to burn.

For long minutes the prince was a flickering beacon of heat. All of the hopping and clicking was drowned out; only his flames and Gray's contraption rose above the din. Then he pulled the energy back to him.

The realm was feeding him back all he'd used. Other than the bites and a bit of soot, he felt up to doing it all over again. A single buzzing hum came from behind him.

Jack turned and caught the creature, his hand locking on to the back of its neck. Its pinchers clicked and wings buzzed, blowing soot in little gusts. He took a moment to look it over. The prince tasted the flavor of the energy within it. It was the same as all the others.

His eyes flashed orange.

**

The sound of the torrent of juicy bodies was deafening, but the noise was muffed within his construct. In seconds all he could see was the assorted gunk and ichor of the diced swarm. He had no way of knowing if he was still doing damage, but there seemed to be a fair amount of liquid running down the sides.

The blades were making enough noise to draw plenty more to him. For long minutes he ran his machine, the air inside his shell growing stale and warm. Finally, the snapping sound grew less constant as the number of creatures slowed in their assault. Then there was silence, only the faint hum of fast-moving air above him.

He shut down the blades and pushed out on his shield, blowing the muck away from him. In a complete circle, there was a mound of parts coated in a blue-green paste. The smell wasn't as bad as he feared, kinda like stale almonds. He looked out at the surrounding area.

Much of the vegetation had still been consumed, but there were some plants untouched. A slow crunch of bare feet approaching caused him to look up.

Jack hadn't escaped unharmed, both arms and one leg beginning to swell from the creatures who got through his defenses. In one hand, he held a still living specimen. Gray spoke in heaving breaths, exhausted from the effort.

"Don't kill it.... I want to... take a closer look later."

The prince seemed not to have exerted himself at all. He nodded and shoved the creature into a sack, pinchers still clicking away. Then Gray noticed the film of ash across the field before him. He looked to his pile of bug corpses and smiled as he chuckled to the prince.

"So... this is my pile. Where's yours?"

The prince looked at the fragments of soot blowing away in the wind and frowned.

**

Gray asked her not to fight! That arrogant, foolish, infuriating, gibberish spouting man! She missed him already. Even if her team was already quite powerful, Claire was going to help defeat this threat.

The small shed was well built, with thick wooden walls and a heavy hinged door. She was about forty paces from the little hound when the howling began. The reaction of the cloud of snapping bodies was instant.

Claire felt a chill up her spine as she remembered what it was like to be attacked all over by them. She had nightmares about that moment the night before, her mental screams waking her bond-mate. The Banshee would have her revenge.

Maeve was covered in snapping jaws and humming wings. They moved into her mouth and nose, attacking her eyes and ears as they all snapped and bit the now large hound. Maeve chewed, chuffed, and rolled around as she tried to clear them off of her. She'd gathered most of the little beasts to her when Claire gave the command.

"Now Harvest!"

From the direction of the sun, a shadow stretched out, flashing across the field. As quickly as it appeared, it began to recede into the distance quietly. No roar of challenge or slamming of the ground to intimidate. Harvest was there, and then he was gone.

If she hadn't felt him through the bond, she would've almost thought it a trick of the eyes. Yet there was evidence of his passing. Maeve now rolled and barked inside a thick cloud of the miasma the dragon spewed onto the field. His passing had gathered little attention as the hound was making quite a spectacle. Almost half the attackers had already given way to the death fog.

Another wave of creatures reared up and came at the hound from higher up. The queen opened the door and stepped forward. Her Banshee Wail was aimed in a wide arc, well above Maeve, who wouldn't be immune to its effects.

Countless thousands of the enemy left the world of the living, wings stopping, and pinchers freezing as tiny ghosts were pushed from their vessels. The sound brought attention, but the door to the shed was closed once more.

Her scream hit twice more. Harvest passed three more times. The threat to Autumn left just as quickly as it appeared.

The last of the swarm was no more.

CHAPTER 4

T he enemy was strange. The tactic was scorched earth. In the end, it was never the direct attack of the Dark Host that was the threat. Gray had the living creature inside a sizeable clear orb of spirited crystal. The tiny claws scuttled against the clear surface as it clicked and jabbed at him.

On a table in Issabol's workshop lie another that was very much dead. The limbs were spread on a large wax plate, pins holding it open. Gray had examined the creature for some time but was having no luck trying to figure out where it came from. He was both frustrated and relieved when the prince came in eating an apple.

"What are you trying to do?" Jack asked after watching for a moment.

Gray sighed. "I don't think this was a natural event. How could a creature have a life cycle that takes place over thousands of years? The first witness said the swarm came from the southeast, meaning it would have flown over Summer. These things eat everything but left the jungles to the south untouched. Does that sound likely to you?"

Jack took another bite and wiped the juice with the back of his hand. He looked at the live creature in the jar. His eyes narrowed.

"No, but they were made not to."

Gray cocked an eyebrow. "Whatcha mean, someone 'made' these?"

Jack walked over and touched the big man's arm, then pulled a small amount of energy from him. The prince formed a ball of power, free of aspect in his hand, then reabsorbed the fuel and returned it back where it came from.

Transition was a unique ability, Jack being the only person born with it who lived past childhood. He swallowed his bite of apple and tried to explain.

"You have an aspect of air. No specialization, just a basic air spirit. Air is rare enough around here that you make a poor example."

The prince paused in thought. "Hmmm, let's take some of the guards. About half have an earth aspect; of those most are basic. But even all the basic earth aspects taste different: old leaves, copper coins, or garden soil. Everyone's unique. As is every gnome, every brownie, and every sprite."

Jack nodded to the bug in the orb. "I've touched several of those creatures."

Gray looked at the boy's arms; the swelling had gone down, but he'd never bothered to go see Bloom. The prince touched several indeed. Jack picked up the jar, looked at the little beast, and spoke again.

"Pine needles. Every one exactly the same. All sharing a portion of the exact same aspect of earth. One person created the first of these, and then they multiplied unnaturally. This isn't a pest."

Jack looked Gray straight in the eyes, his own flashing orange as he finished.

"This... is a weapon."

***

Claire looked over the ledgers that she used to help keep her spending within reason. Ghamep sat across from her, his raised platform allowing him to sit at an appropriate level. She tapped her quill to her lower lip as she looked at the estimates.

"You believe the yield will be this high?"

The gnome nodded. "I be lookin it over twice and then again, my queen. The Blushing Maiden will eat anything ye give her and then give you back just over half that much in bounty."

Ghamep leaned forward as she sat looking at the numbers once more. He smiled wide and winked.

"Ye are welcome."

The gnomes might very well have saved thousands of lives. Issabol made it clear that the terrible creatures were inedible. Yet, in less than a day, the mushrooms were growing on the waste left behind from the invasion.

All the invading bodies had been gathered and fed into the gnomish caverns. It was tilled with soil and seeded with spores. Now tiny red and white stalks quickly grew.

Counting the crops she'd been able to pull in early, and the meat and fish that were already being processed from the Lock and the Wyld, Claire realized no one would be going hungry. She had just a bit more coming in total than before.

Granted, a large part of what they harvested would have to be used to replant, and the price of ale and bread would be going through the roof. Still, Autumn was going to make it. Her people would survive.

There would be no famine, at least as long as no one minded meat and mushrooms for the next few months. She was brimming with joy to the point she almost cried in relief. Claire pulled herself together and looked to the gnome.

"You won't hear me say this often; I'm a firm believer in cooperation. Yet if you hadn't come forward with this, I might have lost nearly twenty percent of my people to starvation. Or had to beg other kingdoms to cover the shortfall."

She paused to grown inwardly; the words almost made her ill.

"I owe you. What boon would you ask of your queen?"

The gnome held up a hand, obviously surprised by the gesture. His small eyes squinted, and the sides of his beard beard shifted, the best evidence that he offered a smile.

"Do ye remember the night you and yours stayed with meh kin? The night we scraped together a meal and hosted a future queen and her companions?"

Claire nodded. It would've been a hard night to forget. She watched a powerful curse get broken, gained a sister, and watched her brother's head catch fire. She gave a slight smile as she replied.

"I think I hold a small recollection."

The gnome nodded. "Aye, I would think ye do. The next morning as ye left, your wee hero of a brother went out and brought five deer, dressed and hung, to the door of our home."

Ghamep looked down, eyes filled with sadness. "We awoke from the dream to bare larders, and our mushroom beds were nearly empty. All we had were some questionable dried meats and pumpkins."

The old gnome's smile returned as he spoke of Jack.

"He might well have saved some of us from a slow death that day. I heard alliances often start with a gift, my queen. The Blushing Maiden is our gift to you."

Claire looked to the sept leader. Of all the people she'd worked with, none were as keen on business as this tiny old man. It was only fair to offer the boon, yet he wasn't taking it.

Jack had indeed provided for the little people when they were no doubt in need. Yet she knew she was missing something here. Her slight nod acknowledged the gift and the giver.

"You are generous, Ghamep. I accept your gift, and I thank you for allowing us to be of one mind when it comes to keeping our kingdom well and fit."

The little man nodded and leaned back as if he had offered but a pittance. He seemed to remember something and leaned forward once more.

"Eh was just thinking, your grace.... With all the empty fields, the farmers might require some top-quality fertilizer. The funny thing about our mushrooms is, after they've been harvested, the soil below is the world's best. I've found myself in possession of a good deal of product, should ya be interested in getting an order in."

Claire was *almost* able to hold back her chuckle.

***

Issabol was in one of her moods. One of the good things about building up legends about yourself being dangerous and strange was that few sought you out. Putting her front door weeks of travel away from the nearest town had given her centuries of peace.

Yet, for the third day in a row, she found her house full of people. The tall man was playing with disgusting dead bugs in her workshop. Her own many greats nephew had eaten every apple in the kitchen. Now her breakfast was consumed with a constant stream of words.

"...so I told him, silly prince, you have to chew it first. Then he still almost choked, but then he was ok so we met with the pixies, and they were helping move the icky bits to the mushroom beds, but they needed tiny shovels, so we had to go back to the gnomes and—"

This had gone on for the better part of two hours. The ancient girl was already exhausted and still hadn't even entered her workshop. Areena had found an excuse to go fly around the Vale and left her alone. Finally, she decided if the information was going to roll in, it could at least be useful.

Issabol cleared her throat. "Say, Joobel dear, have you spoken to Claire about the recovery efforts?"

The gnome nodded, bright eyes sparkling. "Oh yes, she's meeting with Papa today. I looked at his numbers. He always gets them mixed up and I had to fix them. Everyone's going to be ok. I do hope you like mushrooms, though."

Issabol sighed. She hated mushrooms, but they would go down easier knowing that there wouldn't be a repeat of the last time the Dark Host arrived.

"I see your ears are better already. Were you hurt too badly yesterday?"

Joobel smiled. "Oh, I am fine. I'm glad I got as far away as possible though. If the silly sea dragon ever sneezes, the death toll will be in the thousands."

Issabol hadn't thought of that. She felt a shudder run up her spine. Suddenly she was glad she lived so far from the dark waters of Loch Mozeg.

Her conversation with the gnome was interrupted by an infuriating young prince and the tall man who followed him into the room. Gray seemed quite upset and was close to shaking as he spoke.

"We have another problem. Jack and I have talked... and I think these things were made and sent into Autumn to attack us."

There was a hush in the room. Jack's raiding of some shortbread cookies from a jar on the counter only added to the tension.

Issabol was afraid when Gray came to speak to her about the Dark Host. She was the one who had explained the aftermath from the last time. She warned him that the enemy would grow in numbers and split into more groups, but the man had impressed her.

His plan hit all three swarms at the same time. To top it all off, he'd cleaned her kitchen this very morning. Yet the idea that this attack was somehow planned... it was unthinkable. Her words held a wave of anger that had brewed for hundreds of years.

"Do you... mean to tell me... that these THINGS were brought to my home on purpose?" Issabol growled.

Everyone else froze. They'd often heard the girl flustered or annoyed. Jack was a master of poking the bear, but this was different. Her next words did nothing to ease the tension.

"WHO did this? Do you know? TELL ME!"

Her small hands were clenched, her knuckles white. The ancient child's eyes took on a lavender glow and the orbs inside spun in a blur. Gray stumbled over his words, oddly intimidated by the small girl.

"The spirit is of earth aspect. The first accounts said they came from the southeast. From the kingdom of—"

Issabol stood abruptly, her chair tipping to the floor.

"SUMMER!" The tiny girl roared as much as a preteen girl can. "I watched my kingdom fall to ruin. I saw a friend, a good queen, crawl on her knees and drain the treasury to keep a scant few of her people alive. We watched helplessly as our lands went fallow. As people starved in the streets and the *bodies*...."

Issabol broke into tears. In an instant Joobel had her arms around the girl's narrow shoulders. The gnome's power eased the outburst, relaxing the pain of terrible memories. The girl took deep breaths, her age and wisdom still trapped inside a child's fevered emotions.

Finally, she calmed. Issabol moved to sit at the table and gestured for the others to do the same. She brushed several strands of lavender and blond hair from her moist eyes and spoke once more, her tone now even and calm.

"I have always suspected as much. It's... difficult... to confirm such evil exists in our world. Tell me, Grayson, what do you intend to do with this information?"

The tall man stared at the table for a long moment, then looked up.

"Nothing. There's nothing we can do. Not yet. Claire will be informed, and we will safeguard against such attacks in the future. This whole affair was probably meant to weaken a growing threat, but the fact remains that we're sitting between two stronger kingdoms. If we retaliate openly, then we will certainly end up in a war we can't win."

The words sparked anger from all. The ancient girl who'd seen so much hardship from the last attack felt it. The gnome who revered life and saw how fragile it had become felt it. The prince who was always on the edge of catching fire to begin with felt it.

Issabol sighed. "You're wise for one so young, Grayson. Your words are true. We aren't equipped to openly face such an enemy. Please let me know if I can help with the safeguards you spoke of. I'm quite motivated to prevent this from happening a third time."

Gray nodded, then winced. "So... Summer attempted to destroy her kingdom and her people. One of us has to give the news to the Banshee of Autumn. Who would like to draw..."

The sound of chairs being moved quickly was punctuated by a loud hum. There was a slight blur, and both the prince and his gnome were gone.

Gray frowned as he finished. "...straws?"

A little brown hound stood and stretched, then padded out of the room, following the scent of her absent master. Gray looked to the ancient girl with pleading eyes.

Issabol gave him a sad smile. "My niece carries the world on her shoulders. I didn't leave my isolation because the kingdom is in peril or because I think I'm so important. She and her brother are special. They're our future, and that future will be a good one because people like you are supporting them. I'm proud of you, Grayson."

She leaned forward and set her folded hands on the table.

"I also don't intend to be in this world when you tell my niece what you just told me."

***

The sea dragon was content in his cave at the bottom of Loch Mozeg. It had been an exciting day of hunting the larger fish in his lake and getting to test his power for the first time in centuries. The tiny morsels who'd given him a home had proven interesting, more than he'd even hoped.

The clever queen had even beaten him at Ganteque once and seemed ready to do it again. He had gladly offered his help and felt no need for payment beyond what they'd done for him.

The short-lived value life. Those who are weak and fragile seek safety; they derive their joy only in the absence of danger. Yet when life is measured by countless centuries, the real enemy isn't danger. Boredom is the greatest threat to those like him.

Depth no longer craved the fear and respect of those around him, only conversation and fellowship. The occasional battle was always a plus. He'd used the breath of his power for the first time in centuries.

So many years conserving energy had almost made him forget what it felt like. He missed it. The presence that joined him was once his only company, yet now they both were able to form new relationships.

The once-great spirit of water was now the reduced spirit of a tiny fraction of the lake. She was all but invisible in the murky darkness, yet he could perceive her though his own power as if she stood in clear daylight. He felt her joy as she greeted him.

"So, my little one, how was your adventure?"

Only Fluvial could call him little. Her power had once been as vast as the oceans that called her mother.

"I destroyed the enemy before me and I helped feed many morsels. It was a good day."

Her presence shifted and moved. He knew she was with him, but in many ways she was all around. She was happy he'd found contentment. It was his turn to ask a question.

"Do you wish for more, my lady? To have more than a single spirit to nourish?"

Her mood darkened only slightly, not in anger but in longing. A great spirit's purpose was to nurture and grow the maturing spirits within her realm. For so long Fluvial had only him. She let the emotion of a sigh through the link as she spoke.

"Time is fluid; the only constant thing is change. Why do you ask me this question?"

"We both feel the change to the north. The time will come when we will be called to assist the little ones again. Will you answer that call?"

The great spirit reached out with her power and also felt a familiar sense of foreboding.

"You and I are both living as guests in a world not our own. I owe my hosts much, and I will fight alongside them when the time comes."

Depth let out a low rumble as he smiled, the darkness hiding his large triangle teeth.

***

Claire had retired from her meetings for the day. The queen now stretched out on the sofa in her sitting room. She hadn't entirely stopped working. A stack of notes and ledgers sat in her hand as she poured over the logistics of the recovery efforts.

The door swung open and then closed with a click. Jack never knocked, and no guard was brave enough to stop him from entering. The prince strode into the room and set a wrinkled scrap of paper on the low table beside her.

It had a name on it: Rychell Balcan. Also, the name of a port town to the northeast and a passphrase. The queen picked it up, scanned it, and then returned it to the table.

Claire kept her eyes on her work as she spoke. "As always, little brother, you've explained yourself completely."

The prince clenched his jaw, eyes flashing orange. "Two hundred and eighteen."

The queen sighed, still staring down. "Jack, I love you, but I'm terribly busy. Who is this person, and two hundred and eighteen what?"

The prince leaned forward and growled. "That's the name of the slaver who's been shipping people to the mines in the north. She's gotten three shipments delivered so far. Two hundred and eighteen people."

Claire set down the ledgers. She looked again at the paper, hands trembling slightly. Her eyes narrowed as she looked up at him.

Jack had been looking for a project, and he was dangerous if you left him to his own entertainment. The queen was well aware that she was missing a mountain, though she'd yet to figure out just how her brother could've done it.

She set the paper down once again; this time, she'd memorized the information. Her words were pure venom.

"Tell me what you need."

Jack began to pace. "I need you to make an exception about your power of Transmutation. For both me and Gray. Maeve's pretty close on her warg form, so she should be fine."

Claire rolled her eyes. "You're still not explaining your plan."

His lips curled in a grin. "I'm going to go live in the Mountain Wyld. In a couple of days, I'll be starting my new career as a slave refugee."

She was both confused and shocked, yet before she could ask for details, a rap sounded from her door. A knock meant Gray or one of the guards. Joobel also just went where she pleased. Maeve scratched the thick wood, or went right through it.

The taller man entered right as Jack seemed to find a reason to leave, only saying he would speak to her again soon. She looked to the tall figure and smiled; she enjoyed spending time with him.

That was all she would allow. Claire liked him enough that she didn't see the need to drag him down with her. Blasted prophecies and all.

"So, to what does the queen owe the honor of a visit from the savior of Autumn?"

Gray winced, waving a hand to push off the title. She gave a wry smile as he answered the question.

"I drew the short straw, which apparently was also the only straw. We need to talk about the invasion. There's something you need to know. I think it's going to upset you."

Claire leaned back in her chair. Her people were going to survive, and the crops would be replanted. Other than a couple of sheep and a missing mountain, nothing had really been lost.

What could he possibly have to tell her that would upset her that much?

***

The farthest recorded witness of the tirade that was thrown by the queen on that night was a stable boy. The young man was cleaning stalls at an inn on the other side of the capital. He was able to repeat both what was said and the tone in which the Banshee said it.

That was just before half the ghosts in the kingdom became visible and started yelling as well. In the following years, this tradition became a celebration known as the Dark Harvest.

People would share food in honor of the cooperation that saved the kingdom and then yell at the people who annoyed them for the rest of the day.

It became quite popular.

***

It's a dangerous game to climb the ranks of those who serve the Queen of Summer. The attendant had been promoted four times in the less than two summers she'd served in the Great Arborium. None of those she replaced had retired. It was how the saying went.

'*You always got one more promotion than you wanted.*'

The package arrived from the Blood Keep of Autumn. The smaller kingdom had recently earned the ire of the southern ruler. Still, Queen Fenn had told her servants that she was expecting correspondence from Autumn any time now.

It was customary for the attendants to check incoming parcels for traps or poisons before they reached the queen. Her most senior servants were even to read correspondence before bothering the busy woman. As the attendant read the letter from the western kingdom, her face paled. This wasn't going to go well.

Dearest Queen of Summer,

I must thank you so very much for your recent gift. We've all feasted on the bounty you have sent us and it would seem we will have extra food stores in the coming months. Should you need fruit, fish, or the most delightful mushrooms, please don't hesitate to contact us.

Unfortunately, the little delicacies were just so scrumptious they were all gone before I was able to store any. If you run across more, please feel free to send them our way. Our dragons are getting awfully big, and they seem to like the texture.

I was able to save just one of the cute little creatures for you, should you want to keep him as a pet. We named him Gerald, but you can feel free to change the title to something you think more appropriate. Hope you're well, and if you are ever traveling this way, do call on me.

We simply must do tea. I even set aside a puree of the delectable treats you sent. We can spread it on crackers.

Stay warm,

The Banshee of Autumn

The attendant read the words several times. Most of the letter was confusing, but inside the box was a large clear globe of spirited crystal. Contained within was a hideous creature with long black pinchers, grasping claws, and humming wings.

It stared at her with glowing white eyes.

***

It's always better to make friends than enemies. Those who've lived long know that it's often those who won't fight you directly that you have most to fear. The kingdom of Summer unleashed a terrible weapon on a peaceful nation that did nothing to deserve the fate that would've befallen them. Those responsible had no way of knowing that the creative use of resources and the aid of powerful allies would mitigate the worst of the damage.

The Summer Queen angered her niece. The Banshee's outrage echoed throughout the land. Still, Claire was responsible for all the people in her care. She'd chosen to send a message that wouldn't justify retaliation.

Issabol wasn't a queen. She was cunning and very long-lived. Despite countless years and the wisdom they'd given her, the ancient child still held the vindictive nature of a preteen girl.

Claire could move on from this with a letter and a skillful message of quiet strength. Issabol had chosen a different path.

There was no one else who'd lived through the trauma of the last time the Dark Host was released into her home. The cries of the hungry and the mass graves still sometimes haunted her dreams.

Her old friend and queen never recovered from watching her kingdom fall to ruin. Only a monster could've wanted to do that to her home again. They tried to hurt Claire and let people die for the sake of pride and profit.

Issabol was the only known person in existence that could make a portal. While it was more difficult, she could even make a doorway to a place she'd never been to. Using some trial and error, she could lock an origin or destination using her viewing portals.

It had taken her almost four full days to build her revenge. It was worth every second. Two windows through space sat above her workbench, each to a location she'd chosen carefully.

The portal control that sat on her table wouldn't open inside her workshop; she was going to connect two remote positions. The destination was the open skylight high above the top floor of the great Arborium, the personal quarters of the Summer Queen.

High in the branches of the magnificent tree, she sat above the world. Untouchable, or so it would seem. Issabol would've put it closer, but some places are so filled with power that the doorway wouldn't stabilize if set too close. This would work well enough.

Issabol looked through the other viewing portal. It looked out on a large pool west of the Autumn bogs. The location for the landmark was carefully chosen. It was the spot Gray set up to treat the waste from all of his 'portal potties.'

The northeastern winds carried the smell far out over the Forbidden Sea, far from the people of Autumn. The plans to convert the waste into fertilizer were put on hold due to the recent invasion.

The pit had continued to fill, as more and more waste piled in. Now Autumn needed to empty the pit, and a certain three-thousand-year-old preteen girl required revenge.

Issabol almost decided against her plan; after all, they would need the fertilizer. Then Joobel told her that the gnomes already had more than would be needed. The control orb was activated to connect the bottom of the pit with the air above the Arborium.

The tiny girl pushed a lavender lock of hair from her eyes, and the corner of her mouth slid into a half-smile.

Not unlike a certain prince.

END

FIRST DAY

The Rise of Fall – Book 2.5

WRITTEN BY

Jeremy Graves

CHAPTER 1

PREPARATIONS

K illing a Banshee requires creativity. The assassin had planned this job for almost three months; taking out impossible targets was her specialty. Now she entered the small tent in search of a particular kind of weapon. The air was thick and heavy. The overbearing heat of Summer's jungle lay against her pale skin, and sweat soaked through her clothes.

She wore her travel leathers or at least a few of them. The heat here had most of her gear packed away. Her dark hair hung damp against her neck, falling short of strong shoulders. Her green eyes took in the inside of the canvas room. It was filled with wonders.

This man sold something unique. Something few would even know about. Fewer yet could afford it. He smiled as she walked in, his voice like a bell chiming.

"You're early."

The assassin glared at his chiseled face. It was rumored he was human and still somehow centuries old. That handsome face was likely a weave of power. Either way, she had to admit it was effective. She found herself smiling back.

"I'm on a tight timetable; I still need to meet a contact in the Wyld. Should I wait outside?"

Her thoughts moved to the asking price of his merchandise. For what she'd be handing over, he should've delivered it to her. She waited several seconds for him to respond, his head moved in quick jerks. Maybe not human after all.

Finally, he gestured to a stool next to a low table. The flat surface was covered by an intricately woven rug. As she set her hands on the soft fabric, a tingle of power flowed through her fingertips. He sat opposite her.

"It's not a problem. A motivated buyer is always welcome."

She felt drowsy. Her sleep had been deep the night before and it was still early in the day. The sun wasn't even overhead. Her head shook slightly as if to toss away the fatigue. She narrowed her eyes.

"You can stop whatever spell that is at work. I deal with a clear head... or not at all."

His head jerked twice at odd angles. Then he gave her a broad grin.

"Impressive. Few would even notice. As you wish."

The blanket of fatigue was lifted in an instant. The woman could feel her edge return, though now there were doubts that it would matter. She felt apprehension of this man. That emotion was hidden away. On the surface, she was calm and collected.

"As I said, I'm in a hurry. You know what I seek?"

The man, or what appeared to be one, reached inside of a chest on the floor at his feet. The polished wood box was set in front of her. She carefully opened the latch and looked inside. Her fingers moved to take a long splinter.

"Careful not to prick your skin!"

His voice was abrupt, the relaxed demeanor let go for an instant. He wanted to get paid before she killed herself. The warning was heeded, though. She carefully picked it up and held it out to the light. It appeared a simple thorn of hardwood. She pursed her lips, one eyebrow coming up in question.

"This will kill the Banshee, Autumn's Queen of Death?"

He grinned, reaching into the chest once again. A small circle of crystal was pulled out, the item clearly precious to him. He placed it in her hand.

"Look through it at the cursed wood."

She felt a tingle from the transparent glass; it must be valuable. Holding it up to one eye, she peered at the splinter. Her naked eye saw only wood, while her fingers felt the grain of the surface and the weight of it. The crystal showed her something else.

The aura around the object seemed to writhe with tendrils of dark-green malice. They moved along the base and seemed to pull for the sharp tip to free them. The man saw her shudder and chuckled.

"A dryad turned all of her anger and pain into that curse. Normally, they impale the cutter with it. This one failed in her attack. That cutter kept both his life and what I paid him for the item. It's of the old magics; nothing can survive being pricked with it."

The woman carefully set the thorn back in the box. He stretched out his hand and reverently accepted the crystal. She nodded; this was exactly what was needed.

"How much?"

His head jerked three times, all at odd angles. Then he gave her a broad smile.

It wasn't comforting in the least.

***

Gray entered the holding cell, his larger frame casting a long shadow into the interrogation room. The woman seated on one side of the thick oak table had her hands shackled in front of her. Her light blonde hair was matted and unkempt; her pale skin almost seemed to glow in the reflected candlelight. Her clothing was still the fitted black leather with streaks of dark-red and grey.

It had been almost four months since she was arrested, yet she refused to accept clean clothes. Only two short weeks ago, he helped put this woman's mark on the throne of Winter. Now it was time for this assassin to pay for her crimes. Pale blue eyes squinted as she tried to focus on the large dark-skinned man, who clearly wasn't a guard. Gray paused for only a moment before he gave a single order to her jailor.

"Remove the shackles and leave us."

Her eyes grew wide as she seemed to run through the many ill intentions that could be directed towards her. Gray let her stew in her terror for only a moment before he waved a hand to show she needn't fear him. From across the table, he studied her in the silence of Autumn's dungeon.

The cells and offices were located deep under the Blood Keep, built from the same red stone as most large structures in the kingdom. The facility could effortlessly house a thousand prisoners. Currently, there were less than thirty.

Only five guards worked shifts in Autumn's prison. The previous queen had little use for long term incarceration. Punishments were either death or aging, with some fines and flogging thrown in.

The current queen was also hesitant to burden the kingdom with many who couldn't help build her vision. She could also be brutal, but not without good cause.

The prisoner before him was a prime example. It took only a little digging to find out who this woman was. Thanks to Queen Raine, Gray knew Makani Sho was once a promising young woman of Winter. Now she seemed to await her death.

Makani no longer ate or bathed. In the middle of the night, the guards often heard her crying. The words were always the same. 'I'm sorry, Noelani.' Gray discovered that it was the name of her younger brother. Makani was only seventeen winters according to the records, her brother barely six.

Claire asked Gray to see if there was a way to salvage the life of one so talented. She'd held out against Jack, at least for a few seconds. Gray knew how impressive that really was. There were matches he didn't make it that long.

His silence had served its purpose. Gray cleared his throat and began.

"My name is Grayson Davis, though most know me as just Gray. I'm here to decide what to do with you."

Her eyes narrowed for an instant, then she made her move. A wave of dense air lashed out from her hand. Her feet bolted to the door before she even looked to see if it had taken the large man down. She jerked back on the handle. It remained in place. The door wasn't locked, and yet it might have as well have been fused stone.

Makani swung her head to see Gray shaking his head slowly. She screamed at him and lashed out again. The air left her grip as a wisp of a breeze. She could have puffed her cheeks and blew more at him. She tried a different tactic as she bared her teeth and lunged at him.

Gray never moved as the woman hit his shield. She swung her limbs like a turtle trying to swim through thick mud. He let her struggle for a few seconds and then sighed.

"Please sit down. I have a lot of things I need to do, and... this is embarrassing."

The woman started to scream. Before she could gather the breath to do so, Gray spoke one more word.

"Noelani."

She froze. Anger and frustration gave way to fear. Her attempt at words was nothing more than a mouth moving around gasps. A tear rolled down her cheek.

Gray was a strong fighter and a loyal friend. Makani intended to kill the young woman he'd saved only hours before that night. He was there to offer a second chance if she could prove she wasn't the monster many thought she was. He gestured to the chair.

"Let's have that conversation."

This time she moved quickly, sitting up straight and setting both hands flat on the table. Her words were almost sobs.

"Is my brother safe?"

Gray cocked an eyebrow and thought out his answer. This was more out of his habit of carefully choosing his words than creating suspense. She stewed in the silent pause.

"I picked him up late yesterday afternoon. He was quite ill, and I had to take him to see our dragon."

Her eyes began to widen, and he realized her interpretation. He held up a hand.

"One of our dragons has an impressive ability to heal. Bloom most likely saved his life. Noelani is recovering upstairs. He seems a bit weak from long inactivity, but I think the boy will fully recover."

The look of relief that passed over her was impossible to miss. Years of stress and struggle seemed to ease from her face as fear and tension left her. She still really needed fresh clothes and a bath. Makani's sigh preceded her shaking words.

"I thank you for that. At least I can die knowing my brother will live."

Gray shook his head. "I don't think you understand. Your death simply gives us another mouth to feed. How does leaving us to care for your brother pay your debt?"

She seemed to hesitate, not quite sure how to reply. Her question hinted a spark of hope.

"You're not going to kill me?"

Gray shrugged. "Well, I mean... it's still early. I'd really prefer not to."

She raised an eyebrow. "I'm a murderer. I was here to kill the queen's own kin."

"I know the story; we have contacts at the assassin's guild. Turns out this was to be your first bounty. Enough to pay for expensive treatments of a long sick brother, perhaps? Either way, you're a poor killer seeing as you actually just tried to kill the Demon Prince and that tank he calls a hound. A far cry from your previous training."

Makani's eyes widened for an instant, then narrowed as she stared at him. He knew too much, and that made her nervous. Her sarcasm didn't hide the fear she still felt.

"Tell me... do you also know my dress size... or perhaps my favorite food? Also, what's a tank?"

Gray gave her a wry smile. "You're a six, though maybe a four now with starving yourself. Your favorite food is cake. A tank is a moving fortress."

Her blue eyes narrowed; voice now an angry hiss. "How could you possibly know that?"

Gray waved a hand at her attire. "Your clothes are a mess, and a friend made you some new ones. She's quite good at guessing measurements. As for the food, everyone loves cake. Lastly, where I'm from, all guys know cool stuff about tanks."

For the first time in months, Makani hinted at a smile. Gray could see that, under the grime and emotional turmoil, she was a lovely girl. He hoped this attempt to save her worked out. She now asked him the question he was waiting for.

"You saved my kin; you bring me clothes, and you're not going to execute a foreign assassin. Who do you want me to kill?"

The tall man shook his head. "As I said, you're a poor assassin. I'm more interested in your potential in other areas."

She frowned, blue eyes narrowing. "I'd rather die than do that."

He smiled back. "Well... I didn't think you would be that opposed to being a teacher."

Her head tilted to one side. "Wait... what?"

***

Even if you can kill a Banshee, it does you little good if you cannot escape. Timing and planning were essential. The movements of Autumn's dragons were somewhat predictable. If the attack hit on the right day and time, she wouldn't have to work around the western kingdom's black terror. The death drake known as Harvest would make this task impossible.

Even so, getting out of the kingdom alive would be complicated. The woman's plan required an extra card up the sleeve. She could use the strange portals to move around the kingdom itself, but she'd still have days of travel into Summer or the Wyld, even from the border towns.

The dragons of the Mountain Wyld could be hired for the right price. If the death drake gave chase outside of his kingdom, then she could collect his bounty as well. Strong as he might be, no lone dragon can take on an entire flight of fire drakes.

This contact was of great value to her. Few could get word to the dragons that roosted on the cliffs of the mountain of caged flame. The woman pulled her strider to the entrance of a cave. The large flightless bird carried her swiftly from the southern jungle. It had still taken almost three weeks to move from Summer, and her back was stiff. She was also sore in places she wouldn't admit.

The elf that walked from the entrance was shorter than those of the far east. Brown skin was adorned with thin tattoos of green and black, his reddish-brown hair hung down his back. He carried two curved swords, one on each hip. His walk was a stalking dance that kept his stance ready to draw and slice in an instant. He stared at her through narrowed dark eyes.

"You risk much entering the territory of the Weyr of the Wyld. What business have you coming onto dragon lands?"

The woman was careful to dismount slowly, keeping her hands in sight and exaggerating her movements. The elf watched every motion with caution and distrust. She held hands to the sides and moved to stand about four paces away.

"I seek to hire the services of the Weyr. I'm told this is where I should go to put forth my petition."

The man tilted his head to one side, seeming to weigh her words against her appearance. Finally, he gave a short nod.

"I don't speak for them; only serve as a gatekeeper. The Weyr doesn't work cheap. If you cannot afford them, then I'd see your back moving away. I won't enjoy you annoying them. You won't survive it."

The woman narrowed her green eyes. She hadn't traded countless blisters and days on the wretched bird to be turned away. Her hand moved into her jacket slowly. The bag of gems was gingerly set on the ground. She took two steps back.

She knew dragons cared little for money. They wanted territory, lands they could purchase and hold. Already the Wyld Hunt encroached to the west, and the desert blocked much of the north. Not even flame drakes could hunt sand squids and burrow worms, the only larger creatures to inhabit the sun-baked sands. The gems on offer would purchase enough to expand their borders without having to fight for every inch.

The elf moved forward, ever cautious. His eyes never left her as one sword moved out to catch the drawstring of the pouch. He moved back far enough to look inside without opening himself up to attack. He nodded and set the bag back on the ground. Then gave her a long hard stare.

"You're sure you wish to bargain with the Weyr? They negotiate under the old laws; this is your last chance."

Without the aid of a drake, this mission would fail. She might hit her mark but would die before collecting. This was a necessary evil. The woman nodded, her dark hair swaying lightly in the breeze.

The elf gave another curt nod and moved into the cave once more. There was a long wait before she heard a loud '*bong*' echo out of the entrance. The pitch was low, and the vibrations lingered in the air for several long seconds. She expected the elf to come back out, to collect the gems, if nothing else. He wasn't seen again.

The shadow moved out from the cliffs above, broad and sweeping in slow circles, getting smaller and darker as the drake approached the ground. The dragon seemed to slow to a stop just before its claws reached the earth.

It still shook the ground under her feet as it thumped down. Great wings folded up, and it focused a sizeable orange eye on her. Pulling in a torrent of air, the drake then blew a stream of smoke just past her head. The words echoed inside her mind.

"We shall bargain."

It wasn't a question.

CHAPTER 2

GETTING READY

Bayu ran through the Keep, grabbing his satchel of parchment and ink as well as the lunch Norim packed for him. As one of what many simply called the seven, Bayu was now a Blood Keep ward. The queen herself had sent him and six other boys with a note to the capital.

A wonderful woman named Norim quickly decided they were her children now and treated them as such. He'd been only twelve autumn's then, now he was fifteen.

As one of the younger boys, he hadn't yet worked as a junior guard like Jugthen. He hadn't even been given the responsibilities of a page. Norim insisted that he and the others get a chance to be young. She made sure he had everything he needed.

He went from being alone and living in the woods with the other orphans to residing in Autumn's castle. He even saw the queen sometimes. Claire would greet him by name when she saw him.

Today he was to be part of the first class to go to the new school. Children from all over the kingdom would be in attendance. Bayu had heard of trolls and brownies but never actually seen any. He'd seen gnomes and sprites around, but never the young ones. Today he would see all of these and more; he would get to learn.

Bayu had only ever met one other person of his aspect in Autumn: the large man who was often seen with the queen. The boy had once hidden his link to air, thinking it weak and embarrassing. That changed when he saw that man duel the Demon Prince and win.

Sure he won one out of three, but honestly, that was incredible. The man used his powers in so many odd and crazy ways, the prince was all over trying to keep up. Bayu wanted to learn to be like that, wanted to be smart and have good ideas. He'd been told his potential was even greater than the Wind Walker's. Today was the day!

He donned the uniform he often wore to help around the Keep. It was a dark-red tunic and black trousers with gold trim on both the collar and cuffs. His boots were soft brown leather. His blonde hair was neatly combed. He'd tried to straighten his crooked nose again today, but it seemed insistent on the previous location.

Bayu almost made it through the door to the main hall when a tall woman in a silky blue dress stepped in front of him. She leaned down and kissed his cheek, hugging him close before speaking.

"I'm quite proud of you. You know how important this school is to the queen. Try and make sure everything goes smoothly."

He blushed slightly at the attention. Norim was like a mother to him, but she was still exceedingly lovely.

"Yes, ma'am."

Bayu then ran through the main hall to the portal hub. There he could reach the central hub, a building that wasn't really in the capital. He stepped through the doorway into a large stone structure with walls covered in doorways. Signs stood above each with the destination and directions to others you might need instead. The one for the school was on the other side of the main walkway.

He saw children coming in through other portals on the walls of the hub. They converged into a line headed for the larger doorway up ahead. Above the door was a sign that read "Ornella School of Autumn." He took a deep breath and entered the line of marching children.

Today was the day.

***

The torchlight hurt her tiny eyes. The gnome awoke before the sun rose, not that she could verify that since her room was under countless tons of red stone. Deep inside of the mountains of western Autumn among the Sept of Fallen Leaves. Wemwi had recently celebrated her seventeenth autumn and was excited at the prospect of her first day at the newly built school.

She'd argued for her own attendance along with about twenty others of the sept. Many adults were skeptical of the idea. The youngest members of the sept out and vulnerable with bigger races of Fairie raised many concerns. Sprites and pixies were also relatively small but could take to the air. Gnomes survived by being cautious and living deep underground.

Wemwi knew that the world was changing. It was up to her generation to help her people find a place in it. In the end, it was the Blessed One who convinced the leaders to allow their attendance. Joobel was at the meeting and gave her personal guarantee that the gnomes would be both safe and respected. As the largest gnome in history and the betrothed of Jack O'Lantern, she was hard to deny.

She quickly put on the flowered dress and coat she'd laid out the night before. Her sept was all of the earth aspect, with one notable exception. Most liked to dress in sedate browns and subtle tones. Wemwi liked colors. Her dress was bright blue and yellow with a white coat with matching yellow sunbursts along the hem. Her long brown hair was braided down her back. She even pinched her cheeks to add a splash of extra color.

A small backpack lay in the sitting room. Wemwi had all the writing tools she needed and a tin that contained some dried pumpkin slices and berries. She also carried a bit of coin in case of an emergency.

Her mother and father saw her off at the door, wishing her well and advising caution. Both had to hug and kiss her more than once. Cautious and affectionate were the gnomes.

She wasn't the first to reach the portal that led to the hub. Two members of the council had insisted on walking the children as a group. Both the two adults and well over a dozen gnome children waited to cross through. It wasn't long before they all passed into the large building that allowed travel within the kingdom.

Gnomes and other small races had a different walkway that allowed them to move about without the risk of being stepped on. It was only a couple of minutes before they reached the portal to the school. The escorts wished them well.

Wemwi stepped into her future.

***

"Get up."

The young troll squinted at the bright light of his window. "Huh?"

The troll woman finally gave up on using words and grabbed his dark-green leg. She pulled her son from his warm fur-hide blankets. He hit the floor with an '*oof*,' and the cold ground had him on his feet instantly. Tedar was a way from joining the hunters at only seventeen cycles. Though here, they measured time by autumns.

Despite his age, he was tall and lean. His skin had lost the spots of youth early, and he was gifted with the blood. Some trolls could use the aspect of fire to 'Boil Blood'; he was one of the most promising at this.

It gave him enhanced strength and bursts of speed in exchange for increased hunger and fatigue. This, combined with his size, had

Chieftain Rakash eyeing him for future leadership. Despite his gifts, Tedar preferred to spend his time reading.

All trolls learned to read early in life. One too many bad treaties had led them to be wary of the goodwill of others. As a recent immigrant to Autumn, his mother was determined to give him a better future than could've been hoped for in the barrens of the Wyld. She was going to see that he didn't waste his chance to attend the new school.

"Get dressed; your clothes are set out. You'll have to warg down your breakfast before it's time to leave."

He rolled his eyes. "Yes, mum."

"Next time you have to get up early, try not to be sitting with a book till the late hours."

Tedar sighed. "Yes, mum."

She hugged him close, the top of her head only coming to his chest. She'd told him he got his size from his father. It was a word they had learned only after coming to this new land. Now that he understood the meaning, he had a picture of who his father was.

He was a great warrior and hunter, killed during a slaver raid a few years back. Tedar swore he'd see that debt paid someday. For now, he needed to move before the smaller woman thumped him.

The tunic and trousers were loose and comfortable. The light tan and brown colors went well with his dark-green skin. A quick splash of water to tame down his coarse black hair, a quick shine of his newly protruding tusks, and he was ready.

He jogged to the house's main room, where strips of meat steamed in the chill air. He grabbed his breakfast, and his pack then ran to the east end of the village. There lay the portal to the school, waiting to send him onwards.

Tedar wasn't the oldest of the trolls in attendance, but he was the largest. He helped keep the younger trolls gather together for the journey. Before his growth spurt, he often was a target for some of the more aggressive trolls. Now with his new size, the tables had turned.

He hadn't lost coordination in gaining proportions, and being bullied made him protective over those weaker than him. As long as he was present, no one would try anything.

Soon the group of over twenty trolls filed into their new adventure. Many more would join them as soon as they were settled. The Stone Spear Tribe was hundreds strong and had spread over much of the Mountain Wyld. Now all were concentrated into Autumn's Twilight Vale.

Tedar herded the young of his tribe to a new way of life.

CHAPTER 3

FIRST HOUR

Bayu squirmed in his seat. The teacher was an older man named Fess, who said he was once a royal tutor who attempted to teach the prince. He wasn't the only one to catch the use of the word 'attempted.' The man had a way of flailing his hands about when he talked.

It was distracting at first, but now Bayu was carefully taking notes in his messy hand. Norim made sure he and his brothers all learned to read and write. The skill allowed him to move ahead of those who would learn that first. The old man turned to the class and waved a hand towards the room.

"Who can tell me the difference between the kingdoms of Fairie and the realms?"

Bayu's hand shot up, but a tiny girl in front was faster.

The gnome folded her hands in front of her. "Realms are the territory of a great spirit; Autumn's aspect is change. Kingdoms are ruled by people. Usually, the borders are the same, but they don't have to be."

"Yes, very good..." Fess looked at the seating chart. "Very good, Wemwi. I see the gnomes are on top of things. As I was saying, spirits gain power with each lifetime. What happens when a spirit is so strong that the vessel it's bound to can no longer hold it?"

Bayu's hand went up again; he lost this time to a very tall troll sitting right behind him.

"Spirits start out as essence, then with time they're born into the older races, such as trolls or sprites. Eventually, they can inhabit a foreigner. Either one born here or somewhere else. When even they cannot contain the power, the person and the bonded spirit can become a great spirit."

Fess waved his hands and nodded. "Ah yes, well done... Tedar. Impressive. Now tell me, what happens when there's no realm for the spirit to take over?"

Bayu had his hand up before the question was even finished.

"A rogue great spirit can seek out new territories or bond with an existing spirit. Some great spirits have many bonded with them, sharing wisdom and power."

"Yes, quite right, Bayu. Norim would be proud. Our world lives or dies on the spirit magic that sustains us. It's our greatest asset and our biggest weakness."

Bayu jotted down every word he could. Most in the room were doing the same. History would be more straightforward for him simply because he'd gotten some exposure to it in the Keep. The queen even had people sitting in the royal meetings to learn how everyday issues can be daunting at a grander scale.

Suddenly the door cracked open. Fess noticed and stepped out to speak to the person outside.

The gnome in front of him turned. "I didn't know about great spirits bonding together. Where did you hear about that?"

Bayu shrugged. "In the Keep, they have books going back centuries. We spend time each day reading them. Some have even been written by the queen."

The girl grinned. "I'm Wemwi, of the Sept of Fallen Leaves. It is nice to meet you."

"Bayu, I'm a ward of the kingdom. I live with Mistress Norim in the Keep."

The tall troll leaned forward and tapped Bayu on the shoulder. The boy almost cringed at the enormous dark-green hand that appeared to be missing a finger. He forced a smile and turned to face his classmate.

"Hi, I'm Bayu."

The troll pointed to himself. "Tedar, of the Stone Spear Tribe. The books you spoke of... do you think I might be able to look at them sometime? I've read most of ours many times."

Bayu had assumed the troll was intelligent from his answer to the earlier question but hadn't expected one so large to be interested in books. He pushed his hand into his blonde hair as he felt a bit guilty. The troll hadn't seemed to notice any slight but waited for an answer about the books.

"Usually, we're supposed to keep them in the study. I'll ask if I can loan you some of them."

Wemwi perked up at that. "Oh, that would be great. Though I'm sure I couldn't carry one."

Bayu shook his head. "Most of the books have several copies. We have small ones for gnomes and pixies and such. I will ask for you as well."

She seemed to blush at this, nodding with a big smile on her tiny face. Before they could speak further, the door opened again, and a pretty woman entered in front of Fess. She had long brown hair that curled at the temples.

Her eyes were the color of falling maple leaves, and her pale skin held only a hint of brown from the dim Autumn sun. She wore a dress of dark brown with gold trim and lighter brown leggings sewn into the skirt. A slim silver band of intricately woven leaves sat upon her head.

Wemwi and Bayu were the only ones who knew to stand and go to one knee as she entered. The queen gave them both a nod. She walked to the head of the room and spoke with a smile.

"Hello my children. I'm Clarissa Ashotok. Claire, to my friends, queen to the people of Autumn, and Banshee to our enemies."

There were several gasps around the room. Bayu had met and even dined with the queen. Being a ward of her advisor had some privileges. Wemwi had recognized Joobel's work on the dress and realized instantly who wore it.

"My queen." Tedar stood and then also went down to one knee. "On behalf of my tribe, let me thank you for allowing us to come here. You saved my people and now offer to teach us. I'll never forget your generosity."

At the largest student's example, several others kneeled as well. The woman nodded, accepting the words and the pledge, no doubt putting it aside for later. She smiled and once again addressed the class.

"You're all here because Autumn's greatest resource is our children. It was no easy thing bargaining for you all to attend classes. I want you to know that I'm committed to seeing this endeavor a success. I ask you all to do what you can to help this experience connect our people in the years to come."

The room was silent for a long moment, then a pixie on Wemwi's right hovered in the air.

"You have my pledge, my queen."

She placed her fist over her heart and held her pose. Soon all the other students had done the same, most doing so while merely standing. The queen smiled.

"All I am asking is for you to all do your best. You are our future."

As Claire began to walk out the door, a ghost appeared in the center of the room. The queen's final words echoed from the specter's open mouth.

"I'll be watching."

Bayu could just make out Wemwi's whispered words.

"I hope those guys don't hang out around the bathroom."

***

The woman arrived in the capital early the night before. It was easy to remain anonymous when you stay on the poorer side of the city. The Blood Keep was actually nice for such an urban area. People were all working cheerfully at their tasks. The smell was of the fruits of the market, not of the typical waste of cities. The red haze that seemed to cover everything had grown thicker as the sun rose.

She'd stayed at a tavern in the southern part of the city. The meeting was now with the people she'd hired for this mission. This inn had a dark interior. There was a group of men sitting at a large table in one corner. The one with his back to the wall was dressed in red; this was probably her team.

The woman noted they'd ordered food but not ale. It was a good sign. People who drink early tended to make mistakes. Four of these men were a mercenary team out of Summer. They were mostly known as bounty hunters, tracking down slaves for the southern kingdom's families and nobles. Two of them were to be from Spring. She gave them all a blank stare.

"Is there enough porridge for a stranger?"

The question was code. Nothing about it would give her away, nor those she was speaking to. The man in red leaned back and gave her a wide grin.

"Only if the strange can spare a coin."

The woman gave a curt nod and took the open seat at the table. Before she bothered with the plan, she wanted to verify the pieces were all on the board.

"The key to all of this is the Spore Weaver and his support. I trust both are present and up to the task?"

One of the men held out a hand, a tiny puff of what appeared to be green smoke wisped from the palm of his hand. The lean man to his right moved his fingers, and the wisp moved deftly through the air and hit a woman across the room. She teetered for a moment and then slumped down in her chair. The assassin turned and snarled in a low tone.

"Don't broadcast what you in this place! We want to do our work and leave no trace. I don't need to tell you who might be coming after us."

Her reference to the Demon Prince hit home. She had a plan for the death drake, but no one wanted the prince to hunt them down. The Spore Weaver nodded.

"Point taken. I've filled my core, but am weak in this realm. I can top off maybe one of the buildings you mentioned. I'll be spent afterward. Then it'll be up to the rest of ya."

She nodded; that would be enough. The air spirit supporting him could push the fog into the rooms and halls, allowing them to work with little resistance. The others were mostly there to help keep control. It was time to go over the plan.

"You were all hired to help me fill a contract. The price for the death of Autumn's Banshee has tripled since Winter signed the treaty. She's well protected in her red fortress, but today is special. Today one of her projects is finished."

She leaned over the table, her mouth moving into a sneer.

"Today is the first day of school."

Chapter 4

Second Hour

Wemwi's second class was designed for those with inborn spirit magic. The small room suited her and her classmates perfectly. Around two dozen miniature desks sat waiting for the gnome, pixie, and sprite students."

Gnomes were slightly larger than pixies, who were, in turn, larger than sprites. There were notable exceptions, but the rule was pretty close to universal. At the front of the class, a plump sprite named Aura addressed the students.

"We are, of course, all of the older races. Our magic is not symbiotic like the queen or the prince. Our power is more subtle. For example, my wings shouldn't be able to lift me."

The plump woman smiled as her thin translucent wings hummed, and she came an inch off the ground. A couple of the other sprites giggled at the joke.

Aura grinned. "Yes, I like to eat, and it shows. My magic allows me to lift myself. Even though if I were a bird, I wouldn't be able to. This is actually true for all of you who fly."

Most were aware of this, but a few murmured surprise.

Aura hummed to hover above the class. "Sprites like myself are of the air aspect. We can have a small effect on the air around us, can fly, of course, and even lift things bigger than we are."

An ember sprite in the back raised a hand and was called on.

"How can we fly then? Our aspect is fire."

Aura touched her chin. "Ah, a good question, does anyone know?"

There was a long pause until Wemwi raised her hand.

"Yes, my dear, what do you think?" Aura asked.

Wemwi leaned forward. She felt a bit odd answering questions about wings when she was one of the few without them. Aura smiled cheerfully, urging her on.

"Your air magic doesn't change the air to let you fly. It changes you. The same goes for all flying creatures of magic. Even dragons."

The room fell quiet. Aura seemed to think about this and then looked to the room.

"That's a bold statement! Have you met a dragon?"

Wemwi nodded, smiling as she thought of Bloom. "Why yes... many times."

"Were you sick?"

Wemwi knew the teacher was referring to the healing the green drake gave all over the kingdom. Blood Mountain was no exception; she healed them as well. Wemwi had met both Bloom and Harvest on their visits to her home. Joobel often came by with her dragon, as she considered Bloom family. That made the drake an honorary gnome. No one was going to argue against having a dragon loyal to the sept.

"I'm related to the queen's advisor. The dragons of Autumn visit my home sometimes."

Aura brightened at this. "So you've seen them up close! Mighty wings, no doubt, but they also need magic to fly."

The room began to erupt with chatter. Wemwi forgot about how few would get to be close to the only two dragons in the kingdom; it made her feel special.

A pixie raised a hand. "What type of power do gnomes have?"

Aura called on a broad gnomish boy in the back of the room. He stood and cleared his throat.

"Gnomes are strong for our size and thrive underground; we're of the earth ye see. Our real talent, is being maker-magic."

Aura almost clapped at this. "Maker magics are such a gift. Gnomes can invent and improve on many of the things we need every day. Our farms started producing more food when gnomish plows started tilling the fields. Why my dress is of gnomish make, and I've never worn finer."

Wemwi took pride in the creations of her people. Still, her dream was to work in the Keep, perhaps in a position like Joobel. Aura went on about the different kinds of inherent powers as Wemwi soaked in all she could.

***

Tedar stood in the expansive room set up for the larger races to study spirit magic applications. They'd changed into loose-fitting clothes that would allow free movement. The space had various objects along the walls that the troll assumed were to test and hone abilities. He chose to stand next to the much shorter blonde boy named Bayu as he seemed both intelligent and well connected.

An older man speaking in front was ranting about how proper use of a person's abilities could save a life one day. This wasn't new information for the trolls, who had survived in the Wyld.

"If you neglect your skills, you could either miss out on opportunities or hurt yourself."

The man who called himself Torg was broad and well-muscled, with short brown hair that was turning grey. He had stubble of the same shades and moved with practiced ease. He stepped forward and motioned for Bayu to move up into a large circle in the room's center.

"People like Bayu and I are descendants of people from other worlds. Our bodies are a blank slate for a spirit to bond with.

Because of that, we can hold the more powerful ones. That doesn't mean we're stronger overall, just that we can cast more energy as our bodies are not infused like say," Torg trailed off and scanned the group. "Gorb, come on over."

Tedar watched as the lumbering ogre moved up. He knew he, of all people, shouldn't judge by appearance, but ogres tended to be relatively slow of thought and quick to anger. This one wasn't changing his mind. The man had both students stand apart and then told the ogre to drag the boy out of the circle. Bayu flinched a bit, but to his credit, didn't protest.

The ogre seemed confused but lumbered forward and then stopped. He began to push toward his foe but found himself against a wall of dense air. Tedar watched as the much smaller Bayu sweated from the effort. Air users were uncommon in most kingdoms but were comparatively rare in Autumn. He had only met the Wind Walker, and that man had blown his village away. Bayu seemed a good deal weaker.

Gorb was starting to get angry now. He stomped hard enough to shake the floor and grunted in frustration. Tedar could see the situation heading down a destructive path; Torg saw it as well.

"Ok, that shows what I was talking about. Bayu and Gorb, you can move back now."

Bayu nodded and dropped his shield. He started to move back with the class; however, the ogre roared and rushed at the boy. Torg stomped his foot and sent up a wall of stone, blocking his path. Gorb never reached the barrier.

Before anyone understood what was happening, the ogre slammed against the far end of the room, shaking the whole building. Tedar stood where the ogre had been. His lean, dark-green body had swollen with dense muscle, spiderwebs of dark-red veins bulged from his arms and neck. His body seemed to deflate as steam rose from his skin.

Torg looked at him in astonishment and then shook off his surprise.

"Yes, um... Bayu and... Tedar was it, yes um... go stand back with the class."

The man walked over to check on Gorb, who seemed to be out cold. Tedar did as he was told, and Bayu stood beside him again. The boy sighed as he ran his hand through his thick blonde hair. Then he looked way up.

"Thanks for that. I'm glad we're friends,"

Tedar stopped to think about that. If he was going to be here for a while, friends might be a good idea.

"I'm sure you'd do the same for me."

Bayu chuckled. "Oh yes, anytime you need an ogre thrown across a room, just call me."

Even with his tusks, Tedar's smile was clear to see.

CHAPTER 5

THIRD HOUR

Bayu wasn't sure about this kind of math. Most people knew the very basic sums needed to exchange money and bargain, but the odd woman in the front of the room was using letters as numbers. It didn't seem natural.

The older woman with a crop of curly grey hair and a rather large nose had just finished putting a sum on the slate for everyone to look at. She called herself Nancy. The woman gave the impression she wasn't originally from Fairie.

"Who can solve this equation?"

Wemwi was the only one who raised a hand.

"Yes, the young lady over here."

The gnome stood. "I'm Wemwi; the answer is seven."

The old woman clapped her wrinkled hands together and wrote it on the board.

"Yes, excellent. You see, all our gnome is doing is changing the equation around."

Nancy turned to see another hand up.

"Yes, you there."

"Bayu, ma'am. I was just wondering why we would want to know how to make letters into numbers? I can't see needing to know this for any reason."

Nancy sighed. "Ah, would you believe it's not the first time I've heard that? Sometimes it's not about learning to know a thing, but learning to think about how to know."

Bayu stared ahead with a blank look. His sentiment was echoed in the faces of most other students as well.

The old woman winced and seemed to struggle with her words. Finally, she appeared to give up.

"You know I told him this wouldn't work."

There was a long pause before Bayu asked the obvious follow up.

"Pardon me, but told who?"

Nancy sighed and leaned against her desk. "That blasted Wind Walker! He told me that innovation was the key to our future. That the children needed to learn to think. Just because he likes algebra doesn't mean I can—"

Tedar interrupted her. "Wind Walker? Do you mean the dark man who flies without wings?"

Nancy nodded. "Yes, he said he wanted you to—"

"You mean Gray, the guy who sometimes wins against the prince?" Bayu asked.

"Yes, he wanted me too—" Nancy began.

Bayu tilted his head. "He likes this strange math?"

"Of course, he wanted me to—"

"It helps him fight?" The troll interrupted.

The old woman was now ready to pummel them both. Her eyes began to glow blue, and water seemed to pull from the air into her hand. Her voice moved to a growl.

"The next person who interrupts me will regret it."

Two hands went up, but Nancy waved them away.

"Gray asked me to teach this class to help you all learn to think in different ways. He's powerful, but his real advantage is always doing something new and unpredictable. He thinks differently, so he can fight differently. If you want to know a secret, it's not his fighting that I respect. This school was his idea, and it took quite an effort to get the queen on board."

She seemed to relax, staring at the room. All had grown silent. Finally, a hand went up.

Nancy rolled her eyes. "Ug, yes, Bayu?"

The young man's eyes were looking past her. "So... looking at that equation, how are you rearranging it to get seven?"

As Nancy turned back to her explanation, her wrinkled face shifted into a wide grin.

***

The woman looked to the man in red. From his reputation, he was an earth aspect and an incredibly formidable one. They gathered next to the outer wall of the school grounds. Her informants made it clear that some of the instructors left after lunch. At the same time, the second round of combat training would have the instructors and some of the stronger students on the west side of the grounds.

The east wing was far enough away that they would have over an hour to secure the hostages if they played it smart. Then she could make demands before anyone could attack them. They would have the leverage to keep the enemy at a distance. These men knew the plan now.

The man in red never gave his name. No one had done so. After this was over, all would go their separate ways. Anyone who was caught would have nothing to share about the others. Now, the earth aspect proved his reputation was well earned.

His hand touched the school grounds' outer wall, and it shifted around to open into a wide doorway. The air user working with the Spore Weaver pushed his own power out and nodded after a moment.

"It's clear to the side of the building."

They moved as a group, the man in red restoring the wall to the previously smooth surface before following. Then they moved to a spot just next to the east wing. The building was several stories tall. They would need to gather up all inside and move to the fourth floor. It was all coming together now.

The man in red placed his hand on the ground next to the building. A large hole shifted around to allow them to hide. They would need to wait a couple of hours.

Then she was going to slay the Banshee.

CHAPTER 6

LUNCH

W emwi walked through the line to pick out some food. She'd snacked on her berries and pumpkin between classes, but now she was famished. The gnome took the wide tray and walked out into the room. Looking around, she saw that she could sit at the smaller tables or in the center of the room.

There sat tables that people of various sizes could use to intermingle. A large three-fingered hand waved her over. Tedar was seated across from Bayu, who had another much younger boy next to him. Next to Tedar was a young girl with dark brown skin and the prettiest dark eyes. She looked even younger than the boy. The troll greeted her.

"We were hoping you'd find us."

The gnome put her food down on the little table. Her new friends were an odd group, but she had to admit they kept things interesting. She glanced down at the smaller children.

"Who are these fine young people?"

Bayu patted the little boy on the shoulder.

"This is Noelani. He's staying with me at the Keep until he and his sister find a permanent place to live. He was a bit under the weather, so I'm trying to keep an eye on him."

Wemwi gave a gracious curtsy. "Pleased to meet you, Noelani."

The boy looked up and smiled. He lifted one hand and moved the water in his glass around in a mini whirlpool.

Bayu sighed. "Please don't; you always make a mess."

Wemwi smiled at the way her new friend was watching over the younger boy. Then she looked at the girl.

"Who's this enchanting young lady?"

Bayu was busy wiping up the water that had splashed all over the table, so Tedar stepped in.

"She says her name is Laris. So far, that's all we've gotten out of her."

The gnome watched as the girl methodically put a bit of food in her mouth and then chewed it slowly. Her focus was on the sizeable lean arm of the troll sitting beside her. She appeared to be studying him.

Wemwi arched an eyebrow. "I don't suppose she's normal company for you?"

Tedar shook his head. "The three of us were eating and looking for you when she walked up. Then she sat down next to me and started doing this."

Wemwi walked over past Tedar's tray to stand before the girl. She wore a worn purple dress, and her shoes looked too big. Her hair was brushed and clean, though. The gnome thought she might be one of the queen's orphans. Wemwi spoke softly to the girl.

"Hello Laris, my name's Wemwi. How old are you?"

The little girl looked up, her voice a drawn-out sing-song tone. "I dooooon't knooooow." She went back to examining the arm next to her.

Wemwi looked over to the troll. "Does this happen to you often?"

Tedar seemed to be trying to blush, but his dark-green skin made sure no one would ever know either way.

"Honestly, I was more ready for stares and whispers. Most people think trolls stupid and ugly. This is a first."

Wemwi moved on to discuss how everyone was doing in the classes and how they liked the new experience. Bayu was talking about the air techniques he wanted to try when Tedar gasped. All looked over to follow his gaze. On his right arm was a small red sigil, faintly glowing in the brightly lit room.

The gnome gave a low whistle. "I don't suppose it does that normally?"

Tedar slowly shook his head, eyes wide. "No... this also is a first for me." He rubbed at the glowing lines, as if they itched terribly.

Noelani looked up from the wet table, noticing Wemwi for the first time. "You're short."

Wemwi didn't look away from the red sigil as it slowly faded from the big green arm. She absentmindedly answered as she memorized the shape. Her hands already reaching for her parchment.

"Yes... I suppose I am."

***

Tedar had been torn between going to the healer's office and trying to keep the girl Laris from getting in trouble. Wemwi had insisted he find out what was going on. She'd memorized the shape of the sigil and drew it on a bit of parchment. She made her drawing as large as she could, but he felt silly with the tiny slip of paper pinched between two fingers.

He wasn't the only one who needed the services of a healer. A young brownie sat in the corner with a wispy beard that was quite singed. A sprite with a sprained wing awaited her turn after him. Currently, the school's healer was examining an ogre who claimed he tripped and flew into a wall. Tedar made sure to stay out of Grob's view.

The troll passed his time by looking at the arm where the sigil appeared. There was no sign of it now, and he felt no different. He was tempted to just ignore the event and go back to finish his lunch. The food was quite good.

Finally, the healer entered while reading the paper he'd filled out at the front desk. She was a solid-looking woman of middle age with light blue robes and thick red hair curled up short on her round head. She made faint grunts as she scanned the paper. Finally, she looked up and took a step back.

"My now hun, aren't choo just a big fella."

"I'm smaller than many trolls in the Stone Spears."

"Yeah, but I'd say most of those aren't children."

Tedar shrugged. "I'm big for my age, I guess."

The healer looked him over. "I agree, but being big isn't a sickness. It says here you were the victim of a curse from a child named Laris?"

Tedar snorted. "I never said curse. At lunch, one of the younger human girls touched my arm. It left a mark."

The healer tilted her head, one eyebrow up. "I'm not sure a little girl could touch you with a knife blade and leave a mark."

The troll sighed. "No... she didn't hurt me or anything. It left a glowing character of some sort. Here my friend drew this." He awkwardly gave her the tiny drawing. "Sorry, it's small; Wemwi is a gnome."

The woman took the offered paper and tisked, her brow furrowed.

"Did the girl speak any words? Was she holding anything?"

"No, she was just acting really inquisitive. I assumed she was just curious and had never seen a troll before."

The healer made a note. "What form of magic does your tribe have access to?"

"The Stone Spears are of fire. I can boil blood; it's a form of enhancement."

The stout woman nodded with a grin. She moved over to the large stone table in the corner. It weighed more than four men and had been crafted by an earth shaper on location.

She slapped the hard surface. "Could you lift this off the ground?"

Tedar stepped over and called the blood. His arms and legs began to swell, and dark-red veins protruded from his enhanced muscles. He leaned to set one hand under the center of the table and effortlessly hoisted the balanced weight of it off the floor. He felt strong but not really different.

The healer nodded. "Not bad; how long can you hold your enhancement?"

"So far, about one minute. After that, I'll be exhausted for hours."

"Ok, hun, hold it for now. I need to nick you, don't swat at me. In that form, I'd splatter against the wall."

Tedar seemed confused but allowed the woman to put a small shallow cut on his arm below where the sigil had been placed. The small wound hissed as his hot blood ran out. Even he was shocked to see the skin close almost instantly, healing as if the dragon Bloom were attending him. The healer was just as surprised.

"There hasn't been a Battle Shaper for centuries...," the woman stammered.

Tedar didn't understand what that meant or how he'd been able to heal the cut. To his surprise, he had held the boil for his longest time ever and wasn't the least bit tired. He needed answers.

"What does this mean? What has she done to me?"

She gave a low whistle. "Hun, if this means what I think, she didn't curse you. The girl has given you a gift this world hasn't seen for a long, long time."

His green skin paled. "Am I ok? What has the girl done? Why am I not getting tired?"

"My dear troll, you're better than ok. Please head to your next class and come see me if anything seems off. I've something I need to do."

With that, the woman walked out the door and was gone. Tedar took her advice and released the boil, moving on to his next class.

The young troll hoped answers would come in time.

***

Jack had been enjoying a picnic with Joobel when the messenger arrived. It was an urgent summons to the queen's chambers. At seeing the panicked look in his eyes, the tiny man assured the prince that the queen was in no danger as of the time of his departure.

As the sprite disappeared with a slight buzzing sound. Joobel began to quickly gather things up. They'd finished eating and were only lingering until they'd need to leave for afternoon classes.

Claire had asked many to help teach certain subjects. Jack would be coaching combat techniques and teaching energy control, while Joobel would teach about dragons and help in some statecraft lessons. It seems they'd both be a little late today.

They had moved into the shorter grass just outside of Issabol's home. It allowed a lovely setting for the meal and a chance to stop in on his, many great's, aunt. They were only moments from her portals and were back in the Keep in a couple of minutes.

Claire's apartments were a series of rooms with a sitting area, royal bedroom, a small kitchen, and the smaller bedroom Joobel used. As they both moved inside, they could see that Claire and Gray were already sitting and sipping tea. Usually, Issabol and Norim would attend a meeting like this, but the naiad was very involved in the school, and the Portal Master was busy with a project in her time-altered workshop.

Once the four of them were alone, Claire cleared her throat and began.

"We have a bit of a situation."

Everyone stayed silent as it was clear she was working towards something. The smile on her mouth was becoming more and more evident.

"Earlier today, an orphan taken in by the Keep burned a sigil of power into one of the trolls at the school."

Silence hung in the air as Joobel began to smile as well. Jack nodded in understanding, leaving the big man the only one in the dark.

"What does that mean?" Gray asked.

The queen was grinning ear to ear.

"It means there's a Battle Shaper in Autumn."

Gray rolled his eyes. "So glad it has a name. What does it mean?"

Claire sipped her tea and paused before answering. "You're familiar that some spirit powers are rare, some powerful, some both."

Gray nodded as she continued.

"A Battle Shaper can gift the old races with special powers. More importantly, some spirits are dangerous and only thought to be born into the different kingdoms' royal or powerful families. The first time we have all the children together, we stumble upon an orphan with an invaluable skill the kingdom hasn't recorded in centuries. What does that imply?"

Gray thought for a long moment, then his eyes widened.

"Maybe they're not as rare as we thought. Maybe people with these talents simply never find out what they are. They grow up and die in an obscure village with no training or knowledge of their potential."

Jack frowned. "The ones called Hollows?"

"They might just not know what their spirits are!" Joobel answered.

Claire was beaming, her hands clapping lightly.

"If this is true, then who knows how many gifted youngsters we have right under our noses."

Now Jack knew why he'd been brought in. His sister was hunting mushrooms, and he was to be the truffle pig.

"You want me to find the ones with the rare gifts, I assume?" Jack sighed.

Claire jerked her head back, her hand coming to her breast in mock surprise.

"Oh, would you brother? It would be ever so helpful."

Jack rolled his eyes as Joobel kissed his dimpled cheek. The gnome hugged his arm as Claire went on.

"You have a combat class that will begin shortly. You can start there. Do your magic-tasting thing and note the ones who seem different. Also, take notice of others who have an abnormally high amount of energy. Some might have common powers in great quantities. Honestly... just take an inventory of every child in the school."

She looked over to Gray. He nodded and smiled, also growing excited.

Joobel frowned, looking around the room. "We need to be careful."

She waited for everyone to turn and give her their attention. The sound of a serious Joobel could really drain the mirth from a room.

"Some powers are costly. Jack would've died if he'd been born in a village somewhere, I don't have to describe the cost of saving him. What about Issabol, her power has effectively made her an eternal child. Claire, your powers made you an outcast growing up. You still carry the scars of that loneliness."

Joobel paused, meeting everyone's eyes. "My wings made me special but also kept me from making friends. Imagine being called a Hollow and then learning something completely different. If some of these children are special, we'll celebrate that. Being different can also make life harder. We should be prepared to help them deal with that too."

Her words brought a somber mood over the room. Being different, even when it was in good ways, had a cost. They wouldn't just need to reap the bounty of power possibly spread through the classrooms. They would need to protect, nurture, and guide these children.

Claire stood and looked to Jack. "Please let me know what you find, find an excuse to move through the younger classes as well. As Joobel said, some of these powers may require special attention."

Jack nodded and took his beloved's hand as they walked to the portal that would lead them to school.

CHAPTER 7

FOURTH HOUR

Bayu liked school really well so far, despite the scare with the ogre. Now he was finally in the class he dreamed of, combat training. Only humans would train here. This class was to train those with symbiotic spirits, and only humans and elves had those. All of the children present were humans born in the world of Fairie.

The class was held in the same large room where he'd been in the ring with the ogre. The wall still showed the cracked indentation of Grob's impact. Jack, the Prince of Autumn, was the head instructor for this class.

Bayu preferred the larger dark-skinned man who wielded his own element, but he had great respect for Jack. Many saw him as the unstoppable protector of Autumn. Right now, he was walking around and checking in with each student.

There were several smaller groups. Each was led by an instructor of the same aspect. The groups for earth and fire were the largest, followed closely by water. The change group held only a couple of students.

Bayu belonged to the air group. He'd once thought he and his hero might be the only ones, but he could see that air was rare but not entirely unique. Now he was one of seven students learning air techniques, making them the second-smallest group behind change. There wasn't a single user of renewal present.

The air instructor introduced herself as Makani. Bayu knew her as Noelani's sister, but he was surprised to learn she'd be his teacher. She seemed like a lovely woman. Her long blonde hair had a slight curl, and her pale blue eyes were bright and alert. She wore a suit of loose-fitting yellow robes that allowed her legs and bare feet free movement.

The young woman had Noelani's pale skin and had seen even less sun. Makani seemed a bit too thin, but spirit users often didn't train their bodies as much. She scanned her group and began to speak.

"You're all part of a rare group here. We all share an aspect of air. Who can tell me where our great spirit's realm is?"

No hands went up. Few in Fairie traveled to the realm of Dawn, and fewer still knew of anything past the mountain lookout.

Makani waited for only a moment. "Ours is the realm of Dawn. We are orphans in that way. We're welcomed in all realms and kingdoms, but most of us live in Winter."

Bayu raised his hand. "Why Winter?"

"Winter can be a harsh place. As you will learn in time, cold air is lighter and easier to work with. In Summer, where the air is warm and full of moisture, we're reduced in our ability to do battle. This isn't the only reason."

Makani met each student's gaze, as if weighting the potential within. A faint smile passed her lips as she continued.

"Winter is far from the realm of earth, the aspect most common in Fairie. So far from their realm, the aspect of earth is weaker in the north. Change and renewal are rare to start with. Winter welcomes those who can show strength in that land. Air is welcome in Winter."

Makani began walking around the small circle taking in her class. Finally, she stood before an older boy. He was taller and well built, perhaps big for his age like Tedar. She looked up to meet his gaze.

"What spirit do you wield?"

He shrugged. "I don't know, ma'am."

Makani nodded and walked down the line. Only two of the seven knew what specialization, if any, they processed. Bayu was a Tempest, able to wield storms and the aspect of that energy. Another younger girl was a Whirlwind, able to cycle air at incredible speeds. The others weren't sure and had no way to test. Makani seemed to expect this.

"All of us will have access to basic air constructs such as shields and various small conjured items. Some will have specific gifts you can hone to become more powerful. My spirit is Direction. I can alter the path of projectiles to make impossible shots. Some like to use a bow, crossbow, or sling. I prefer these."

She held up two small copper discs, tossing them into the air and causing them to hover. Then she pushed a hand to one side, and each disc hit a different target in perfect center.

"I'm going to test your basic skills and power. I will, either on my own or with help, determine any specific aptitude you might have. We will work as a group to get everyone closer to their potential."

Makani moved over and nodded to Bayu. He took a step forward. She raised one hand slightly, and a large round stone by the wall moved to hover in front of him. She instructed him to make a shield under it and hold it up.

The smooth surface of the rock settled on his construct, and he held it with little effort. Makani went to each student, in turn, giving an equal burden to hold up. Then she seated herself on a stool she conjured from her own power. Bayu felt that was just showing off.

Each student was set up to hold one of the heavy stones. Bayu was the first to start, but the rock was a far cry from the ogre. He was almost bored. Others were having more trouble. Soon a stone thudded against the ground, with another shortly after. A couple more minutes and a third fell, followed closely by a fourth.

Bayu looked around. Only he and another girl, along with the little Whirlwind, remained. Makani looked at each of them. None seemed to be struggling, and each got a second stone. It was a few more minutes before the Whirlwind gave out. Bayu felt the increase but wasn't feeling any strain. A look at the girl told him she wasn't either.

Each got two more stones. Then another shortly after until they had six each. Bayu felt his power starting to fade; the total burden equaled more than two grown men. Sweat trickled into his eyes.

He was on the verge of seeing spots when a light touch on the back of his neck gave him what felt like a day's rest and a good meal. It was as if he'd just started. The voice behind him wasn't precisely deep but was clearly a man.

Bayu turned to see the Prince of Autumn jotting something down and giving him a curt nod. He did the same to the girl he was competing with, and she too seemed refreshed. The lean man with dark hair and eyes went to each student in the air group and seemed to feel their aura. A small brown hound sniffed around and wagged her tail so hard that the back end of her body shook with it.

Finally, he nodded to Makani, who looked genuinely afraid of the man and no less so of the hound. He handed her a slip of parchment and walked away as the little brown shadow followed behind him. The prince never spoke a word.

Bayu lost his contest to the girl with impressive strength, but only by seconds. Makani let each of them know the type of spirit they wielded. Both he and the Whirlwind were confirmed in the skill they'd described. One of the younger children, a boy with bright red hair and a face full of freckles, was also Direction like the teacher.

The others were all of a basic spirit, all except the winner of the contest. Her spirit was given the same name as his: Tempest. He was both excited to have someone to compete against and disappointed to be told once again he wasn't quite as unique as he thought. He had little time to decide how he felt before she came over to speak to him.

"I sure am glad to have ya in our group. Meh pa says that a hound don't get no faster unless he's chasin a hare."

Bayu was a bit thrown. She must be from one of the smaller villages. Despite her way of speaking, she had impressive power. Her long auburn hair hung long around a pretty face, and she had a few freckles on her button nose and the sweetest smile. Bayu thought her eyes were like the water of a deep well. A blue so dark that they almost seemed black when she turned her head.

She was a bit shorter than him. Her clothes looked like she wasn't the first to wear them. Bayu snapped out of his daze and held out a hand. She looked at it and then, after a moment, smiled and gave it a squeeze as he spoke.

"I'm Bayu, pleased to meet you."

The girl smiled. "Oh, my name's Zephyrina, but meh pals just call meh Zef. It's right nice to meet you too."

Her grip was firmer than he expected. Many people spent a good part of the day working. He'd spent enough time as an orphan living in the woods to hold back judgment. He smiled back at her.

Before they could continue any further, Makani finished helping one of the younger students. She moved over and assigned him an exercise to practice holding his concentration at home. Then the instructor broke them up into pairs and had them each stand in the wide circles painted on the floor. Bayu would be up against Zef, while the others were matched up by strength levels. Makani set herself against the little Whirlwind, whom Bayu learned was named Tass.

"Ok, everyone, the objective is simple. Get your opponent out of the circle. The how isn't important. I will step in if it gets too rough." Her eyes narrowed. "Trying to hurt someone outright will put me in a nasty mood."

He and Zef were first. She'd seemed confident before in her strength but now looked out of place and nervous. Bayu decided to ease into his strategy; she seemed nice and likely had used her powers primarily for chores. He had already trained with the junior guards.

Makani made a small puff of dust pop up in the middle of the ring. "Go!"

Bayu set his shield down and began to push towards Zef. The girl seemed relieved he wasn't trying something more violent, and she too put up a barrier. The two met in the center, and again it was a test of strength.

He could see that she was still stronger and decided one loss was enough of a hit against his pride for one day. He whipped his other hand, sending a small blast of air into Zef's hair to distract her. Another tendril of air wrapped around one of her booted feet. He dragged her back to the edge of the circle. She panicked as her foot went out from under her and dropped her shield. Zef tried to regain her footing but couldn't get her hands down in time to catch herself.

Bayu caught her on a platform of dense air, cushioning her fall and gently carrying her outside the ring. He set her down and dissolved his construct. Zef looked ashamed but didn't seem angry. The instructor gave both of them some areas to work on and set up the next match.

Makani gave Bayu a smile and a nod for the gesture toward his classmate as the next pair got into their stances. Autumn would make sure they all had a chance to learn the valuable skill of fighting. After the matchups, they were each set to building skills that would directly affect the type of air they possessed.

The Direction boy had a bow and arrow. The teacher had him aim it off-center and then try to use a stream of air to set it in the bullseye. The Whirlwind, Tass, tried to hold her vortex with a dozen stone balls spinning around inside. Both Bayu and Zef were set to blow a focused gale of wind at a stone cube on one end of the room. The rock would only move with massive amounts of energy.

The class went on for twice the standard time. By dismissal, Bayu was ready for a chair and a book. This was intensely fun, but he was exhausted. Makani gave them all exercises that would help them move forward before the next session. Soon he was walking out into the hall.

Zef decided to walk with him.

***

Jack looked down at the parchment in front of him. Combat classes had two double sessions, back-to-back in the afternoon. The first class revealed over a dozen human children with rare and powerful abilities that neither the kingdom or the children themselves had known about.

The Battle Shaper, Laris, wasn't the only special case. The prince had discovered another gifted young man that left Jack's hands shaking. Emotions were usually not an issue for him, but the boy's magic tasted just like someone he knew. Autumn had another Portal Master.

The group also contained a Mimic, whose magic tasted like spicy copper. The girl would be able to make copies of complicated constructs with only raw materials. Claire was right, both children were thought to be Hollow. Two rare users of maker magic, not to mention Laris.

None of them had any awareness of their power other than the incident with the troll. The two older students failed terribly at the instructor's tasks. Of course, they did; makers weren't built for combat. Most of the children in the room could take Issabol in a fight, yet she was invaluable to Autumn.

The fire group had a girl named Edana who wielded Inferno, the power his father was once gifted with. Another boy used Backdraft, the signs faint at only five Autumn's. Two others had basic fire abilities with power levels that rivaled the strongest of the guards.

The earth group had a girl wielding Sunder and two powerful basic spirits. The water group had another Purification user, a boy of about ten who didn't seem to know what that was. Another boy could use Flood. Both of these were powerful spirits held by the current Winter Queen.

The air group had feisty scrap of a girl who could use Whirlwind. As well as not one, but two Tempests. They were a boy and girl who were both quite powerful for being just fifteen Autumns.

One of them Jack recognized as a former bandit Claire had sent back to the Keep to keep Norim busy. That decision had paid dividends. He also knew the air instructor. Jack was not one to question his sister, but he'd be keeping a close eye on the failed assassin.

It was no surprise that not a single child of renewal was present. Still, Autumn had gained assets this day. He still had another session to go.

What surprises would the next class hold?

CHAPTER 8

LAST PERIOD

Wemwi was pleasantly surprised to find both Tedar and Bayu in her statecraft class. Autumn was a land of agriculture and trade. With all the upcoming changes, the kingdom had shifted priorities. Change brings opportunity, something the gnomes saw coming from the day the dark dream ended.

The gnome wanted to learn how to help govern. Smaller races had gotten overlooked in past years. She wanted to make sure the future kept up the momentum the kingdom had gained in allowing that opportunity for everyone.

Much like before, the smaller desks were in front with the tallest individuals in the back. That put her in the front, Bayu in the middle, and Tedar in the back. They had time to all get in the same row. It was always nice to have friends with you in a new environment.

Wemwi looked back at Bayu, who looked like he'd run to Summer and back.

Her eyes widened at his appearance. "What happened to you?"

Bayu smiled, his cheeks turning red. "I got beat by a girl."

"Tell me there's more to that," Tedar snorted.

Bayu gave a brief recounting of his combat class and the other Tempest who'd beat him in raw power. Wemwi stared at him for a moment, noticing his smile.

"You like her! She must've made an impression."

The boy's face shifted to a brighter shade of red. "She seemed really nice."

Wemwi looked over at Tedar. She thought he also had combat after lunch, yet he looked as if he'd done nothing.

"Tedar, didn't you have combat as well?"

The troll shrugged. "Yep, we did weapons training and wrestling."

Bayu looked back at the unphased troll and shook his head.

"You look like you took a nap. Why am I damp with sweat and feeling like I was run over by a rock wagon while you seem like you just woke up?"

Tedar shrugged his dark-green shoulders. "Trolls are well built."

Wemwi talked about her textiles class for a short bit. Despite not wanting to work in crafting, the Sept leader had insisted all gnome students take at least one manufacturing class. It was either learn to sew, tan leathers, or work a smithy. Wemwi chose the least smelly option.

Despite her best efforts and Bayu's support, Tedar gave no answers to what happened to his arm at lunch. Wemwi had been about to make one more attempt when the door opened. Parchment blew all over the room.

All three of the group knew of Joobel. Wemwi was in the same sept and saw her around Blood Mountain on occasion. Bayu had seen the lovely woman around the Keep, where she served as an emissary and advisor to the queen. Tedar was there the day his tribe accidentally kidnapped her.

Now, by far the largest gnome in Fairie history zipped into the room. Her wings hummed so loud in the confined space that it sounded like the inside of a stampede. She landed on top of her desk and gave the class a slight bow.

"Hello everyone! I'm so very pleased to meet you all. Some of you I know, some of you I've not met yet. I'm quite excited to be here today. Isn't this all so wonderful?"

She zipped around the room and greeted each person by name. Not a single individual was left out. As she identified them, she spoke about the places they lived and the family members they had. It was a tremendous amount of information to even have written down.

Yet, Joobel never looked at any of the papers that were still flying around the room. Once she was finished, she sat on the desk and crossed her legs. They were really nice legs, and it was clear that some of the older boys had noticed. She either didn't see their stares or didn't care.

"How did it make each of you feel to be acknowledged? For someone you think important to remember details of you and your family, village, and kingdom?" Joobel asked.

A sprite in front raised her hand. "You made me feel big; like I really mattered."

The tall gnome gave an excited clap. "This class is about statecraft, the art of negotiating on behalf of the kingdom or the townships within it. Some of you live in racial groups. I've lived in the gnome sept for most of my life." She made a little wave. "Hi, Wemwi."

The little gnome blushed but waved back as Joobel continued.

"Some of you live in towns or villages where many races coexist."

Then she pointed out a tall, dark girl with long braided hair. The girl nodded and smiled back.

"The key to statecraft is finding the balance between groups of people and individuals. A good statesman, or woman, understands the needs and wants of the group you are dealing with. A great one understands the motivations of the people negotiating as well."

Wemwi was writing furiously; she felt like she had a long road to travel to reach her goal. This was like water to a woman lost in the desert. Joobel continued with the theme of the class for a bit and then began discussing the kingdoms.

"For instance, we have an abysmal relationship with Summer. Why is that?"

Wemwi waited for a moment; when no one else stepped forward, she raised a hand. Joobel smiled at her.

"Summer has conflicting motivations. On the one hand, they have more land and sun than any kingdom but refuse to use it for crops. They need our grain but feel superior to our people."

"That describes Summer, one point. Why are they so against us in recent years?"

Tedar's eyes narrowed. "Slavers."

Joobel nodded at this and expanded on his answer.

"Tedar is right for one point, though that's only another part of why. Autumn is pushing a progressive form of government. Winter is already following a similar example. Summer doesn't grow crops or make many goods; their primary export comes from the mines they work near the Wyld. That and the slaves themselves."

Joobel crinkled her nose at the bitter taste of the words and then continued.

"Autumn shut down its own slave markets under Queen Ornella. Under Queen Claire, we've started tracking down those who move slaves through our lands. Not to mention Winter is doing the same as part of our treaty. We're attacking Summer's way of life."

Wemwi nodded and spoke out of turn. "I support her doing so; we gnomes owe much to the queen and her brother."

Joobel did a little clap and then walked, so no papers moved, to the slate. She began to draw a map of Fairie. The gnome's hands were quick and sure plotting out an impressive model of the kingdoms, the Wyld, and the shoreline surrounding them.

Autumn primarily rested in the southwest, Winter took up all of the north with twice the land of Autumn, though mush was covered with snow capped mountains and frozen lakes. Spring was to the far east and was also about half the size of Winter.

Summer covered the southern part of the map and was largest of all. The Mountain Wyld stood in the center. Deserts, badlands, and the high mountain that led to the realm of Dawn.

The whole thing took her agile hands two minutes or so. When she finished, Wemwi could see that the border between Winter and Autumn was drawn with a dotted line instead of the solid one the others had. Her hand went up, and Joobel nodded.

"Why's the border to our north marked differently?"

"Good catch Wemwi, two points for you. We currently have a formal alliance with Winter. Both kingdoms have set favorable trade conditions and have vowed no aggression with one another. Most importantly, we have an agreement to aid one another should either be attacked by another kingdom. Can anyone tell me why this is so important?"

A brownie jumped in to answer. "It allows us to patrol less border."

Joobel frowned before she clarified. "We still patrol our Winter border; no treaty is an excuse to ignore possible threats. You're partially right for one point; we do patrol our northern border less than before. Any other guesses?"

"The combined power of both kingdoms makes up the strongest military power in the world. It makes attacking either of the two kingdoms quite risky," Tedar answered.

Joobel smiled, clapping her hands. "Three points for you, Tedar. The best kind of battle is the one you don't have to fight.

The treaty is formal, and copies of it were sent to the other kingdoms. As a courtesy, so it's said, but truly it protects us from our enemies."

Bayu raised his hand, and Joobel pointed at him. "Pardon me, but what are the points for?"

Joobel gave him a wink. "When you get one hundred points, you get to ride on a dragon."

The entire class perked up at this. The gnome had the most attentive class in the short history of Autumn's school. The session was the second to have a long double period.

That time was almost half over when the sound of coughing came in from the hall.

***

Bayu was still relatively young to be progressing so well with his powers. The earlier combat class really wound him up, and the prospect of training with his heroes excited him. Not to mention the country girl who'd given him both a rival and a possible friend. Though he was interested in statecraft, his true passion was training.

His self-inflicted regimen was inspired by the one they called Gray. Bayu strived to build stamina with his power and skill in how he used it. Over the past few months, he'd come a long way. This extra control and power allowed him to counter the attack. Both from under the door and from the vent high in the wall.

The sound of coughing preceded a thick cloud of green fog that flooded in after only a couple of seconds. The echoes of people falling and desks turning over came from the nearby rooms immediately. Joobel's class was at the end of the hall, and it gave him a crucial moment to react.

Bayu was the first to realize that this was an attack. His power felt the change in pressure. As the expanding gasses pushed into the room, the young Tempest sealed the openings.

A thick green cloud rolled up against his barrier. He held the cloud back as he looked to his teacher.

"We're under attack... something is being blown in. We need to get out of here!"

Joobel stood and looked around at the walls of thick red stone. She noted windows high on the wall, but they were grated to keep pests away and prevent an attack from the outside. She thought through the situation and spoke in a loud whisper.

"This is an attack on the school, not the kingdom. We need to get out of this room and find help!"

Joobel finished speaking and froze, her gaze becoming distant.

Tedar heard all he needed to; the troll looked up at the windows. They were too far up to be of use to most of the class. Then he looked at the wall. As his blood boiled, he began to swell, muscles thickening, his strength multiplied many times over. Protruding veins spiderwebbed over his bulk; the sigil on his arm appeared as a faint, red glow.

Tedar punched and ripped away rock until he made a new door to the room. They were three stories up. He stared at the drop clearly visible through the sizeable jagged hole he made. Joobel was beside him in an instant. She wasted no time in giving instructions.

"The gas might be sleep or poison. Help is on the way. I just spoke to Claire, but I need to get all the students out. Bayu, how long can you hold?"

Bayu looked up, holding the shield with little effort.

"Indefinitely, but that sound will let them know we're busy in here."

Joobel took a slender band of pale blue; there were several adorning her wrist. She snapped one on Bayu, then hooked two together and put them on the thick wrist of Tedar.

"These will protect you from poison. Can you hold the room until I can get those who cannot fly to the courtyard?"

Bayu nodded and reset his focus on the door. Tedar gave the gnome a wide smile. Joobel was the tallest gnome in history; the troll was nearly twice her height in this state.

Wemwi began lining up students. Some of the pixies and sprites could help move the gnomes, but the brownies and humans could only be carried by Joobel. They started the evacuation. Soon only a handful of humans needed help from the gnome to get down.

The door gave way. Three tall men entered the space. One was spewing green fog from his hands as he moved. The other two had coverings over their face and looked for the one who'd stopped the attack from reaching this room. Bayu stood with his palms up; he'd pulled back and was protecting the other students. The first man pulled out a club and spoke.

"Yoos are putting dem at risk. Let the gas through, and dis will all be over when yoos wake up."

Bayu shook his head slowly. He'd die before he gave in. The man started to raise his club to rush forward when a small voice came from near his feet.

"If you turn and leave our school right now, you might survive this day!"

The man looked down at the tiny Wemwi, her face red in fierce anger. He laughed and pulled up his club for a backhand swing. Wemwi refused to move and instead only pointed straight up.

The man sneered. "Like I be fallin for da—"

Tedar landed on the man like a falling boulder. The smaller body crumbled as the troll hit. The large three-fingered hand grabbed the club; it looked like a quill in his grasp. He swung up and caught the man who was spreading the fog in the stomach. The cloud ceased as he wheezed and doubled over.

The third man slammed his foot down. A slim spear of red stone shot out of the floor to run through the body of the troll. The impact threw Tedar up and into the far wall in a wide arch.

Bayu whipped a tendril of air around the spear, pulling from his friend, and threw it back at the man. The enemy merely held up a hand, and the shaft of stone slid past him to shatter on the far wall.

Wemwi screamed; the sight of her friend impaled was too much for her. She lunged at the man; tiny fists clenched in rage. A cloud rushed over her as she jumped. Her limp body hit the floor.

Bayu turned to see the last of the other students were gone, carried by Joobel to the safety of the ground. He and his friends had lasted long enough. These men hadn't gotten them all, and help would be on the way. Bayu decided to stall.

"So... what do you hope to—"

The ball of stone hit him in the head before he finished his question. The room faded as he slid to the floor.

CHAPTER 9

SABOTAGE

Tedar woke up on the cool stone floor. His three-fingered hand moved up to an aching head, while the other went to a faint scar on the left side of his ribcage. For a few seconds, he tried to put together what happened and why he felt an icy stab in his chest.

The memories flooded back to him. He shot up, running to the door where the strange men had entered the room. A steady hand grabbed his arm. The troll looked down to see a lean young man with light tan skin and dark shaggy hair. Beside him was his own teacher, the gnome Joobel. It was the man who spoke, his calm words contrasting the rage in his eyes.

"Tell me what you know."

Tedar wanted to rush in to help his friends, but he didn't know where they'd gone. Then the realization hit him.

"You're the Demon Prince?"

The young man shrugged. "It's not my favorite title, but it's not as annoying as some. I need to know what we're dealing with."

Tedar gave a short version of events. When he mentioned the spear hitting him, Joobel began prodding at his chest with her small hands.

"Oh, it must have hurt so—" Joobel stopped in confusion, " wait... how did you heal so fast? I only thought Bloom could heal someone that fast and—"

Jack put a hand on her shoulder, and she calmed down, focused again on the task at hand. The prince kneeled on the floor and put his fingers against the stone. His eyes closed for a moment, a look of concentration crossing his face.

"The fog was made by a Spore Weaver. Renewal magic... potent. It causes a deep sleep."

Tedar touched the bracelet on his wrist.

"The talisman you gave me worked. I was defeated, but the cloud didn't affect me."

Joobel nodded as Jack crept to the door, listening carefully. He turned back.

"Help is on the way. Torg is gathering the guards, and they will be coming from below. The attackers would know that. I think they're trying to shut down the school. It was a close thing for this project to happen at all. If students die on the first day, there would be a huge amount of pressure to kill the project."

Joobel shook her head, disagreeing with the assessment. "If that was the plan, they wouldn't have bothered putting them to sleep. They will want to set a ransom. My guess is, regardless of what Claire does, the children will be killed then."

Jack's eyes grew wide; Tedar could see why. The attackers must have close to a hundred students from this wing now. They would all die, including Wemwi and Bayu. Tedar's fist clenched as he looked up.

"That can't happen! My tribe is sworn to protect this kingdom. Those students are my people too."

Jack looked at him carefully, eyes moving to the healed wound. "Are you able to fight?"

Tedar nodded. "I'm only a little fatigued. I will be ready to battle ag—"

Jack slammed his palm into the troll's chest, just below the neck. A flood of pure fire aspect rolled into him. Tedar's eyes gained a faint red glow, and he fought the urge to cry his bloodlust to the heavens. He smiled around his short tusks.

"I could take on a dragon now. Let's destroy these cowards."

Jack gave a half-smile; he seemed to like the troll. He put one finger to his lips, and they began to move silently through the doorway. Tedar wasn't built for stealth and the power in his core made him want to boil his blood. Still, he followed the lead of the man.

The prince that gave Autumn's enemies nightmares.

***

Bayu woke with the worst headache of his life. He glanced around the room and noticed that he was the only student awake. Half a dozen men and one woman stood nearby. One of the men was crying out in pain. His screams came to a high-pitched wail as the snapping click of setting bone echoed in the room. A harsh deep voice snapped from near the window.

"Cease your screaming, you fool. If the guards rush us, we may as well jump from the roof."

The injured man groaned. "Yoos wasn't the one crushed by da blasted troll. I thought dees were children."

Another man snarled. "They are children. Did ya think trolls started out tiny?"

The woman's voice hushed them. "Quiet down; you're getting paid for the risk. With both dragons on the other side of the kingdom, we'll make it out of here right nice. You'll be able to afford a healer for your time as a troll's chair."

Another man grumbled at her words. "Only if yah makes good on da ride."

She shrugged. "The dragon won't betray us now. His help was hired under the old laws. He's honor-bound to bring my team and me safely out long as we're alive. The fire drake should be here within the hour. We need to complete the mission first."

A deeper voice came from a man dressed in red. "Where's the thorn?"

Bayu watched motionless as the women reached into a small wooden box. She removed a long thin shard of what looked to be wood. Or a very large bramble. The women held it up to the light and smiled wide. One of the men moved over to look, careful not to touch.

"Are you sure it will kill her? I know a man who said the Banshee pulled an arrow out of her own heart and laughed."

The woman nodded before correcting him. "It was a crossbow bolt. The thorn will kill anything. It's the manifest curse of a slain dryad. Nothing survives the old magic."

Bayu listened as they argued, and the injured man whined, though more softly now. Then he noticed that none of them were wearing masks. The sleeping poison of the cloud must not be present.

The other students were still knocked out from the initial dose. Bayu knew he was in trouble; he couldn't allow them to hurt the queen. That woman had saved him from a life of dishonesty and poverty. He'd been part of a group of bandits who tried to rob her. The prince alone had easily defeated them all. Jack was younger then than he was now.

The queen was only Autumn Maiden then but still could have killed them. No one would have thought twice about it. Those who didn't run away were spared and given a home with Norim at the Keep. She was a mother to him. He had brothers and a family. His queen was worthy, and he'd protect her no matter the cost.

Bayu looked around at the students lying near him. He saw no teachers close by, but the boy near his feet seemed pretty strong. Yet he wouldn't be able to fight against this many foes. The earth user alone had stopped Tedar dead. Bayu almost sobbed at the thought of his slain friend. They would pay for that.

He had the bracelet. It had done its work on him; he was awake. Now he could wake someone else with it. No one close was going to stand a chance against these people. Maybe strength wasn't what he needed; perhaps stealth was the key. He spotted Wemwi lying near his leg.

Her little yellow dress was crumpled; the braid that held her long brown hair had started to unravel. She'd proven to be brave and clever. Perhaps she might help think through this mess.

Bayu moved slowly as he unclasped the bracelet. He pushed it against Wemwi's neck and upper arm. He closed his eyes and evened his breathing.

All he could do now was wait.

***

Joobel was utterly silent as she moved through the halls of the school's east wing. This plan was hers, and she was determined to play her part well. She needed to distract the enemy and allow Jack and Tedar to even the odds. The gnome was well aware that she wasn't the fighter Jack was, but no one else was either. She was graceful, extremely fast, and could fly like no one else.

Magic was thick in her blood, and by all accounts, she should be a great warrior. Yet, she couldn't bear the thought of hurting someone. Her nature wouldn't allow it, though she was no coward. The gnome shed her stylish boots for the silence of bare feet. She was close now.

The ceilings of every classroom were flat, except for the top floor. The roof needed to be pitched at an angle for when it rained. The high ceiling this created was left by the builders in case it was useful later. Joobel was grateful; this allowed her to work in three dimensions. She stepped into the room next to the hostages and silently vaulted up to the rafters in only two flaps of her paper-thin wings.

The gnome waited in a long moment of silence until confident the enemy hadn't noticed. Joobel walked on the beam with fluid grace. She slid through the vent between rooms and spotted the children and teachers lying stretched out on the floor. Anger wasn't an emotion she often entertained, but she wouldn't mourn what her betrothed would do this day.

Joobel's Naming had awakened powers within her. Now she could push power into her eyes and see life force. Everyone appeared to be alive, though some hadn't coped well with the spores.

She could also take away pain, a skill she'd found useful on many occasions. Her blessings were no longer practical. They were so powerful that they bonded her to the one she blessed, so tightly that it felt intimate. Joobel would only share that with one person. Even now, she could feel him moving down the hall. One other skill had manifested since receiving the gift of power from Claire.

Joobel inhaled slowly and cast her spell. A song flowed into the room that housed both the hostages and their captors. The tune was mournful, carrying a depth of sadness. The kind that could only be felt by genuine empathy. Joobel knew the pain of all she met. The gnome had stored that aching grief in her heart. She wove all the hurt and discomfort she'd taken away into the melody.

The sound began so soft as to not even be noticeable, faint as a rustle of leaves in a slow breeze. As she poured more and more of her emotion into the chilling tune, the volume increased. The music began its work in those below.

Their own pain, memories, and insecurities began to rise to the surface. Soon all were lost in a fog of internal despair. Once they realized they were being attacked, they would start to return to themselves.

It would have to be enough.

***

Claire stood outside the east wing of the school. The ransom report came shortly after she heard of the hostages. There was only one demand: the Queen of Autumn must enter the building alone. Only then would all the children be released.

She fought the urge to do just that. Deep down, she knew that this was about the changes she'd worked in her kingdom. Equality doesn't sound good when you already have most of the money, land, and power.

Whether this was an attack from within her own kingdom or another who was afraid her methods would gain favor and spread, she didn't know. Claire was sure that if she did as the ransom demanded, she'd be killed. With her passing, so would go her dream of the future. She had no heir, and Autumn might well fall to ruin.

A thick cloud of green gas covered the wing's lower level; no living thing could enter that much poison unaffected. Even the silver bracelets from Raine wouldn't hold out long with that much clouding the air. Perhaps if Raine herself was here, things would be different.

Claire happened to have allies who were not alive. Ghosts answered her call, and she learned that the children were being held in a large central classroom on the fourth floor. The information was valuable but wouldn't translate well to the little brown hound leaning against her leg. Maeve's tail wagged so hard that her own leg was bouncing around in a manner that wasn't quite regal. Currently, she didn't care.

The Queen of Autumn had a connection with the dead. Maeve might seem full of life, but the hound's spirit fell within her power. She leaned over and whispered in a floppy ear, pushing the images through her spirit of Death into the mind of the loyal

Named hound. As pictures of children in danger entered Maeve's simple mind, words left Claire's lips.

"Protect my little ones."

The hound's stance shifted, her head lowering. Her wiggling tail ceased its motion. No sooner had she let go than Maeve was a brown blur streaking towards the building. The cloud of fog stirred as she ran unaffected through the door.

Torg leaned towards the queen he still thought of as a niece, his tone worried and cautious.

"Do you think the hound will be enough?"

Claire wiped her eye as her angry words came in a whisper. "I fear if any of those children have been harmed, I won't get to question our attackers."

The older man nodded slowly; he'd seen what the strange construct from another world could do when she was excited. It was terrible to think of Maeve as angry. The queen and her guards waited within plain view of the top floor. She hoped the enemy would think her making preparations in case she didn't return.

Jack would need time.

CHAPTER 10

SACRIFICE

Tedar had been warned. The song of the unique gnome, who only a short time ago was teaching him statecraft, would test his mind. It would bring to the surface his fear and pain. He would have to fight through it to save his classmates.

Much like any teenager, Tedar had felt invincible. Now he felt small. He was the young troll who was big enough to be a target while too small to defend himself.

He was standing next to his mother. The funeral pyre was stacked with all the dry wood the tribe could find. In the Stone Spear Tribe, all men carry the responsibility of the women and children. This man had taught him, protected him, and loved him.

When he came home with his eyes thick with shameful tears, that man had wiped them away. He showed Tedar that the only real shame is turning your back on those who trust you. It was years later when he even learned the word 'father.' He knew that this man had been that to him.

That memory broke the spell. The pain was almost sweet, but the people here needed him. He wouldn't fail his friends. As Jack turned the corner, Tedar saw the most frightening thing he'd ever witnessed.

Even in his tribe, way out in the Mountain Wyld, they had heard the legend of the Lantern. The man whose anger burned so hot that his face became living flame. Most believed the stories were told to frighten Autumn's enemies. Tedar learned that the stories fell far short of the sheer terror the young man radiated.

Jack was angry at the attack on his sister's school. His face darkened when Tedar had explained the attack. These people had assaulted a classroom where his betrothed was teaching. Now, as they walked into the room with rows of unconscious children, the Demon lost his composure.

His eyes began to glow a blazing yellow. Tears of liquid flame ran down his cheeks and seemed to ignite his chin. The bright orange fire moved up his face, and instantly everything from the neck up was a ball of orange flames. Only glowing yellow eyes could be seen. They weren't comforting in the least.

One of the attackers turned to see the Demon of Autumn only two steps away. The prince stepped forward and popped a ball of pure heat into the man's gaping mouth. The man wasn't able to scream.

Tedar began to boil his blood as they neared the enemy. He didn't want to risk the strange regeneration only working if his blood was active. Now he wondered if he'd even be needed. Jack stepped past the bubbling mass of boiling flesh and made a quick slash with his extended hand.

The man Tedar crushed back in the classroom had his head removed at the neck. The gaping skull rolled past his own feet. Ahead a woman turned, her eyes filled with tears from the song. She seemed to snap out of her trance and screamed. The sound startled one of her allies.

He turned and shot her with a crossbow. The shot had been impossible; the bolt slid sideways and turned midair. Jack aimed two fingers at the man, did seemingly nothing, and a corpse crumpled to the floor.

Now the other men seemed to realize they were under attack. The woman was injured but not down. She stumbled back then seemed to flip up into the air, slamming against the ceiling. Her form was motionless, held in place by a layer of dense air. Bayu stumbled to his feet and smiled. His focus was still on the woman he held as he spoke to his rescuers.

"This one seems to be the leader. She should be kept alive for questioning."

Bayu turned and saw the flaming visage. The startled young man almost dropped his captive. Jack winked at Bayu, who nodded with wide eyes. His pale face looked away as he fought his terror.

Tedar watched three enemies die in a handful of seconds. One more seemed to be out of the fight. Looking towards the window, he saw the man who killed him. He growled around his tusks.

"The tall man in red is the earth aspect!"

Jack would need to deal with him. The song was loud now. He could tell Bayu was struggling, but to his credit, the young man held his captive firm against the high ceiling of the room. Then a short, stocky man with thick black hair rushed at the Tempest. Tedar moved with speed born of his boiling blood. A leaping punch connected with the man and the troll could feel bone crunch under his fist.

The move had separated him from Jack, who fought the earth user and another man. The second enemy began to produce a cloud of poison. Jack slapped away two spears made of the red stone of the building itself. The fog of sleep, however, wasn't so easy to dodge.

The thick green smoke engulfed the prince; his bright visage of flame lighting up the cloudy air around him. A third stone spear went right through the ball of fire and slammed into the back wall. The song came to an abrupt halt.

Tedar heard an anguished scream.

***

Wemwi awoke to the sound of the saddest tune she'd ever heard. Visions of her time in the dark dream came to her. Broken images of blood and savagery assaulted her mind, but she fought her way back. That time was not her. She was Wemwi of the Sept of Fallen Leaves. She was a citizen of Autumn and wouldn't be haunted by the sins of another.

Her tiny eyes flashed open to see a battle going on around her. Sitting next to her was the bracelet. She guessed it was Bayu's. The plan was for her to leave with the others, but she'd stayed to try and help.

She looked up to see another cloud of poison a few feet away. A ball of flame was dancing around inside. Then a spear flew through it, and it stilled. On her side of the cloud, a young man with dark hair was crawling toward her. It was the prince.

Wemwi had seen him with Joobel at Blood Mountain a few times. He was an ally and was hit with the poison. The little gnome moved swiftly to him and snapped the clasp of the bracelet around his wrist. She looked around to take in her situation.

The cloud was dissipating. The air clearing before the haze could knockout the other kidnappers. Standing in the middle of the floor was a clear ice statue; it had a fading ball of flame sitting on top its neck. The earth user began to laugh, the sound deep and guttural. His shot had missed after all.

On the floor before him was the strange wielder of fire spirit. The man in red lifted his hand, and a spear of stone flowed up from the floor. He grabbed it and stepped forward. Right as he was about to thrust, a woman landed just in front of him. Joobel spun around, slammed her elbow hard against his nose, then flipped up through the air and landed next to the unconscious Jack.

Tears filled Joobel's eyes, and Wemwi could see she was afraid. She'd thought Joobel was past fear. The Blessed One was the most famous and powerful of the gnomes. If she was scared, what could someone as small as Wemwi hope to accomplish?

Then she heard a whisper behind her. As Bayu stood holding a furious woman in place against the ceiling, he waved a hand. A little box slid towards her, lightly bumping against her leg. The gnome opened it to see look inside.

Wemwi found a long splinter of wood.

***

Maeve didn't understand most words. She knew some hand signs. She knew that 'Maeve' meant 'best dog' and that 'oof get off me' meant 'I enjoy you showing your love by sitting on my lap.' Only Her Boy's first girl could show Maeve pictures. She was the one who smelled of apples and dry leaves. Her Boy's good girl smelled like strawberries and rain.

The first girl had shown pictures of family pups being hurt. Maeve had wanted family, now Maeve had a big family. Her Boy's first girl showed a family in danger. Maeve wasn't afraid of danger. Maeve would save family pups.

Maeve couldn't understand where the room she was looking for was. Now she was forced to use her nose to track everyone. Though the haze of poison didn't hurt her, it did make it hard to track. She moved quickly through each floor, searching for those who needed her.

Good dogs get treats.

Maeve was the very best dog.

***

Tedar turned to see Jack battling two foes next to the wall. The troll struck his last opponent so hard that the man might not live. He quickly focused on his role in the plan and started using his speed to safely move the children away from Jack's fighting.

Just as he finished, he saw the prince go down, and Joobel step in to fight. That couldn't be a good sign. Tedar changed the plan.

The troll rushed from one side just as the winged gnome had jumped away from her impressive strike to the earth's user's nose. Tedar was hit full in the face with the cloud of green-tinged gas. His wrist felt warm as the bracelet did its work. That man was getting annoying.

He slammed into the Spore Weaver and lifted him above his head. The throw was hard enough to shatter the lattice covering the room's high window. A trail of green haze arched after the departing man.

Tedar turned his attention to the earth user just as two barbs of rock slammed into him for the second time. He really didn't like that guy. The troll's vast body was pinned to the wall.

Once again, his world went dark.

***

Generally, Bayu could hold this much weight for hours without much effort. So far today, he'd drained himself several times, gotten a rock to the head, received no small dose of the strange poison, and he really needed to use the bathroom. His anger and exhaustion were getting the best of him.

He watched Jack fall and Joobel's desperate attempt to save them all. Now his troll friend got speared through the chest... again. Bayu decided enough was enough.

Instead of dropping the shield and letting the woman fall, he reversed it and swatted her to the floor like a bug. She didn't move. His energy reserves were dangerously low, but his mood had brought a different power to him. A power that frightened him.

For months now, he could feel the tingle of the storm. Distant clouds called to him. The Tempest moved to stand by Joobel. His eyes were sparking yellow energy as he looked at the man who'd hurt his friends. His rage burned inside him, but his words were even. He almost spoke in a whisper.

"You deserve this."

Some spirits require long practice, others an intense level of control. Bayu wasn't experienced enough to properly wield some of the abilities of a Tempest. This particular skill was fueled by emotion. He was entirely done with today.

The song had drawn out a good deal of emotional baggage. Years of being alone and hungry. He needed to vent his anger and frustration. This formed a rather ominous thundercloud directly above the east wing of the Ornella School of Autumn.

Even with all that built up power, the young student of air was happy to let others finish the fight. Bayu was content to make sure they could interrogate the leader of the band. Events didn't play out that way. He really disliked this man who hit him in the head with a rock.

All that anger and fear came together in his core and reached into the sky, calling the storm that served him. He felt the tingle of that power and reached up as if to grab the storm itself. He formed a fist, jerking it down as if to pull the heavens to earth.

The crash of lightning slammed through the roof of the school and into the man in red. He exploded in a glorious display of smoke and ash. The sound thundered into the space and he staggered at the impact of his own attack.

Bayu had no idea how powerful the lightning would be. He had little control or finesse with his powers. He just threw everything into one shot.

Gray would later tell him that what he did was overkill, like swatting a fly with a predator drone. Jack further explained that Gray was a bit crazy and just to smile and nod when he talked like that.

Either way, the entire roof caved in on the enemy, the children, and everyone else. Bayu looked up to see a layer of ice forming above him. It covered much of the room. Bayu looked to see Jack being held up by Joobel. With a wave of his hand, he used the ice to push rubble aside.

The children were neatly piled against one wall where Tedar had set them to be safe. Jack stumbled over to where the troll was pinned to the wall. A knife of fire cut the barbs holding him in place, and Jack slid the troll to the floor. The wounds began to close as soon as the spears were removed.

Bayu started to smile, but he didn't get to finish. A shadow covered the floor of the classroom. A massive figure landed just below the open hole he'd made. He looked up into the face of a dark red dragon. The echo in his mind hurt his already sore head.

"You've interfered! For that, you must die."

Jack calmly stumbled forward, making no motion to summon power. The prince looked up at the dragon and made a sign with one hand. His words were calm despite the threat before him.

"There's something you should know."

The drake's orange eyes narrowed. "What is that human?"

Jack pointed off to his right. The dragon turned his gaze around just in time to see the red stone hound slam into him. Her momentum pinned him to the wall, her long sharp teeth sank deep into the base of the dragon's neck. The creature roared in fury.

Bayu wasn't sure what Maeve was, but he didn't know she could do this. As powerful as the hound was, she started to falter. The gout of flame that poured over her head forced Bayu to cover his eyes even from this distance.

The hound's head and neck began to turn molten and melt away, the nose and mouth falling back until an orb the size of a large apple was visible.

Jack cried out. "Maeve, no!"

The prince shot a blast of ice at the fire, but the dragon's breath was far too hot. The attack continued as the orb started to change color. Then the dragon froze.

It wasn't from the ice.

**

Wemwi had never spent so much time in complete terror. Magic poison, enemy casters, and her friends were taking a beating. Even the unstoppable prince had been taken down.

She was looking for something that she could do to help. Gnomes were just too small. She knew if she got herself hurt, it would only make things more difficult for those fighting.

Then Bayu had sent her the box. She had no idea what it was for but had little difficulty opening it with her agile fingers. The gnome looked inside and frowned. All it contained was a long bramble. The thorn of hardwood slimmed into a needle-sharp point.

She was about to toss it away, but at her touch, her own inborne earth aspect recoiled. It was pure malice. Wemwi was no stranger to curses. Autumn's gnomes had been the victim of one for many years. The thorn was powerful magic. It was also just her size.

Her first target had been the powerful earth user. She'd been working her way around the room when Bayu lost his temper. The explosion had tossed her near the other students. Her tiny body was stunned by the hard landing. She rose to her feet again just as the dragon arrived.

With most of the roof gone, they had no cover. Most of her allies were either exhausted or down. There was little hope. Wemwi wanted to help but couldn't get to a weak spot in time to stop the attack. The hound bought her precious seconds to act.

As the stone construct pinned the dragon to the far wall, Wemwi moved unnoticed through the path of broken stone and ice. She jumped up and pushed the spike between the flame drake's thick red scales.

The plates were so close together that she couldn't get it between them. The dragon shifted to launch the fire from its mouth. The scales parted slightly, and the gnome heaved. It didn't go in deep, but she felt the curse leave her little lance and flow into the dragon.

Wemwi stumbled and fell away.

***

The drake's orange eyes went wide. From every inch of the thick, red hide sprouted shards of wood. Sharp, angry brambles grew out at odd angles. It barely held the shape of a dragon. In only a few seconds, it looked more like an incredibly dense briar patch.

The hound began to reform while dumping most of the red stone to the floor. Maeve moved to Jack's side and started wagging so hard it shook his leg. The prince smiled and worked hard to convince the hound that she was, in fact, the very best girl.

Bayu stepped forward and kneeled down near the dragon. Joobel joined him, curious at what he was looking at. The tiny form of Wemwi, long hair mostly burned away, crawled to Bayu from the brambles that were recently a dragon.

Her dress was torn and burned, her skin was red and blistered from the heat. Bayu handed her a handkerchief to cover herself with and smiled at his friend.

"I see you found the thorn."

CHAPTER 11

SECOND DAY

Claire almost closed the school down herself after what Jack had so eloquently called 'The Situation.' Only one day in, and she had over eighty students taken hostage, a troll twice dead, one of Norim's wards blew a roof off, her own brother almost died, and Autumn was now home to the world's smallest Dragon Slayer. She'd been biting her nails and wringing her hands when she finally got to talk to Bayu.

Despite everything, all the boy would say was, "I learned a lot today, I'm looking forward to tomorrow."

She simply couldn't handle another Jack! The world couldn't handle another Jack. She was entirely out of Joobels. Though if she Named the little Dragon Slayer....

The Queen of Autumn let out a sigh of frustration. Claire sat alone in the war room. There was so much work to catch up on that she could use the extra time this place provided. The others would join her soon. All things considered; Jack had given her a long list of the spirits that stood out among the students.

Claire was shocked at how much potential they'd been wasting. If nothing else, she needed a way to train and nurture the future. She made a mental note to form a roof replacement budget. There was apparently another Tempest in the air class. It would be a long night. She and Issabol still had items to craft.

The first to join her was Gray. The man was livid this all happened while he'd been making preparations for his trials. It was nice to spend some time with him. Claire was starting to feel he could handle the insane amount of baggage she would come with.

Only a few minutes later, Issabol walked in with Raine and Hurley. The Queen of Winter would need to be informed of the attack, and Claire liked Raine's chief advisor. Jack and Joobel soon entered with Myrin and Norim.

The Queen of Autumn stood and looked to the group. She sighed and forced a wide smile.

"So, our first day was *technically* a success."

***

The queen addressed the entire student body in place of the first class of the next day. Students and teachers sat in neat rows. At least as neatly as they can be when the children varied from the size of a sandwich to that of an ox. The stage beside her held three of the new students.

Claire took a deep breath and spoke, her words entering the minds of everyone present.

"As you know, some foolish brigands thought to attack the children of Autumn on their own land. Seven people and a dragon attempted to use you like a game piece to change our way of life. The last I checked, three of those are still breathing. I doubt they are happy."

There was a restrained chuckle from the crowd. Claire waited a moment before continuing.

"You know that part of the agreement for coming to our new school is to leave violence behind. I have with me three students who broke that rule. I find myself in a difficult position. Should I punish these students... or reward them?"

The room went silent. No one wanted to offend the queen. No one spoke up in case they chose wrong. Finally, a brave sprite flew up, hovering above the crowd.

"The boy of air stopped the poison from our room. He saved us and stayed behind!"

A human stood, adding his own voice. "Tedar, the troll protected us when we were attacked."

An ogre stood proudly. "Your dragon is big!"

Everyone looked at Grob for a long moment. Then a shout of 'pardon' began to rise from the crowd.

Claire smiled; she wanted this to come from the students. It was the first victory of their generation, and it needed to inspire them. Her hands went up, and a hush came over the crowd once again. The words carried with her power; this would be official.

"I Clarissa Ashotok, Queen of Autumn, do pardon Tedar of the Stone Spear Tribe, Bayu of the Blood Keep, and Wemwi of the Sept of Fallen Leaves. They are forgiven the crime of deadly violence within school grounds." She smiled back at them. "Just this once."

The whoops and cheers rose loud from the students for these heroes of Autumn. Again the queen's hands went up. Silence spread throughout as Claire continued.

"That takes care of their crimes, but what of their heroism? These among you risked much to save not only you but the prince and his betrothed. What gift could a ruler bestow to show appreciation for such a deed?"

No one stepped up this time. Standing up for a classmate was one thing; telling a queen the proper reward was another. Claire smiled and held out one hand. Joobel landed gracefully beside her and handed her a long spear.

It was crafted of Autumn's red stone, but its core contained the might of a great sea dragon. Issabol had helped her craft the powerful weapon. Claire looked to the troll.

"Tedar of the Stone Spears, step forward."

The tall, lean troll took only half a step; it wasn't a very big stage. He kneeled before the much shorter woman.

"It is said that one who would lay down their life for a friend is best of us. I'm told you did just that. Twice." Claire chuckled. "I know the dead better than most... I must say you took it pretty well."

He smiled around dark tusks. "Mine are a resilient people."

"Understatement, I think. For your deeds, you're presented with this spear of stone, the namesake of your clan. Even with your impressive strength, you'd be hard-pressed to break it. It's called Tremor." She paused, biting her lower lip. "Oh, it packs quite a punch. Practice with it away from my people and buildings."

Claire turned and shouted, "Now rise, Tedar the Unbreakable, Hero of Autumn!"

The queen lifted the troll's large hand as high as she could. It came up level with his head, but the crowd still cheered. Tedar moved back to his spot, and Claire called up the next student.

"Bayu of the Blood Keep, step forward."

The blonde boy with the crooked nose took two whole steps forward; the stage allowed him plenty of room. He kneeled as a tall, dark man stepped onto the stage. The Wind Walker wore frayed travel clothes and looked tired. His hero stood before him, and Bayu was enthralled.

Gray smiled at him and handed two small bands of purplish metal to the queen. He bowed deeply to Bayu and then stepped away without a word. The queen continued speaking to the crowd as the boy knelt before her.

"Power is a blade with no handle. It can harm both friend and foe. You've been gifted with more power than control, yet you used that gift to protect your fellows and your kingdom. I have no weapon that would make you stronger, nor would I give you one if I did."

Claire paused and glanced at the roof of the large room as if worried it might explode.

"I offer you control. Your adopted mother has the power to bring calm to those close to her. I took the liberty to have that power woven into these bracelets. While wearing one, you'll find your emotions are calmer and your power more precise. Also... my buildings will be less at risk."

Bayu looked at the gift and paused. He seemed honored but confused. Before he could ask, Claire leaned down and whispered.

"I'm told another Tempest is walking around just waiting to blow something up. Don't you think the second band would make a lovely gift?"

Bayu broke into a wide grin as his queen stood and proclaimed, "Rise Bayu Stormcloud, Hero of Autumn!"

Claire lifted the boy's hand. This time she was a bit taller than the student she honored. The crowd cheered. Bayu moved back to his spot, and Claire called up the last student.

"Wemwi of the Sept of Fallen Leaves, step forward."

It took well over a dozen steps for the little gnome to move to the front of the stage; the platform was huge. She now wore a white dress with blue flowers. Her short brown hair had the burns trimmed away and was now styled in a bob cut.

She was shocked as her queen moved to sit cross-legged before her, the old sign of respect for the smaller races. It was something done for a sept leader, not a mere girl. Her eyes began to tear. Claire's words were no less audible for her position.

"It's easy to be brave when you wield power. To enter a battle with a strong arm or a powerful spirit. It's much harder when you don't hold a Tempest's lightning or the hulking body of a troll. You stood with them anyway. In the end, it was you who saved all. I'm told you slew a rogue fire drake?"

Wemwi was overwhelmed by the sentiment. She didn't feel worthy of this moment and the attention of the queen. The gnome wiped her cheeks and met Claire's gaze.

"I only did what I could to help my friends and kingdom. No gnome would do any less."

Claire smiled at this; the girl lifted up her race by crediting her nature. She'd make a good diplomat someday. For now, the gnome deserved to be young.

"I don't doubt your words. Yet it was you who did the deed, and it is you who will receive the reward. Kneel Wemwi."

The gnome did so, and Jack stepped up to the stage. The prince wasn't known for words; he spoke with purpose or not at all. Jack never addressed a crowd. He had Claire and Joobel for that. Yet he was impressed by someone who should be so weak but did something he hadn't.

Maeve had defeated a dragon once, as had Depth on accident. Most dragons were not to be harmed, having an essential role in the kingdoms they served. The fire drake had invaded another realm and threatened innocents. The old magic allowed execution with no threat of reprisal.

Jack stood on stage in front of the gnome, turned in military fashion, and gave a deep bow. His words were few but carried significant meaning.

"You have my respect... Dragon Slayer."

Then the prince handed a small box to the queen and gave a nod of acknowledgment to both Tedar and Bayu. They had fought by his side and were given a warrior's esteem. He walked off the stage and out of the room.

Claire opened the box. Tedar's gift had been a natural choice, and Bayu's had been a necessity. The queen had thought hard about what to make for the gnome. Despite her great act of courage, she'd never be a warrior.

No one would command one such as her to the front lines. She needed people like Wemwi, though. With the changes to the kingdom came the need for talented people to help manage the society she was building. This girl had potential.

She pinched a small dagger made of the same purplish gleaming metal that made up the bracelets and the core of the spear. A similar construct sat near her own breastbone. It was a source of power when she was away from home.

The knife was housed in a sheath that had the same properties as another scabbard. One that had been made for another blade. The dagger was infused with the remnants of the spores that had been used against them. The smallest wound would bring deep sleep.

"I present to you a weapon of my own making. The properties I will discuss privately, as it is a statecraft tool, something to protect yourself when others aren't able. I present this to you on behalf of a grateful kingdom. I call it Thorn. Rise Wemwi Dragon Slayer!"

The students stood and cheered. Both Tedar and Bayu walked up to congratulate the gnome. Tedar set a hand down so she could climb up and be lifted high. She could just hear Bayu's whisper to the troll.

"You're now free to use any of the books in the Keep. It seems they're being moved to the school. We're going to have a library."

The troll smiled wide. Claire nodded her approval and let the moment linger. At the proper time, she subtly cleared her throat. Her power lifted her final words to all present.

"Ok... we're done. Now get to class. There will be no more pardons today!"

The students filed away to continue their voyage into this thing called education.

END

TRANSFER STUDENT

STUDENT

The Rise of Fall – Book 3.5

WRITTEN BY

Jeremy Graves

CHAPTER 1

The desert sun crept just below the horizon to the west. The air was already beginning to cool as a musical voice rang out from their shared bed.

"Won't you tell us a story?"

Kila had to make one more attempt. Jari rolled her bright aquamarine eyes at what must have been her sister's twentieth effort to delay bedtime. She never saw the point in dragging out the ritual. You were going to sleep about the same amount either way. Still, she wasn't going to say no to a story should Mother give in.

Kamini smiled as she chided her daughters but, as she often did, stretched out the time the three would spend together. She moved her hands to describe the scene of the tale she began to tell.

"In the desert we live in, there was once a little girl—"

Kila's face brightened. "Was it me, Mother?"

Kamini shook her head. "No sweetie, this was long ago—"

The girl's head tilted. "Was it you?"

Kamini rolled her eyes and smiled. "No, it wasn't me and no more questions, dear. Now, this little girl loved to run and play near the southern oasis. She often came upon the animals that would come to drink the crystal waters."

Mother made a plodding motion with her hands as she described the first creature.

"One day, she met a large creature who looked like a rock, but when she sat on it, it shook her off into the sand. It looked down and said, 'Not all is as it appears!'"

Kila chuckled at Mother's attempt to make a deep voice. Now the woman made one hand hop around on top of the other.

"Then one day the girl found a cactus, but when she got close, it spit blood at her face. Hopping away, it said, 'Not all is as it appears!'"

Then she moved her hand in a waving motion. Her pitch lowered as her voice slowed, and she leaned down and spoke in a hissing whisper.

"Then one day... the little girl found a stick... and she reached down and grabbed it!" Kila squeaked as her mother rushed forward. "Then... it... kissed her on the nose!"

Kamini grabbed the younger sister and planted wet kisses on the girl's face. Giggles rose up as Kila was tickled, and even Jari had to laugh at the trick. Now thoroughly exhausted, both girls were soon tucked under the thick woven blankets.

The hut was made from dried clay bricks and would reflect much of the desert heat throughout the day. The stone held some of that warmth even as the sun dropped below the horizon. Still, the sisters would snuggle up to stay cozy. The desert nights were cold.

The village lay on the hills overlooking the oasis. In the sands of the desert, nothing held value like water. This was one of the few places that people could survive for any length of time. The family was blessed in that both parents held spirits strong in the aspect of renewal.

Mother was a renowned healer, and people would travel the sands to seek her aid. Father was a Beast Speaker and could communicate with the creatures of the land. The village could fend off sickness, and no one had been hurt by viper or scorpion in many years.

There was only a tiny bit of distant light trickling in from the campfires outside. The high window faced out to where the adults would gather. Wood was scarce enough that the flames were kept low. Much of the cooking was done by a woman who lived just down the hill. Her aspect of fire was strong in this land.

Jari was just drifting off to sleep when a musical snore rolled out of her sister. A moment later, Kila's small brown foot found its way next to her face. Jari was almost fifteen now and hoped to talk her parents into getting her own bed soon.

Kila was eleven and still had dreams that sometimes required someone to calm her. After Jari pushed the foot back down and rolled her sister into something resembling a normal position, she got comfortable once again.

She'd almost drifted to sleep when she heard the shouting. It was distant. Tall black ears shimmered out of her raven hair and flicked toward the sound. Screaming, perhaps on the edge of the village.

Jari slid out from under the blankets and slipped her nightgown to the floor. Her lean form shimmered and, in her place, stood a very large, gangly-looking feline. Caracals weren't the largest of cats, but a Fawnin's size is based on the size of the human that's transforming. Jari wasn't a large girl, but she made for a big cat.

The fur of most of her body was a toasted brown. Her well-shaped face was cream-colored at the chin with black stripes leading from an ebony nose to her large aquamarine eyes. The true mark of the caracal was the ears. They were large and stood high off her head, black as shadows, with long tufts of hair that aimed straight up as if reaching to the sky.

She wasn't supposed to leave the hut after bedtime. The village was mostly safe, but there were rumors of raids taking place just to the south. Bandits would sometimes even try to hit the homes on the edge of the community.

Curiosity and cats are often grouped together, and Jari was no exception. Besides, it was only an issue if she got caught; it hadn't happened yet.

She retracted her long curved claws on both her front and back feet. They were useful for climbing, but there were few places she couldn't just jump to in a town where everything was one story tall.

A silent leap carried her to the high window, then another out into the dark night. The fires had burned low. She was confused that there was no one sitting around them.

The chill of the night air was already trying to push into her brown fur. Few would linger away from warm beds or flickering flames. Large black ears ticked back and forth, listening, waiting. Another shout. Sounds of fighting.

She hopped lightly onto a nearby roof. It was nothing compared to the heights she was capable of. Caracals could leap high enough to hunt birds from the sky. The clay tile roof felt warm on the pads of her paws, the last reminder of the blazing sun that had passed over the horizon. From rooftop to rooftop she moved, silent as a whisper and alert as a nervous cat.

It was on the south end of the village she saw her world fall to ruin. Jari watched as both the men and women of the village fought a raiding party. The dark greens of their clothes and spirited wooden weapons would mean Summer most likely.

The raiders would usually capture any they could take alive. What they wanted most were the children. Those who couldn't remember freedom were less likely to fight for it.

Her paws moved like arrows in flight, leaping and dashing, running to find her father and mother. They'd gone with the other adults to sit in the firelight and discuss trade and work. Now both would be helping defend their home.

The roar of challenge rolled across the sands and echoed between the clay walls of the houses. A minotaur stood head and shoulders above the man who was wielding a spear of shaped clay, the man's earth aspect pulsing in the weapon.

The point struck the colossal challenger's armored chest, but it left no mark on the thick bronze. The flat of the minotaur's ax swatted the man to the ground. He didn't get back up.

Jari looked around, but the chaos made seeing her parents like trying to find a single grain of sand. Most of the men and women here shared the dark hair and eyes, as well as the deep brown skin of her people. She was one of the few who stood out, her eyes a bright aquamarine no matter what form she took.

Again it was those large ears that served her well. She heard her father's voice to the left, just past the woman using her fire for something other than cooking.

He was holding off four men. The ground and sky were filled with creatures answering his call. Vipers whipped across the sands and struck at the legs of the raiders. Small owls clawed at eyes while scorpions scampered up armored legs.

He held a long copper dagger and darted in and out of the fray, adding his own efforts to the attack. Jari shifted back to her two-legged form as she landed beside him. She worried little for her nakedness, only for the man she loved so dearly.

Her hands ended in long claws, and her ears and tail remained visible. The gifts of the cat weren't to be ignored. Her long tail added balance and the ears twitched to let her hear in every direction. The claws were for something else.

The thrust of the spear meant for her father's side was tossed away as she leaped at the raider. Long claws raked his face, and he was blinded in one eye. She hopped back and the wide swing swept by her head. He started to attack again as a scorpion stung him in the neck.

She felt a firm hand on her arm as she was swung around. His eyes held love and fear as they met hers. Father's words would haunt her.

"Jari! You shouldn't be here!"

Jari didn't understand. She was strong, her power so similar to the pride of the royal family of Spring! She shouldn't cower in the shadows while they fought for her home.

"I came to help, Father! I want to—"

His slap tore across her face. The tears in her father's eyes told her that he wasn't angry, but afraid. Terrified for her and for Kila. He rushed his words as he eyed the fight around him, animals still coming to his call.

"Look around us, Marjaria! We cannot win. They've almost two hundred fighters, and we've less than half that, most far from warriors. You must take Kokila and run from this place. Keep her safe; she mustn't be taken!"

Tear began to run down her cheeks. "But Father, I—"

He grabbed her shoulders and shook hard. "Promise me, Jari!"

Her heart broke. She knew he would stay. Her father and the others would buy time, and they would pay with their lives or freedom.

It was up to her. Her large aquamarine eyes shed more tears as Jari knew she would make the promise. He was right. Even now, the lines were falling. She hugged him tightly.

"I promise, Father. I will make you proud."

He wiped his eyes and turned back to the battle. "I have always been proud of you. Now go!"

His back was to her now. One hand sent a swarm of hornets into the face of a raider while he parried a spear with his dagger. Her naked body shimmered as she took to her caracal form once again.

Her claws ripped at the hard clay of the rooftops as she ran. Jari never found her mother and might never see her father again. As she skidded across the roof next to her own hut, she let her momentum carry her off the edge. Her coiled feline legs hit the ground in a bounce that launched her straight through the open window.

She had to get Kila out of the village.

***

Jari landed on human feet and grabbed the blankets, tearing them from her sister. The younger girl groaned and whimpered before falling back into a musical snore. Jari grabbed Kila's brown foot and slid it toward her as she pinched the leg above it.

"Ouuuch! What's that—"

Kila wasn't a stupid girl. The picture of Jari quickly pulling on clothes, with cat ears and tail still out, told her to panic. She rolled out of bed and began to pull her own clothes on. Jari explained what she could.

"Raiders are in the village. Most of the adults are holding them off, but we need to hurry."

Kila trembled, her voice squeaking. "What about Mother and Father?"

Jari only shook her head. "We'll try to find them later. For now, we must get moving. Bring the sand shroud. We'll need it."

The shroud was a large blanket woven by a weaver in the village with the earth aspect. When laid out on the sand, it would blend in, allowing a person to hide in the open. All families had one, a testament to the dangers their people faced.

Both girls quickly threw some clothes and travel food into a bag. Jari would carry it unless she needed to shift. Her spirit did much to fuel strength and endurance.

They rushed out the door, and instantly raiders were running after them. Even with the heavy bag and a slow-moving sister, Jari gained ground as she dragged Kila along, weaving through the houses. She wasn't heading north. The enemy would likely have people waiting to ambush those who ran straight from the fighting to the south.

To the west was weeks of travel with little to no water, not to mention the sand squids and burrow worms. Jari might have a chance alone, but Kila would never make that journey.

Their aspects were both of renewal; Spring would make them both stronger. Perhaps they could make a home there. Kila's spirit was in high demand in Spring's military.

They moved to the east. Twice more, the raiders spotted the two girls in a full run out of the village. Jari was pushing her strides to the edge of endurance. The claws extended on her feet gave her purchase on the smooth clay bricks of the path.

As they reached the edge of town, her eyes began to meld to those of her caracal. Her vision lost color but allowed her to see in the pitch-black night. There were raiders here too, but they were fewer. She could fight a few.

Fawnin weren't so uncommon that she was one of a kind. It was a spirit ability that allowed an animal form and was held by several hundred every generation. It was uncommon to have a spirit as strong as hers with a predator form. Most received the shape of creatures like bulls or goats. Jari thought of the minotaur and shuddered. Those were something else altogether.

Her father knew she was special and had trained her for years. Her body was a weapon, claws her swords, and teeth her daggers. Jari could move at speeds few could even track. It was this speed that allowed her to use the tactic her mother had her practice with Kila.

As they left the torchlight near the village, she slung off the pack and set it on the ground. Kila lay down beside it and pulled the shroud over her and the bag, pushing herself low and blending into the desert sands. To Jari's cat eyes, it was a poor disguise. To her human ones, Kila was all but invisible.

Without a sister to worry about, she could clear a path. This time she kept her hybrid form, taking the claws, ears, and caracal tail while maintaining a generally human shape. She would need clothes later, and they would fall off her cat form.

Jari darted to her right, blending into shadows and moving as quickly as her powered legs could carry her. The posted raiders were looking in her sister's direction but seemed confused as to where she went. As she flew past them, razor claws severed the tendons just below the knees on all four of the enemies.

They'd stood facing the village, and she had no trouble sneaking behind them. It took her only a few seconds. The last was cut just as the first cried out.

A talented healer might fix the damage. Her mother could have done so. But healers that powerful were expensive.

Maybe it will eat into the profits of selling our people, Jari thought darkly.

The screams from the raiders blended into the sounds of fighting to the south. The heat of the battle was now fading as most had been killed or subdued. Jari never slowed as she dashed back to her sister, seeing the shroud from a good way off with feline eyes.

Kila was crying, but she instantly stood and followed. Jari moved them swiftly, once again holding the heavy bag of supplies. They ran for their lives.

The pair were deep into the sands of the desert when they stopped to allow Kila to rest. Jari set down the pack and moved to scout a perimeter.

As she returned, the two of them looked at the faint glow of their distant village, the only home they'd ever known. A place where their parents and friends still remained.

"I will... get them back. The raiders will pay for this night... I swear it!"

Jari was speaking to herself, an oath to repay the blood debt created with the destruction of her home. Kila's voice held none of the resolve and little of the anger. Her words carried grief and longing.

"I just want them back."

Her father's words echoed in her mind.

'Keep her safe; she must not be taken.'

Jari had another oath to keep. This one was more urgent.

As cold as night travel in the desert is, it is much preferred to the day's heat. Kila had wrapped up in the sand shroud as they moved swiftly across the dunes. After only two hours, the younger girl faded, having only had a scant half-hour sleep. Her young body wasn't able to keep pace.

Jari could go three days without sleep if she had to and didn't want to be caught in the open when the sun rose. Her pack was strapped to the front of her torso as she had Kila wrap arms around her neck and legs around her waist. She tied the light tan shroud around the younger girl to help hold her in place. Jari took off at a quick run.

Soon her smooth lope through the sands was accompanied by Kila's rhythmic snores. At least her foot wasn't in Jari's face this time. Even with the pack and her sibling's weight, the older sister ran faster than most could unhindered.

As the sun began to rise, cat eyes could make out dark-brown mountains. They would need to pass through them to leave the desert. She pictured her father's map in her mind.

Once past the rocky hills, they would enter the eastern Mountain Wyld. If they moved at night and weren't seen, they could avoid most of the area's dangers. Then they would pass through the far end and into the kingdom of Spring.

Even in the dim light of morning, she could feel the sand under her feet beginning to warm. Soon it would burn her soles, and the warm air would drain the moisture from her body.

Jari drew the edge of the tan shroud over her head and kept up the quick pace. The ground grew uncomfortable just as she reached the brown stone of the mountains. It would be simple to climb directly over the dark rock of the cliffs. Sadly, it would be dangerous for Kila to try.

She moved south along the ridgeline until she spotted an overhang. Jari stepped inside, out of the bright sun, and far enough down to find cooler air.

There could be no fire. Smoke would attract unwanted attention. Instead, she opened the pack and pulled out a strip of dried meat. She liked other foods, but her predator wanted to eat several meat servings per day. That same predator was hungry from the recent exertions.

The distance to the village would have taken a group of provisioned travelers two full days. They would have needed a shaded camp during the day and swift travel at night. She'd made the trip in part of one night, carrying both the provisions and her sister. Despite her stamina, Jari was growing sleepy.

She finished the meat and moved to where Kila still dozed on the hard stone. She wrapped her arms around the girl and pulled the shroud around them both. The exhaustion and emotion she'd held back caught up to her. As Jari wept quietly, she held her precious little sister tight.

For once, she was grateful to not sleep alone.

***

Kila was able to sleep for several hours before Jari had gotten to lie down. It was no surprise she woke up first. Jari jumped from her makeshift pallet and ran toward the opening of the cliffs. She didn't need to go far.

Her little sister sat in the shade at the edge of their shelter, looking out at the ocean of light brown sand. Dunes formed just to the north. The sloping hills seemed to go on forever to the west.

Jari moved to sit next to the girl, her strong arms wrapping around Kila's slim shoulders. Her younger sister asked the question she'd been dreading.

"Do you think we will ever see them again?"

Logic told her no; if either of their parents survived, they would be prized by their captors. Father's skills were exceedingly rare. Beast Speakers were much less common than Fawnin, perhaps even unique. Her mother's abilities weren't as rare but just as prized.

There was no scenario Jari could think of where they would be rescued, even if she could find them. These were thoughts she couldn't share with Kila. The girl was already heartbroken. Her attempt at deflection fooled no one.

"Little sister, we see them every time we glance into a pool of water. I'm looking at our mother even now. We're their legacy."

The younger girl sniffed but didn't cry. By the looks of her puffy eyes and streaked cheeks, Kila had wept all she was able. Now she just sat coping with her new reality. Jari almost sobbed on her behalf as the child spoke again.

"Father will make a poor slave. He's proud and a leader. They have grabbed a viper but left enough of the neck free for it to turn and strike."

Jari nodded as she thought of the man. He wasn't tall or brawny, but he was so very strong. Father changed the air when he entered a room. She missed him already and tried to change the subject.

"Have you been practicing your power?"

The younger girl turned to meet her eyes. She really was the image of their mother, with soft round features and long, silky black hair. As Kila's dark-brown eyes met the aquamarine of her own, Jari almost felt as if she was with the dear woman once again.

A sound began to move through the air. It flowed slow and thick, like honey slowly sliding into her ears. Sweetness poured into her mind. She felt relaxed, at peace.

Jari fought the temptation to lie down on the stone and sleep. She tried to move her limbs, but the signal was lost before it passed through her thoughts. She was frozen, unable to move or act.

Then as smoothly as it began, the song started to change. The melody shifted, and the tones became harsher as the tempo sped up. Now she could move, and she felt strong. Energy flowed from the very air and into her core.

She wanted to shift, to wield claw and fang! To fight and hunt! The predator inside her needed to kill. Then once again, the song transformed.

Now she felt the soreness from her night's exertions leave her limbs. The stiffness in her neck and shoulders earned by carrying her sister long hours left her. Then the sound faded into the breeze. The little girl who sang the tune was once again looking into the distance, toward the home she couldn't return to.

Jari gave a strained smile. "Well, that's an answer. You're getting much stronger. Mother has been teaching you to flex your core, I see?"

The younger girl nodded, a hand moving up to just below her neck. The mention of her mother brought pain again. Jari cursed herself for the reminder. Kila really was getting stronger, though.

Sirens were exceedingly rare. Most were born to strong parents who were both of the aspect of renewal. Sirens themselves weren't powerful in the sense that they could fight or kill. Yet having one in a group allowed others to fight enemies who were confused or paralyzed.

Kila could heal minor aches and injuries constantly. She could strengthen the flow of power to all who could hear the call. There were other songs as well, powers you shouldn't teach a child. Kila was a prize that any slaver would've killed for. The single girl would have been worth more than the entire rest of the village combined.

Her abilities were kept a secret from all except a few close friends and her own family. Jari knew why her father wanted the younger child far away from the raiders. One like her would've been doomed to the battlefield, a tool for those who enslaved her.

Jari wouldn't let that happen. Kila might be weak in a fight, but her older sister was not. She'd protect the girl with her life. When her sister came of age, she could sign on with the Spring military. Kila could have her pick of assignments and live well. Jari just needed to keep her safe for a few years, then they could rebuild their lives.

She glanced out at the sky; the sun was past its peak. There would be less than half a day of light. Travel with her sister would be safer with daylight for now. The heat of the sands was behind them. She stood and gave her orders.

"Eat a bit and pack up. We need to get moving so we can let you walk during the day."

Kila nodded and obeyed. Mother often left Jari in charge, and the two were accustomed to the dynamic. Jari moved off to one side and answered nature's call before returning to grab a bit more of the meat and dark bread.

Jari folded the shroud and put it in the pack. Sifting through the sack, she pulled out some sandals and a ribbon for herself. The biggest challenge as she saw it was the fact that they were two young girls traveling alone.

While not helpless, anyone who saw them would assume they were. Appearing weak would bring trouble. Jari thought up the lie as she laced the sandals to her feet and pulled the ribbon into a bow.

They were sisters traveling with their father, who was hunting in the Wyld. That would explain why they were alone but let others know help was just around the corner. Of course, large animals wouldn't care and might attack outright. Best to avoid encounters. If forced, her claws would make it clear they weren't easy prey.

Again Jari carried all the supplies so that Kila wouldn't tire out as quickly. They had a sparking stone and could start a fire, but the weather was warm, and other than cooking, it would be unwise. Daytime fire could be seen for miles.

They moved along the hot stone of the cliffs. This close to the sands still made for warm travel. It would be less safe in the dark. If Kila slipped and cut herself on the jagged rocks, they would have no good way to treat her.

The pace was painfully slow, but it was only a few hours before they saw the pass. The air around Jari's head shimmered as her caracal ears formed again. Tall black tufts reached high above her raven hair. The large ears twitched in various directions, searching for danger.

Jari could hear a mouse scampering in its burrow several inches below the soil. A large bird was feeding hatchlings in a nest far up and to her left. A snake rustled some dry grass a few paces ahead.

A few people were bustling around in an outpost within the pass. The maps hadn't shown any type of settlement. Her body went rigid as she considered the safest way to get across. They could try to climb the rocks, they could sneak by in the darkness, they could—

"Hello, girls. It's not safe to wander away from the perimeter."

Jari almost jumped to the sky. How could someone have gotten so close? The man was tall, broad, and had the most enormous mustache she'd ever seen.

A pressure at her side told her Kila was intimidated. Jari looked the man up and down, seeing eight ways to kill him. She narrowed it down to a slice through his throat or claw across his gut.

Then he disarmed her.

CHAPTER 2

J ari didn't really use standard weapons. Her tools of battle couldn't be taken away, but his smile was wide, and his blue eyes were kind. He continued speaking in hopes of one of them answering.

"I gotta be honest, those ears are about the best thing I've seen in a while. Haven't seen a Fawnin pass through in some time. Cat or bear, I should think."

Jari looked him up and down again. His clothes were worn but mostly clean, and he sported a leather vest and a wide-brimmed hat. A slice to the throat could muffle his scream.... She told the lie she'd chosen earlier.

"We're traveling with our father. He's hunting nearby. We can just wait for him here."

The man's eyes twinkled, and he looked around with clear doubts.

"Well, if it were me and I had two pretty gals to be watching over, I wouldn't be wandering around without them. Slavers are passing through in all directions."

The man looked meaningfully to Kila before shifting his gaze back to Jari.

"I'm going to throw out an idea. If yah find it to your liking, then just nod. See, I know of a raid that was heading through the desert a few days ago. Don't care much for the practice myself. I sell rare herbs, and the Wylds is where yeh be finding them."

He looked around again and then leaned down to lower his voice.

"Now, should yah need to pass through this area and need to keep from drawing attention, yah are welcome to travel with me as far as Spring's border. I'm a terrible cook who's willing to share. Most around here know me well enough to not go botherin. Name's Kurch."

Jari listened to the words. Her caracal ears shimmered back into her head, and she retracted her claws. His heart rate hadn't sped up. He was either telling the truth or what he believed it to be. She pondered whether the man was so evil he could speak lies with no change.

Options were limited, and Kila would need to rest soon. Jari sighed inwardly and held up a finger. A long claw slid out as she pointed to herself.

"Jari... and this is Kila. We will accept your offer, though we have our own provisions. We simply wish to pass through without incident. I accept your words but be aware that any attempt to harm either of us will end in blood. I will kill any who try to take my sister." Her eyes shifted to slits. "It will hurt while I'm doing it."

The claw slid back in, and the man's eyes went wide for only a moment before he smiled once again.

"Now then, I'd say this will be interesting if nothing else. For now, just walk with me, two steps behind and off to one side. You're Kurch's nieces, on my wife's side. No one would believe you're my daughters with my lighter skin. I have a tent up ahead. You two can use it if yah like. It's not supposed to rain, and I don't mind the stars."

Jari listened as the man went on and on. The best place to find the spice bulbs in the south. The best time to look for the herbs that grow on the mountains and his favorite color of tree bark. By the spirits, the man never stopped!

They reached his small campsite in only a few minutes. On the side of the tent and on a board hammered into the dirt was a symbol. It was a leaf that had well-defined veins, all leading down to the stem.

Jari pointed at the sign as they approached. "What's the symbol?"

Kurch rubbed his chin and nodded. "It's the symbol of someone under contract with the royal court of Summer. In my case, it's with the kitchens of the Arborium. There's a princess there who's one of my biggest buyers. Displaying that means that few would try to harass or rob me and that raiders need to steer clear."

Jari's eyes narrowed. "Summer is evil. They attack and enslave people. You would sell to them?"

Kurch laughed a hearty sound that made her feel at ease, despite the hair on her neck still standing at attention. He shook his head.

"Sorry... I'm not trying to disagree. Far as I can tell, all the kingdoms are evil. Summer is grabbing anyone who isn't protected to work the mines or fill the armies' ranks. Winter's new queen stabbed her own sister in the heart and called up monsters to help her do it. Spring's king lives in luxury while half his people starve."

Jari waited for a moment, then tilted her head. "That's three kingdoms. What of the fourth?"

Kurch rolled his eyes as if she were crazy. "Autumn's Queen turned her own dragon into a zombie. I heard she eats babies and then raises the bones to entertain herself. The prince is said to be ten feet tall and half-demon. I do business with Summer because I have to make a living. I won't even set foot in Autumn."

Jari listened to his words. Her cat ears were often used to listen to the stories around the night fires. If she didn't leave her bed, no rules were broken.

Stories told of all these rumors and more. Well, not all. The zombie dragon was a new one. A shiver ran up her spine as she looked at the symbol and then back to the man.

"You knew where we came from, didn't you?"

Kurch nodded. "I hoped some would get away. Summer is getting desperate. Normally they wouldn't have gone so far north as the deserts. I heard rumors that there was a Siren near the southern oasis. The bounty in Summer for a young one is insane."

Kila squeezed tight against her arm. Jari only flinched slightly, then lied to cover her reaction.

"The Siren was a friend of mine. She headed west. I don't know if she made it out. I'm Fawnin, as you guessed. My sister has Healing, though she's weak and not well trained. We hope to make it to Spring and try our luck there."

Kurch nodded, seeming to see the logic in that.

"I was watching for any who might have made it out. I can't do much for people, but this symbol lets me help one or two on occasion. Yah let people know you're with me, and ya'll be left alone as far as the Spring border. Now, I'm going to see if my stew is done. Either of you want some?"

Again she felt Kila squeeze her arm. The girl very much preferred a warm meal to the provisions in the pack. Jari sighed; this could still be a trap. Her compromise gave her sister a tiny bit of joy. That, in turn, gave her some as well.

"I prefer my own food, but if you allow a bowl for Kila, we will share some stone bread for you to have with yours."

Kurch grinned. "Well now, that sounds fine and fair to me. I see yah're cautious." He gave her a knowing smile. "Making sure if I drugged the soup, the fighter would still be fit. I won't try to talk yah out of good sense. Yah're right not to trust."

He scooped two bowls of the thick liquid and set both before the younger girl.

"Yah pick one. I'll take the first bite of the other."

Kila chose at random, and true to his word, the man took a big bite of his without hesitation. Kurch then realized he'd failed to blow on it. He quickly drank from his canteen to soothe his scorched tongue. Her sister laughed at the antics, and Jari felt a bit of hope run through her. Perhaps her sister would find happiness again someday.

She sat next to Kila and pulled out two small loaves of stone bread. Handing one to the man, she tore the other in half for Kila. She ate another of the strips of dried meat and some toasted sand crickets. Kurch tried not to cringe, but the crunch made him shudder.

Jari grinned at his discomfort. "You're not the first to act as if these are so terrible. Have you ever tried one?"

She held a cricket to the man. He paused for only a moment before, to his credit, he reached out and took it. Kurch looked it over for a moment and popped the insect into his mouth. At first, the crunch seemed to make him go pale.

After a moment, he nodded. "Tastes kinda like smoked nuts. They aren't bad. I hope I didn't offend."

Jari let her fangs slide out just a bit. "If I'd been offended, you'd be dead already."

Kurch seemed to flinch, then winced as he moved one shoulder. Perhaps an old injury. The air around the small camp grew silent as she let the words hang for long moments. Then she gave the man her best smile.

He let out the breath he'd been holding and then paused again before saying, "Yah know... the smile would've been more effective if yah didn't still have the fangs out."

Jari let her teeth recede back into her mouth. The ability to control different aspects of her caracal form were hard-earned. Months of practice were needed just to be able to work only her claws.

Now she could mix and match however best suited her. The man had recognized her as a Fawnin. He might also realize she was a powerful one.

In the end, she accepted his offer for the two girls to use the tent. The night would still be cold, and some privacy would make both sisters feel more at ease.

Kurch seemed to respect her caution, never trying to talk her out of the protectiveness she showed toward Kila or her insistence on being in control. They slept soundly that night.

Jari only woke up when someone walked too close to the small camp or when Kurch got up to relieve himself. Her caracal ears heard all, and she was ever alert. Yet the night blessed them with peaceful rest.

The morning wasn't so kind.

***

Jari had to admit that the mustached man had been true to his word so far. The night passed without incident. No one tried to bother her or her sister. Kurch had packed up his things and paid the fee for his campsite to the outpost guards. Having a night's rest with someone else keeping watch wasn't without value.

Kurch had a small donkey and cart. Soon all was ready for travel. Kila spoke for the first time since they'd arrived as he was hitching up the animal.

"So... what's his name?"

"She..." Kurch gave Kila a wink. "...is named Callie."

Kila grinned, stroking Callie's gray fur. "I always wanted a horse."

Despite his offer to stow her supplies on the cart, Jari decided it best to keep them with her. Again he made no complaint to her precautions. He may also have been aware the burden was no concern to her. She could have pulled the cart with no real effort.

They made their way onto the main path when a group of men came past. They were all mounted on striders. The large flightless birds were quite comfortable in the desert as well as the jungles of their home. Jari kept her head down, but one of the men spotted Kila.

"Ho! You there! Where did you come across these wenches?"

Jari watched in astonishment as Kurch leaped up, his fist collided with the face of the man. The punch removed the fellow from his bird and left him on the ground without air in his lungs. The mustached man was screaming as he put a boot to the raider's throat.

"The spirits gave my wife one sister! One! Yah would call her daughters wenches right to my face? I should skin yah here and now!"

There was the scrape of metal as Kurch whipped out a long bronze dagger and held it out. The other two men pulled their own weapons and moved to flank the man. Jari looked at Kurch. He met her eyes and shook his head slightly. The man didn't want her to interfere. As the first of the men started to move to attack, the other saw the cart's symbol.

"Hold on! He's under contract for the queen. Kill him, and you will just as likely end up dead yourself." The raider held up his hands and spoke to Kurch. "What do you sell? Silks?"

Kurch removed his foot from the first man's throat and then backed up three steps. He sheathed the dagger as he spoke.

"Spices. I've a delivery to the Spring outpost at Tuethna and then am heading south to Summer. I'm teaching my nieces my trade. Both of their parents are soldiers in Summer's military."

The first man finally got enough air in him to get back on his strider. The raider gritted his teeth and spoke in a tone that said he didn't mean his words.

"Sorry I disrespected your kin. We're looking for a girl of the desert tribes with dark hair and eyes just like her. Seems one of the villages was hiding a Siren."

The only reason the raiders didn't see Kila almost fall off the cart was Kurch's move to stand in front of her. He waved his hat as he acted shocked.

"Seriously? A real Siren was born out in the blasted desert? What's one of those worth now?"

The raiders looked at each other for a moment, then began to move off toward the other end of the pass.

"To the Summer Queen... more than our lives are worth," one chuckled grimly as they walked by.

Kurch went on like nothing had happened, leading Callie down the path and dusting off his trousers. Jari moved next to him, her voice low.

"Why did you attack them? I've been called far worse and not acted so."

Kurch looked around out of the corners of his eyes. When he saw they weren't to be overheard, he responded.

"If I'd acted meek, they would've pushed. A closer inspection would've made it hard to convince anyone we were kin. Even if yah aren't who they're looking for, a Healer and a Fawnin are worth more than my spices. When I punched him, they stopped looking at her..." he gestured at Kila, "and started watching me."

Jari was going to be painfully slow to trust anyone, but this man had earned a bit by risking his life for the sake of her little sister. The path carried them to a waypoint, a small gate opening to allow them through the pass.

Despite her fears of the Wyld, they traveled close to a week without another incident. She never left her sister's side during that time. Unfortunately, the food they'd brought was running low. It was time to help earn their keep.

It was time for her to hunt.

***

Her cat form would have more success at night. As Kila moved into the tent to change clothes, Jari sat in front of Kurch. She allowed enough teeth to show to remind him of what she was willing to do. Her words were a bit more kind.

"You've been good to your word, and I thank you. I have seen your food stores, and you cannot afford to feed yourself and us. If you can get a fire going, I will bring us back dinner."

He tilted his head. "Wait, what do yah mean—"

There was a shimmer in the air around Jari. A large cat stepped out of her clothes. Kila stepped out of the tent and walked over to pick up and fold her clothing as the caracal padded off into the night.

As she left the little camp, she could hear the man ask her sister, "Does she do that often?"

Kila giggled. "Yup."

Black ears flicked back and forth. Jari stretched her limbs. It had been too long since she'd used her caracal form; her ears seemed to grow stiff. Long dark claws extended and then retracted. A long yawn flashed her sharp teeth in the dim twilight.

Her aquamarine eyes peered through the darkness falling over the land as her ebony nose sniffed the air. The area was mostly quiet. She could've made a meal out of any of a dozen creatures.

Jari learned she could eat as a cat and be fine as long as she stayed a cat for a couple of hours afterward. If she were to consume a snake and shift back too soon, her human digestion would be displeased. She'd made that mistake once. She wouldn't do so a second time.

It only took a few minutes to find the trail of a large hare. It had bounded through recently. Her black nose sniffed the ground, then again at the next point that held the scent. The distance apart was almost two paces. This prey would feed the three of them nicely.

Her padded feet were silent on the cooling ground. Black ears twitched to hear what she couldn't yet see. It was several minutes of following the dotted trail of scent before she could hear the animal.

Twitching and scraping drifted to her tall ears. There was a sound of little teeth chewing the short blades of grass. Then she could hear the heartbeat, rapidly pumping its lifeblood.

Jari loved animals. She'd begged for a pet for years, but life in the desert allowed little excess to be shared with an animal whose only purpose was friendship. Father once had a thunder lizard companion, but it passed years ago. Still, she paused to watch when the creature was close enough to see.

Its coat blended well with the brush of the area. Long ears extended high and turned back and forth, an oscillating detector not so unlike her own. Jari sniffed the air again.

A male, so no litter would go hungry from this hunt. She took a moment to thank the creature for its sacrifice. It was a gesture that would mean little to the animal. At least it made her feel better about the kill.

Jari was only about four paces away when she leaped. Her teeth sank into the back of the hare's neck before it even knew she was there. A twisting snap ended the pain of death. Then leaning down and moving her teeth to the middle of its back for balance, she bounded back toward the camp.

She heard the danger before drawing near. The campsite wasn't far, and she could hear Kila humming as she stirred the cookpot. Kurch was splitting a small stack of wood for a fire. Neither had spotted the redcaps.

Redcaps were often mistaken for brownies. They were nothing like the short honorable clans they resembled only in size. The creatures would come just above her waist when in human form.

Most of the redcap families worked as mercenaries. There were some with the raiders that attacked her village. The creatures were so violent that the hats they wore were dipped in the blood of their kills. They wouldn't be deterred by the symbols on the tent and cart.

Jari set down her kill and pawed forward, ears twitching as she counted the enemy. One was stalking near the cart. Another two were just over the crest of a bank next to the tent. Two more were moving up the path.

It wasn't an uncommon hunting tactic. Two would allow themselves to be seen and would either distract or drive the prey into the ambush waiting behind them. If she'd read this correctly, then there were maybe thirty seconds to halt the slaughter.

Jari moved behind the wagon even as she shimmered into her hybrid form. Her ears scanned for more enemies. These five were the only ones close.

The air was chill on her bare flesh, but Fawnin learned early that modesty is a luxury during a life and death fight. The first redcap died with only a slight gurgle as she put a firm hand over his mouth and sliced his windpipe open.

She leaned down to muffle the thrashing for a few seconds and then shimmered back into a cat. Humans weren't built for sneaking, and her padded paws would serve her better. The two near the tent went down the same, the second not noticing her dispatch the first. Jari allowed the bodies to stay in their hiding place and once again moved unseen.

She couldn't kill the last two before they entered the small clearing next to the path. Each held a long copper knife and smiled a vicious grin. Jari had hoped to spare her sister even seeing the threat, but was lucky to have made it back when she did.

The two invaders strolled into the camp, making no effort to hide their presence or intentions. The look one gave to her sister sent fire through Jari's veins. She wouldn't risk trying to get behind them.

Her father had told her that learning to fight without clothes would one day help keep her alive. Her caracal form couldn't fight as well as the hybrid. Instead of walking back into camp as a caracal, she entered the ring of flickering firelight as a nude girl.

Her tall black ears were still on her head, the toasted brown tail twitching behind her. Her aquamarine eyes held the narrow pupils of a cat and long claws extended from her fingers and toes. Kurch saw her before he noticed the redcaps.

To his credit, he started to look away. Then the mustached man also saw the threat. Kila was frozen in fear as she watched the macabre creatures approach. She hadn't yet seen her sister enter the area.

The first of the redcaps spoke in a gravelly voice that seemed too deep for the squat form.

"Ye can surrender if ye like. We will take ye gear and supplies, but leave ye unharmed."

The second redcap's snarling grin made it clear that it wasn't a real offer. These things would kill for sport even if people had nothing to steal. Jari's own voice had a slight yowl to it, her mouth still holding long fangs.

"You may leave now or die. There won't be another warning."

Jari leaned forward and swayed slightly; muscles tensed for the inevitable battle. The first enemy spoke again.

"Ye chose your fate, lil kitty. Now ye will regret it!"

Then the creature made a sound in the back of his throat, a whooping high-pitched keen that sent shivers up her spine. His expected help didn't arrive.

Jari had given the warning in an attempt to prevent her sister from seeing this, seeing what she really was. She spoke four more words in that yowling voice before she moved in a blur.

"Close your eyes, Kila!"

The redcaps she'd fought before weren't expecting her. She hadn't known just how vicious and quick they could be. Had there been only one, she would've won handily. Yet as she slammed into the closest enemy and tore him apart, the second managed to thrust his dagger into her hip.

The sharp blade stabbed all the way down to the bone. Jari yowled in pain and surprise, then sidestepped a second thrust before she moved into his guard. Her claws slid into his throat; the flesh pulled away with a sickening pop.

Jari was panting now. Not from the exertion, but from the pain shooting up her thigh. She shifted back to her fully human form and fell as the leg refused to hold her weight. Her body should be healing even now.

She'd been cut dozens of times. Father used real swords when they trained for a good while. Why wasn't it—? By the spirits, it hurt!

Kurch was at her side in an instant. His words came fast, and he seemed afraid for her.

"Jari, I'm sorry! They poison their blades. I didn't know any of the redcaps would be this far north. I've never seen them attack in a pair before. There will be more of—"

She waved her hand to interrupt him. He poured water from the canteen into the wound, squeezing it gently. Her voice was now that of a frightened young woman.

"There were five in all. I got the rest before those two got—Aaaaauuugh!"

The rinsing seemed to help, but her breaths were coming in short gasps from the pain. Her spirit fought the poison and tried to close the wound. It was agony.

Then sound started to fill the camp. Slowly at first; no words but a mix of sounds and emotions. The pain was all but gone, and Jari felt her core overflow with energy.

Kila stepped forward, holding the sand shroud and gently draping it over Jari's still naked body. Then the tempo moved as Jari felt that little bit of healing seep through her. Her body warmed as the tingling sensation moved throughout her, beginning to focus on her leg.

Her own regeneration was increased by the flow of energy, and the song's healing bolstered it even further. The exposed puncture wound began to close. A greenish-red liquid pushed out of the opening as it sealed into smooth brown skin once more. Her breathing slowed, and she sighed in relief.

Kurch looked at the younger sister, his eyes wide. He moved his shoulder and smiled before he stood and took Kila's hand. For a long moment all was silent, then he kneeled before the younger girl.

"That shoulder's been tender for years. My dear girl, yah're a treasure. Thank yah for trusting me with this secret. Hearing that song was worth more than any help I could give to yah."

Jari stood with the blanket still wrapped around her. She eyed the man suspiciously but said nothing as she moved to the tent. Her hands were shaking as she dressed. Then she moved to the redcaps, pulling them away from the camp and stacking them downwind of the tent.

The smell of blood might well bring more trouble. The mustached man sensed her intentions and moved to help. After all the bodies were hidden, he helped dress the hare. They stashed the gore with the dead redcaps. While she set up the spit, he looted the copper weapons from the bodies. He found daggers and a couple of small knives, as well as some buckles and buttons.

One at a time, Kurch threw them into the fire. Both girls looked at him inquisitively as he worked.

Jari's curiosity won out. "Why are you burning the weapons?"

He nodded and poked the fire with a stick.

"Something will come to scavenge the meat. Most likely it would've cut itself on one of the blades. This way, some critters need not die for being hungry. Besides, when we get to Spring, I can sell the copper. Jari here earned the profits. If yah're going to get a new start, a bit of coin won't go to waste."

Kila seemed to accept this, but Jari was disappointed in herself. How was she to provide for both of them if she'd never handled money? She had no idea what a fair wage would be or what a loaf of bread should cost. They would need a place to stay and food.

As the meat began roasting, she moved to sit by Kurch.

"I want to thank you for helping us. I've been... cautious, and you've been kind. I have another favor to ask of you."

His mustache moved in a wide upward arc.

"Yah're smart to be cautious, and yah just saved my life, too. I'd no chance against five redcaps by myself. What would yah like for me to do?"

Jari looked down to her feet. "Teach me about money. I've never seen more than a few coins. We gathered our own food and supplies in our village. Mother would've taught me eventually—"

"Say no more," Kurch said with a wide grin. "I'd be happy to." He reached in and pulled out a coin purse and some parchment.

Spring was another week away. Every night for the next seven days they spent time learning how to add, subtract, and estimate prices. Kila seemed to pick the concepts up faster. In time Jari also began to understand how to buy essential goods. They both memorized what things should cost.

True to his word, Kurch accompanied them both to the Tuethna Outpost on the western edge of the kingdom of Spring. There he haggled the sale of his spices and also sold the copper from the redcaps. He put her share of the coin in a pouch and even added a bit of his own. He handed Jari the bag and then surprised her with a hug.

He whispered into her ear. "I'm glad I met yah, and I wish yah well. Perhaps we will meet again someday."

Jari cringed at first but gave in to the embrace.

"I wish you good fortune as well."

Then she watched as Kila gave him a tight hug. Her sister had to hug the donkey, too; the girl had grown attached to Callie. Then the first kind stranger they'd met moved back into the Wyld.

Kurch headed south to deliver his goods to Summer.

CHAPTER 3

J ari and her sister went about buying supplies. It quickly became
   evident just how important it was to understand the value of
things. She bought a tent and some dried food as well as a travel
cloak for each of them.

The covering might help to hide that they were both young
human girls. Many races wouldn't be much larger than them, even
fully grown. It might help avoid trouble.

They still had a good deal of coin left. Jari was careful to only
take out what she needed within the view of others. No need to set
out a sign inviting thieves. Kurch had been quite clear about the
risks. It was while she was bundling up their new items that she
overheard someone speaking.

"... said it was going to be open to any who can fight. My cousin
is going to sign up for the melee competition," a tall man said.

"I heard the prizes will be enough to set you up for life if you
place high enough," replied a short, cheerful woman.

Jari was unsure of the subject and moved to stand near the
conversation. She nodded respectfully and tried to get more
information.

"Pardon me, good people. Are you talking about a fighting
ring?"

The woman shook her head. "Oh no, child. The Contest of Champions is only a couple of weeks away. There are adult and junior divisions. Each of those is split up into melee and casting. It's the talk of the land. Have you not heard of it?"

The lady seemed a likable sort. Jari thought it over; she was no slouch when it came to fighting. If she could earn enough to allow her and Kila to live on, that would solve many problems.

Jari looked to the woman once more. "How old to fight in the junior division?"

"Well, you're supposed to be at least fourteen." The woman gave her a playful wink. "I know of a few who might have fibbed on the forms a bit if ya catch my meaning."

Jari thanked her for the information. The nearest place she could sign up was a city east of Tuethna. Shaneh was large, second only to the capital of Amaya. The road north out of town would lead them there, but they'd only have six days for her to make the tryouts.

Asking around, Jari learned that she could purchase passage with a merchant transport. Alas, that would take almost as long as walking. In the end, she decided to travel as she had the night they'd escaped.

Jari's only compromise was buying a thick leather belt she could use to help hold Kila in place. Her sister would be asleep in the first few minutes of running. If she wasn't hanging on, Kila tended to slide down her back.

The pair waited for nightfall, and then Jari was off. To her excitement, the miles flew by. Never had she stood on the realm of her aspect! Her spirit was strong, and she practically flew up the dark roads.

Twice they got the attention of forest wolves. Jari left them far behind, the pack panting as it was forced to let her go. Several times they would leave the road to avoid the curious travelers heading south. No doubt her pace would draw no small amount of attention.

Jari slept for a few hours each morning, and they walked during the afternoon. At night she ran. The wagons would've taken well over a week to reach the city of Shaneh. It took her three days to get there and an afternoon to find a suitable inn.

It wasn't difficult to find the fields where the trials were being held. People were lined up to watch the matches. It seemed almost as many would be trying out. She moved to the line and waited for several hours as the contestants went up.

It was almost dark when Jari was finally called up to compete. The slits in her eyes made it clear she'd be happy to fight on a new moon if needed. There was little ceremony, and she walked out to the center field to find she would be facing a tall boy who seemed a couple of years older than her.

She sniffed the air but couldn't scent his aspect. It wasn't of concern; only a few would give her any clues anyway. The young man took a clumsy fighting stance, clearly early in his training. He spoke across the field.

"I'd rather you surrender. I'll take no pleasure in hurting a pretty girl."

Jari paused; she should've been offended. Most of the boys in the village were afraid of her. None would spar with her for the last three springs or so.

Despite the slight, she pulled her claws in and tightened her fists. She intended to win but wouldn't bleed the boy. He'd called her pretty, after all. Her words held respect, and she gave him a slight bow.

"I'm afraid I am set on the fight. Do as you must."

The small gong rang out to one side, and she waited to see what he'd do. The boy also just waited. She shrugged and extended the claws on her bare feet. Moving at really high speeds would have her sliding around if she didn't grip the soil.

Her strong legs launched her straight at the boy, speed nearly a blur. Just before she reached him, his fists caught flame. He dropped low and swung out at her.

Jari spun as she dodged to the side. At the odd angle, she couldn't get a solid swing in. Had her claws been out, she could've sliced his face. She settled for a quick jab, snapping her knuckles against the side of his head.

Her momentum carried her several paces past him. Clawed toes tore long furrows in the ground. Her guard was up, and she turned with fists raised.

The boy lay sprawled on the ground, knocked out cold. There was a cheer from the crowd, though most seemed disappointed it was over so fast. How'd he gone down so easily? Jari was strong and had little doubt she would win. But one tap?

One light punch had laid the much bigger opponent out on the ground. She thought it might be a fluke. Perhaps he was prone to such things?

Her round was up, and her next wouldn't be until the following morning. Kila was waiting for her in the stands, and they headed back into town. There she found she had access to something she hadn't enjoyed in years.

In the desert, water is life. Both girls bathed daily but mostly used oils and scrubs. Jari only used water to wash maybe once a week, and then only a small pail. Sitting in her room was a large tub filled nearly to the brim with hot, soapy water. Kila tugged at her arm and spoke in a reverent tone.

"Is that for us?"

Jari remembered she'd asked for a room they could bathe in. This city sat on a large lake of crystal water. To her, this was the height of wealth. The inn saw it as an afterthought.

Both girls giggled as they stripped down and sank into the warm bubbles. The feel of the liquid heat working into her limbs pushed her into a state of bliss.

The siblings lingered for long hours, only leaving the tub to eat the plates of food that were laid out. They did so while dripping on the floor and then got right back in. Finally, the window showed only dark night, and they were long past clean.

After they'd dried off and slipped into their nightgowns, Jari took out a comb of carved bone. Nimble fingers began to pull the wet tangles out of her sister's hair. Kila hummed a slow, sad tune as the older sister worked her long black hair into straight lines.

Jari spoke in a whisper. "Do you think we could be happy here, little sister?"

The song faded out as Kila thought the question over. Her answer gave Jari more hope than she'd felt in some time.

"I miss them so very much. I think you are right, though. We're their legacy. As long as we're together and follow what they have taught us, we will honor Mother and Father."

As the words ended, the humming tune began once again.

Kila took a turn on her hair but only got about halfway through before musical snores rose up from the younger girl. Jari finished as best she could and moved her sister to a comfortable position on the bed. Then she also snuggled up, and they both faded to sleep. Kila's snores continued to carry a sweet melody.

Jari only woke up twice to find a small brown foot in her face.

***

It was the best night of sleep Jari had experienced in weeks. Even with Kurch, she'd been on edge. Her paranoid mind always felt afraid of the betrayal outsiders would surely be planning.

Yet most of the people she'd met had been polite. They answered her questions with pleasant words. None in this kingdom had meant them harm. Hope began to form in her. Jari fought it back, even as it worked to wear her down.

Now she must focus on her next round. She was called up, and it seemed she'd made an enemy of whoever had set up the matches.

Across the field from her stood a young sasquatch.

The tall furry creatures lived in family groups called troops. The vast majority lived inside the borders of Summer, but this one must have found a home in Spring. She tried hard to remember what her father had told her of the creatures.

They were intelligent, and most held an aspect of earth. Whatever its abilities, her opponent was almost twice as tall as she was. Jari could only hope that most of the bulk was fur. She spoke no words, only took her stance.

Once again, the gong rang. This time Jari didn't wait for her opponent to move, using the claws at her feet to charge quickly forward. She dodged a gripping hand and threw a fast jab at the arm that reached out. The crack of snapping bone was loud even in her human ears.

Her shock at the damage the weak punch caused made her pause. Unfortunately, she paused next to a furious sasquatch. The low rumble of its voice didn't tell her if it was male or female. She'd tried to move at the last second, but its good arm grabbed her leg just above the ankle.

The power of the response confirmed it was insanely strong. The first swing slammed Jari to the packed earth, and the second threw her across the field. She landed a pace from the edge of the ring. Her claws dug deep trenches to stop the momentum.

A little further and she would've been disqualified. Her leg was dislocated, and she couldn't pull in a breath. She gripped her knee and pulled hard. The snap of bone into the joint made a loud 'pop' just as she rolled. An enormous foot missed her by a whisper. She leaped away, still lightheaded from her lack of air.

Jari landed just as the creature charged again. She couldn't think of a way to end the fight without killing her opponent. Then she remembered the line behind her. Her hand claws extended and gripped into thick muscle as she rolled onto her back and pushed out with all the strength in her legs.

The sasquatch flew past the line. Then past the wall enclosing the field. The brown furry body landed in the sixth row of the spectator stands, narrowly missing a group of elves who seemed to think she did it on purpose. Jari looked in horror as she realized the toss might have killed her opponent.

It seemed sasquatch were more durable than she knew. In seconds this one was looking at her with dark, angry eyes. The crowd stood and clapped as she walked off the field. The judges decided they need not test her further. Her spot on the Spring team of the junior melee was assured.

Kila squealed and hugged her as they met in the stands once more. They stayed for a while watching the bouts, Jari conceding that it would be wise for her to see others competing. The last round had shaken her. She hadn't meant to break the arm or throw her opponent so far.

Once back at the inn, she decided that her roll in the dirt justified another tub of hot water. They'd gained more money than she expected for the copper, though she'd held back one small knife that Kila now carried in a sheath at her belt.

The younger girl didn't have any real power to defend herself and was vulnerable any time Jari had to leave her side. Using her song to paralyze an opponent would do more harm than good. The power of a Siren would be unmistakable in this land.

The water was everything Jari had remembered, and again they soaked until the liquid grew cold. They slept well and still had enough time to get to the capital by wagon if they left by midday.

The issue with paid transport was the price. Staying at inns and buying meals was eating into their funds quickly. Kurch had been generous with both his purse and their lessons on how to spend wisely. Even so, spending without income was starting to make her nervous.

In the end, she decided to travel overland and aim for the road west of the ferry. The raft would carry them across the mere southwest of Amaya. That would give them plenty of time to get there. Sleeping in the tent until then would stretch her purse.

Jari had her qualifying certificate and their provisions packed and ready. After a big breakfast, they were off. They walked the roads during the day and slept through the night. She still ran for a couple of hours before daybreak to keep their pace up.

The roads were more traveled now. Though they saw no predators, there were many more people. One morning a kind merchant let them hop on his cart for most of the day until he had to take a route to the south. Kila had napped most of the time, leaving Jari again alone with her thoughts.

She realized her hand was stroking Kila's silky black hair. The sleeping girl smiled slightly and started her musical snore once more. How she loved the girl. Could she ever leave her? Even if she had found a safe place in Spring?

Part of her still wanted to look for her parents. Jari was fast and strong. There was a small chance to find them if she was careful. Once discovered, they could work together to fight their way back to the Wylds or even back to Spring.

Kila's spirit was so valuable she would no doubt find a place of wealth and live well. There would be no way to take her on the search. A Siren would be captured for sure. Then her sister would never be free again.

Her father's words came to her thoughts.

'You must take Kokila and run from this place. Keep her safe; she must not be taken.'

Keep her safe? How was that even possible? The only reason she was safe now was the secret they kept. As long as they were just two girls traveling with little to steal, they were mostly left alone. Father had told her of the world, of the dangers of being young and a girl. Her hand stroked her sister's hair and she let the thoughts consume her.

Until they had to hop off the wagon to continue west.

***

To a young woman of the desert, the city of Shaneh was like walking into one of mother's stories. The streets of paved stone, the tall buildings, and—ohhhh, the bathtubs! As the two girls entered the city gates into Amaya, the Jewel of Spring, they were nearly overwhelmed.

The streets and sidewalks were all paved with polished white stone. All the shops and homes were made of various hues of colored marble. In the distance, they could see the home of the royal family.

The Beryl Gardens were a picture of what perfection hoped to be someday. Nature and civilization were brought together, each somehow complemented by the presence of the other. The display of wealth and beauty was enchanting. It was the most beautiful place either of them had either seen.

"Get off the path!"

The words came from a tall man. No... it was an elf. He was well dressed and looked at Jari as if she were nothing more than a stain on his shirt. The contrast of the city's beauty and the rudeness of this man felt almost surreal. Both girls stood confused at why someone would speak to them so.

"See here, you urchins, the walkways are for the citizenry! Your kind isn't needed or welcome. Be gone with you!"

Jari started to slap the man. 'Your kind?' Did he mean the fact that they were human? She was about to leap at him when Kila pulled out the form that proved Jari was to compete in the competition and held it up.

The man rolled his eyes and pointed to a walkway leading to the arena.

"If that is why you're here, then go mingle with the brutes."

Then he walked past, careful not to let his clothes brush against them. Jari looked to her sister and growled.

"Pay that fool no mind. Never let anyone tell you what you're worth. That's for you to decide, little sister."

Kila reached out and slid the form back into her pack. She gripped Jari's hand tightly as they made their way to the fields.

The crowd began to grow more and more dense as the two got closer. Once they reached the registration area, it only took moments to get her name on the roster and be scheduled for her first match.

The games wouldn't begin for a couple of days yet, and there was time to walk the city's paths. Jari's first concern was the price of everything. An apple was priced several times what it was in the smaller towns, and she feared what a room might cost her at one of the fine inns in the capital.

Her first inquiry didn't go well.

"You? Street urchins aren't allowed to stay at our establishment."

Jari narrowed her eyes. "We have money. I'm only asking about the cost. What is your rate?"

"More than you can afford. Off with you."

It was the same at several other places as well. They roamed for some time until the two found themselves outside the city limits. Amaya hadn't solved the poor and homeless problems. The great city had simply pushed them far from the bustle of the main areas.

The path led through a wooded area. In a large clearing, there was a camp set up. People of every race were milling about. Several tents were lined against the edges of the space.

Jari felt the press of her little sister leaning in close, afraid of the atmosphere of desperation. An older woman walked over and greeted them.

"Peace, daughters. We look out for one another, and all are welcome. My name is Keffi. What brings you to our camp?"

Jari looked the woman up and down. Her slitted eyes spotted seven ways to kill the woman before she'd spoken her first word.

She thought of the well-dressed elf and the keepers of fine inns. This was the first person to speak kindly to them since they'd reached the capital. Jari let her pupils round out as she gave a slight bow.

"You speak with kindness, and we thank you. My sister and I are here for the Contest of Champions. I'm competing in the junior division."

Keffi nodded; her back stooped slightly even as she stretched. A callused hand waved them over to the central fire. A thin man was spooning some sort of stew into makeshift bowls and handing them out to those walking by.

The kind woman took two and handed one to each of the girls. She motioned to a rough bench that had once been a log. The old woman sat on a stump across from them and smiled as she spoke.

"Your story is yours to share if you choose. You owe us nothing, and we won't ask for more than that. If you have a tent, you may choose a spot and set it up. Our only rule is that you show everyone respect while you're here. If you have more than you need and want to share, well, let's just say that's the only way some get to eat. We keep a patrol. Three people watching over us at all times. If you can take a shift, it lets others rest."

Jari felt her suspicion rise. Yet many were eating the stew from the same pot. She sniffed the bowl with her cat's nose and could smell nothing wrong with it. It actually seemed quite appetizing, it held various mushrooms.

She looked to her sister. Kila's eyes were longing to dig in, but she waited for permission. The sister in her hated that it was a needed precaution; Kila deserved so much better. With Jari's nod of approval, the girl began to eat with relish. Jari looked back to the stooped woman.

"We're only looking for a safe place to stay until the games. We have some provisions we will share and won't eat more than we return. I can serve a watch every night except, if you will allow, the night before my matches. If your kindness is genuine, I'm grateful and offer our thanks."

Jari leaned down and let her fangs peek from between her lips, her words going low.

"Understand if any offer either of us harm, they won't survive the encounter."

Keffi blinked twice at the last words. She seemed to absorb the teeth and extended claws. The old woman looked around and then nodded.

"I would think so. Your sister is precious. There's another girl about her age near the fire. Would it be ok if I introduced them? Ninazu seems quite lonely and might enjoy a friend while you're here."

Jari looked to the fire, the orange light flickering to fight off the dimming twilight. There was a girl there who might be about eleven as well. She had skin much darker than her own, with curly black hair in tight ringlets and dark eyes. The girl looked to Kila, who seemed hesitant to leave Jari's side.

Jari sighed and looked to her sister. "Kokila... it has been too long since you got to be a child. Go and introduce yourself. I will be right here, and nothing will bother you."

Kila moved slowly over to the fire and sat next to the dark-skinned girl. After only a moment, Ninazu looked at the newcomer and smiled bright white teeth. Then she hugged Kila tight. Jari almost laughed as her sister froze and then slowly hugged the girl back. Her gaze was drawn by the old woman's words.

"Ninazu is special. We all look after her. She's a different kind of healer. One who can bring back a broken mind. We don't even have a name for it, but she's precious."

Keffi's expression fell, pain haunting her features.

"Many who come here have had some bad experiences. The girl can take the pain out of them. She leaves the memories but releases the fear and dread. If you ask her, I've no doubt she'd do so for you."

Jari thought of the pain of her parents. The attack on her home. The hard life her sister was forced to live even now.

She knew she wouldn't let it go. That pain would drive her to find her family. To get justice for those hurt in the raid. That pain was hers to keep.

"I've nothing I need to let go of. My sister isn't so talented, but she's dear to me. Kila is lonely as well. It's nice they may have each other for a time." The lie was comfortable now, no hesitation or guilt. Jari would do so much worse to protect Kila.

Keffi nodded and slowly stood up, moving toward her spot near the fire.

"You may stay as long as you like. All are welcome here."

Jari looked to the rough ground around the campfire, then to the tents and the poor bedraggled people moving in and out of them. Her eyes settled on the two girls laughing and talking a few paces from where she sat.

Now she saw beyond the veneer of the capital. Jari knew in her heart that the real Jewel of Spring was here in this place. With those who had little sharing freely. Few would ever know the truth of it.

She quickly downed the stew. It took little time to set up the tent in the spot she chose next to a large log. When finished, she moved to sit next to Kila, who'd made fast friends with the other girl.

Her sister squealed as Ninazu softly told her a story. From what Jari gathered, the girl had gotten a copper talon from her mother. It was spending money for the fair. Ninazu seemed shy and spoke to Kila in only a faint whisper.

"... I looked all over the place but couldn't find anything I wanted. So... I bought a duck!"

Kila was giggling and dangerously close to rolling over. "You bought a duck?"

"Yes, they tossed in a little basket, and I carried him home. Mama didn't know what was inside till we got to our cottage. The little head popped up, and he quacked at her!"

More giggles. Jari was also interested in finding out what happened to this new pet. She was too ashamed to ask what a duck was, but it sounded funny.

"So my mom dropped the plates she was holding, and the duck got scared and started flapping around the room." Ninazu giggled as she waved her hands around.

Kila was laughing so hard she couldn't ask what happened next. Jari had to step in.

"Did your mother let you keep it?"

"Yeah, we named him Turnip. He was my best friend until the bad men came."

Jari's face darkened. It would seem they weren't the only ones who'd been orphaned by raiders. Kila hadn't registered the last words, but the older sister reached out a hand and squeezed the little girl's arm gently. She tried to hold back her own grief as she spoke.

"You aren't alone, little one. You must hold hope."

A warm feeling stretched up her own arm. It covered Jari like a blanket. She felt some of the tension leave her. Just a bit of the anger and fear. She whipped back her hand before the child could work any more of her strange power.

Ninazu shrugged. "Sorry." The girl looked to Kila. "I'm not alone... I have Kila now."

Jari let the girls have their time together. The odd girl had done something. She felt better but wasn't sure if anything had been taken.

As night approached, she decided to offer the girls a sleepover in the tent. She took a night's watch. The others patrolling were both men, one relatively young and the other older.

She stayed out of the firelight, walking the darkness with her ears out. Even as she listened for intruders, she kept the hum of musical snoring in the back of her mind.

This night passed without incident.

CHAPTER 4

The morning sun peeked over the hills just as she grabbed a couple hours of sleep. Kila promised to stay near the tent till she woke up. The nap did much to refresh her, and Jari decided she needed to address the food stores.

The trip to the market was disappointing. Jari had thought her purse sufficient but found that even the price of modest food would leave it empty in just a few days. She returned to the camp empty-handed.

On the third day, it was clear that they needed to contribute. Soon they'd be taking food out of the mouths of people who couldn't afford it. Her first match was still two days off, and a conversation with Keffi allowed her to skip part of her watch.

Jari moved past the firelight to a safe distance from the others. She undressed and set her folded clothes under a low bush. There was a shimmer, and she was once more fully in her caracal form. Her long toasted brown legs covered the distance quickly. Soon she found a game trail.

Her ebony nose sniffed the ground. A herd of deer had passed through earlier in the evening. They might be bedded down nearby. Jari twitched her tall black ears, the long tufts of hair swaying in the gentle breeze.

The soft pads of her paws carried her to the animals in minutes. She could hear their gentle breathing, the heartbeats inside the chests of each animal. One was much older. Its disappearance wouldn't harm the herd.

The pounce carried her far through the air, fangs closing on the back of the target's neck. The others shot up and scattered. Her jaws tensed and crushed the base of the animal's skull. Its death was instant. A normal caracal couldn't have hunted such large game.

Jari's cat size was based on her human body, making her much larger than her type of cat. Her spirit-powered physique was much faster and stronger than any normal animal.

There was a shimmer in the air as she took her human form to dress the creature. She only took the meat and left the parts that might attract other predators' attention. She stayed in her human form to allow her to carry the load without dragging it along the ground.

Jari moved quickly through the forest, finding her clothes and getting dressed before moving the last few hundred paces. She was still a good way off when she heard crying. Large black ears shimmered from her head.

It wasn't just one or two who were upset. Most of the people inside the camp were groaning or crying. Her feet extended long claws as she bolted toward the firelight. As she cleared the thick brush and the trees, she looked out to see the aftermath of a fight. She dropped the deer carcass, her face now a mask of fear and terror.

"Kila! Kila, where are you? Speak to me, little sister!"

Jari was fully melding into her hybrid form as she let out a yowl of anger. She turned to see Keffi laid out on a mat of old blankets. She was injured, and tears streaked her face. Others were moving around in confusion and fear. One woman was curled up in a ball and rocking back and forth, her words unintelligible. Jari moved in a blur and stood at the old woman's side.

"Keffi, what's happened? Where's my sister? Where's Kila?"

The woman had a trickle of blood down the side of her face. Another spot was drying on her leg. She reached out and gripped the still clawed hand, her raspy voice fighting the tears.

"The city guards came. They sometimes do. They said we couldn't stay here. That we had no right! One of the guards pulled out a club and hit one of the men. I tried to stop him, but he hit me too."

The old woman paused to wipe the blood from one eye. Her face was distant as she remembered what happened.

"Ninazu saw him hit me, and she jumped up and bit his hand. He slapped her and lifted his club. Your sister pulled out a knife and stabbed the man in the leg. They took both girls for crimes against the crown. They've been imprisoned in the city. I'm so sorry, child, I...."

Jari watched the woman break down. Her sobs wracked her body as the cut on her head reopened. A man pushed her down and put pressure on it once more. Jari wanted to slice her open, to punish all these people for failing to protect the only person she loved in this foul place.

Then she looked around. Most of these people were weak. If they were strong, they wouldn't be poor and living like this. Of all those here, she was the only strong one. She was the one who could fight. This was her fault. Standing slowly, she spoke in a loud, clear tone.

"I'm going to get my sister back. I will try to get Ninazu as well. Thank you for trying to help us."

Jari fought back her own tears, leaving the meat for whoever wanted to deal with it. She moved into her tent and shed her clothes. The night was well underway as the large cat moved toward the city, aquamarine eyes piercing the darkness. At the same time, ebony ears flicked in all directions.

She would get her sister back.

***

The city of Amaya didn't truly sleep. Despite the veneer of respectful business evident in the capital layout, there was a seedier side to the place. Jari moved along the rooftops, silent as whispers and swift as an arrow.

Her nose wasn't as good as a wolf or hunting hound, but she'd scented the blood of the guard Kila had stabbed. The trickle on the ground was distinct: it was elven. No elves lived in the camp of the destitute. That blood could only have come from one source, and she had the scent.

Ninazu had touched her arm and slept in her tent. Her scent was remembered, and Kila she would know anywhere. Now Jari moved through the city, seeking evidence of either girl or the guard who hurt them.

Her search was swift, but the city was extensive. It was several long hours before she found herself near the Beryl Gardens. Jari would admit she was afraid of the place. Word around town told of two foreign queens who'd come for the Contest. They were up in the towers above where she crept.

Jari was going to move back away when she scented the blood. The blood of an elf and a specific city guard. The man who'd struck a tiny girl. Her desperation to find Kila drove her past the fear of the terrible people who had come to Spring.

She moved in the shadows, the soft pads of her paws making no sound on the stone path. It led to a wall near the base of the central dome. The scent seemed to move down with the breeze. Her strong legs pushed her into the air, and she landed on the sill of a barred window. She couldn't fit through, but her tall ebony ears made out voices.

"... how was I to know the little wretch would have a knife. The other one bit me, so I gave her the back of my hand."

"You still could have shown a bit of restraint. They were just a couple of urchins."

The first guard huffed. "You go to the dungeons and let one bite you. Then let me know how much restraint you show."

Jari's ears were focused on the conversation. She'd assumed the girls were in some sort of dungeon but had no idea where it was. Her ears twitched as the tufts of black hair fluttered in the breeze pushing out of the window.

"Well, it won't matter whether I show it or not. Those girls have been added to the reenactment tomorrow morning."

The injured guard winced at those words. A look of guilt replaced the grimace of pain he'd been wearing. His voice held a hint of regret now.

"I... I had no way of knowing they'd get caught up in that. I just thought they could spend a few nights fretting and then get set loose."

"You knew it was possible! Even so, it isn't right to separate children from their families, even for a short time. You're going to have to live with sending those girls to their deaths."

Jari's claws began to dig into the stone of the wall. She heard those words, and the thought of her sister being killed robbed her of better judgment. She turned her head and bit down on one of the bars.

They were thick shafts made of the same white marble as the walls. Stone shapers had made it seamless and smooth, as if it were cut and polished from one giant piece. She clenched her teeth in rage.

Her sharp claws scratched furiously at the marble, producing a high-pitched screech. Both guards stared at the window in alarm as the wall gave way to a series of large cracks. The bar shattered and crumbled to the ground, followed by a large cat pushing through the opening. She opened her sharply fanged teeth, and a large chunk of marble tumbled out.

Both guards ran for the exit. One was fast enough to clear the threshold and moved quickly down the hall. The other limped due to his injured leg. Jari moved swiftly to the heavy wooden door and hit it hard enough to slam it closed.

A low yowl escaped her lips as she stalked toward the guard. He turned and ran for a rack of spears on the far wall. The impact against his back drove him to the floor. There was a shimmer in the air as caracal became girl and a firm hand held his head down. The side of his face pressed hard against the cool marble floor.

Jari slowly let her other hand's claws dig deep furrows in the polished surface just in front of his face. She could feel the renting screech send shivers up his spine. Her lips hovered over his ear.

"The girls you took… they belong with me. I'm going to ask you some questions. If you lie, I will know, and you will bleed. If you answer them honestly, I'll let you live. Do you understand?"

The elf moved his head in a nod as best he could. She let her ears flick toward the hall; the other man was still running. She had time.

"Where's the dungeon? In what part are they held?"

His voice tremored as he spoke in short, gasping breaths.

"It's under the barracks. I don't know where they're held, but it's likely on the north end of the building."

Jari focused her ears on his words and on his heartbeat. He was telling the truth as he knew it.

"Why did you harass the camp?"

"I didn't, we—"

One claw sliced into his arm. It was far from the arteries under the armpit but would still be painful. He screamed and stammered before giving her the truth.

"Ok… ok… we were told to clean up the area. The Alder King wants the other kingdoms to see things are perfect here. He thinks the camps make him look bad."

She thought for a moment, then heard footsteps approaching. There were many coming now. Her voice hissed with urgency.

"What's the reenactment you spoke of before?"

"It's a live show of the battle against the Ardon tribes. The defenders will face some of the military."

Jari's eyes narrowed. "You said it was a death sentence. What did you mean?"

He was slow to answer, and her claws scraped once more in front of his face.

"The defenders aren't supposed to win! The soldiers will be well equipped and have greater numbers. There's even to be a dragon at the end. I... I'm sorry.... There won't be any survivors."

Jari felt the rage flow through her. She looked down at the man and remembered that look of regret. She wouldn't kill him. She'd given her word, and he might yet find redemption.

A clawed hand pulled his head up and thumped it to the floor. He would live but have quite a headache when he woke up. She shifted back to caracal and leaped for the window just as the other guards burst in.

The cat wiggled through the remaining bars and into the night. She heard spears hit the wall where her back had been moments before. One even went through the opening and stuck in the manicured lawn a few paces from her.

They couldn't hope to catch her.

***

The barracks weren't so far from the arena. She had passed by them a few times with Kila. The only one who knew where Jari was headed wouldn't be talking for a few hours.

She moved swiftly through the night. The cat stalked the shadows, keeping her eyes and ears busy as she scanned the gloom for threats. She moved in nearly a straight line with a destination in mind and reached the barracks in minutes.

Now that Jari could see the structure up close, it was clear this wouldn't be easy. She moved as close as she could to the wide door without being seen. The broad swath of light gleaming on the blades of grass moved to the edge of her shadows.

Jari sniffed the air, twitched her large ears, and peered inside. The scent wasn't one she could be sure of, and no soldiers were in view. Yet among the throng of noises below, she could make out the faint but familiar sound of musical snoring. Her cat's mouth would've done a poor job on the words that passed through her mind.

'Oh, Kila... you're alive!'

The caracal pawed against the edge of the light. When Jari heard no footsteps for long moments, she moved inside. There was a large main room that had stairwells that branched off to head both up and down. The dungeons were underneath.

She moved to the descending stairs and was already three steps down when the sound of footsteps came up from below. Jari turned and moved back into the main room just as she perceived another group coming down from above. Glancing around, she ran under a wide oak table and froze.

The men were speaking of the Contest and some of the contestants. Some had even placed bets on their favorites. More than a few were rooting for someone named Ohkami.

Jari watched their booted feet move around the room until finally they sat at a table a few paces away. She would've been able to sneak around them if one of the men hadn't moved out to fill a tankard. The guard turned to see her black and brown form. He lifted his hand and began to speak as Jari shot across the room.

"Intruder!"

There were cries of warning and the sound of scraping chairs. A fireball flew past her head on the left, long tufts of black hair singed as the heat moved by. She ran forward as a section of floor moved to block her path and she leaped high to fly over it. A thick cloud of a dark-green fog shot at the ground below her.

"No, Garken! You'll knock us out as w—" one guard began.

Jari could move in a blur, but her speed and strength could do nothing to halt her descent into the gas. Her lungs gasped a breath in before she entered. She hoped she hadn't taken much into her lungs.

The caracal ran full speed for the door as the spirit fog began to take effect. She had some resistance to such attacks, but this was too strong. It was only a matter of time before she'd fade to unconsciousness.

As Jari moved out of the building, she turned right into the shadows, then pivoted and leaped over the light coming out of the doorway. As she hoped, the men who hadn't passed out moved to the last place they'd seen her.

In her panic, Jari was growing dizzy and jumped into the branches of a large elm tree. Her claws pulled her high into the thick leaves. She wouldn't be found. It wasn't for herself she wept as the spores forced her into sleep.

Jari hoped she'd wake in time to help Kila.

***

The sun was already past the eastern horizon when her Fawnin body finally countered the toxins. Jari was disoriented at first. Her stomach rumbled, and she felt stiff from her bed in the forked branch of the tall elm.

The events of the previous night were like a dream. She remembered hunting the deer and the scent of the animals in the woods. She remembered the kill and her walk back to the camp.

The rest seeped into her thoughts as panic rose in her chest. Aquamarine eyes went wide as Jari remembered why she'd come into the city. The brown and black cat hit the ground in a quick run as she moved back to the barracks.

The smell of Kila was fresh in the air, but not the path. Ninazu was there as well. How could they move without leaving a scent on the ground? Her eyes widened as the answer came into her mind.

A cart! They were moving in a cart through the city. Her heart broke as she realized where they would be going. Jari knew what in store for her sister. Her paws moved quickly across the field. She leaped up to travel by rooftops, quickly moving into sight of the arena.

She needed to get inside, but no one would allow a cat to enter the place. If she shifted back, she'd have no money to pay for entrance. Not to mention she'd gather unwanted attention being completely naked. There wasn't enough time to get to the camp and back. Jari looked around. If she could get to an inn, she could steal some clothes.

Her feline eyes looked again to the arena. The stands rose high into the air, yet the top level had a slight overhang to allow shade for those beneath. The stone platform should hold her weight. Slitted eyes studied the construction, and she planned a path to the top. Her paws moved her quickly around the side of the structure.

There were vents at every level. These openings allowed the heat of the crowd to carry out on the breeze. The lowest was maybe four paces up in the air. The stone's light brown wasn't a perfect match for her own darker coat, but she wouldn't stand out much.

Jari's strong legs launched her into the air, and her claws caught the edge of the vent. Back paws sprang up to launch her to the next level. This process repeated two more times; her last leap put her on top of the stands.

Just as she looked over the edge, a slight hum moved in front of her. She extended one paw ahead of her, but a painful shock drew some of her energy. She hissed in surprise and discomfort. Down below, Jari could see the wagon pulling away from the small fort at the center of the field.

She peered with slitted eyes to the people inside. A few men were moving to the low walls. Two women stood protectively over a group of several children. Among them were both Ninazu and her dear sister.

Both were crying and huddled with others who were doing the same. Most were a bit older than Kila, with a couple even younger. A deep voice came from the air overhead.

"Many years have passed since the last Contest of Champions. They are, of course, our way of testing the very best of each generation. This year's games will be a tremendous affair, with battles like you have never seen. My own son competes for Spring this time around. Before we begin the games, I have prepared a special presentation for our guests from the other kingdoms."

A group of elves was playing some sort of music, the tones sending shivers up her spine. Down below, she could see the edge of the king's platform. He was smiling as the south gate began to open. Soldiers poured onto the field as the guard's words replayed through her mind.

'The defenders aren't supposed to win.'

The Alder King spoke again. "You are all familiar with the great victory over the Ardon tribes on the very spot the Beryl Gardens now stand. Today we have recreated that battle. Rest assured, the defenders are all convicted criminals, and no innocent blood will be spilled."

The word innocent grated across her mind. Jari fumed and readied her long legs for a leap. Maybe she could push through the barrier. She would take a shock if it allowed her to help Kila. Another voice suddenly rang through the air. This one was eerie and sent a resounding shudder through her feline body.

"What is the meaning of this? You would have us sit by and watch as you kill innocents in the name of entertainment?"

It took a few seconds before she could make out who was speaking. Down below in a viewing box, or two that were crudely made into one, stood a young woman with long brown hair. It was far enough away that even cat eyes couldn't make out much detail. She was wearing a strange dress of dark brown and gold.

There was a tall, dark-green man behind her and some other women were beside her. One of the queens? She didn't seem happy, and the sound of her voice made Jari want to run. She wouldn't leave Kila, though. Perhaps this woman was going to stop this terrible act.

The voice of the Alder King rang out in response.

"As I said, these people are all criminals. If they were not to die in honor of our history, they would only await a different form of punishment."

The woman seemed to pause. She spoke to the other women with her for a moment. Then that strange voice creeped out once more.

"I understand. It seems I will have to let this reenactment play out. I suppose I might even learn some of your great histories."

The king's reply drove a knife through Jari's heart.

"Let us begin!"

***

Jari leaped at the barrier. The shock hurt like a hundred bees stinging her all over at once. The large cat lay panting as she watched the scene below. She could hear people speaking; they overheard the loud pop of her attempt to get through. Jari pulled on her power. Even now, she was recovering and would try again soon.

The temporary structure below was surrounded by dozens of well-equipped troops marching to besiege the place. Defenders stood on the low walls. None had more than a dull bronze blade.

Jari was pulling herself up just as the first few soldiers made the walls. Shields blocked the flying stones the prisoners threw, and one swung to stab the first of the defending men. As the prisoner fell from the wall, the cat leaped again.

The man below died as the caracal felt that she might join him. Energy tore from her and left her feline body weak and limp. She could barely drag herself to the edge to peer down.

There were murmurs through the crowd. The man she'd seen stabbed now stood back up and began fighting with much more skill than he'd shown before. Two of the soldiers were quickly dispatched, stabbed in the back as they attempted to climb the low walls.

Both of them were knocked down, but they got up again. The former soldiers began fighting the attackers. For the first time, Jari felt a tiny spark of hope.

The woman! She must be the necromancer, the Banshee of Autumn. The cat's body twitched as it slowly regained strength. If the evil queen decided to embarrass the Alder King, Jari could live with that.

Several of the prisoners were dead, but many more had risen to take their place. The two women were still watching over the children. With each passing moment, more of the soldiers were killed. Each rose back up to fight, protecting Kila and Ninazu.

All around the stands, Jari could hear cheers. Her aquamarine eyes grew moist as she understood the girls might live through this. The fear she was fighting back of the dead walking was more than met by the joy of her sister's possible survival.

Long cat legs pulled her caracal body up once more. Jari didn't leap at the barrier now, only gazed at the spectacle in awe. It only took another minute to see that the remaining soldiers had no hope of winning. They pulled back. If the defenders won, Kila might even be released!

Her fears returned as a low rumble shook the platform she stood on. Jari had heard of the massive dragons of Spring, but the serpentine spore wyrms were so much more impressive to see in person. The horned heads of the two enormous creatures looked right at the small enclosure, right at Kila and Ninazu.

The cat leaped a third time. As strong as the necromancer might be, no one could stand against a dragon. As her limp body slumped, once more drained, she heard a roar of challenge rise from the field below.

The first dragon slither-stomped right through the undead soldiers. Pale yellow-green scales deflected the attacks as if they were blades of grass. It breathed a mist of tinted fog at the men fighting before them.

Yet the undead kept fighting around the spouting yellow mushrooms growing all over them. Jari was horrified to see the beast working to destroy those protecting her sister.

Most of her attention was on the second dragon. This creature moved around the fighting and headed straight for Kila and the other children. Strange white roots shot up from the ground and grabbed at the huge slithering beast. It was much too powerful, and the white strands did little more than slow it.

Her large slitted eyes watched the helpless children inside the pitiful structure. Jari gasped as the blast poured from the dragon. She exhaled as, at the last second, a giant red mushroom burst from the soil and spewed a white fog that met the yellow breath of the dragon.

Jari pulled herself up more with will than energy. She weakly lined up for another leap. Then a dark shadow passed above her.

By the spirits, another dragon? This one was in flight. The bright green of its scales left dancing green specks on her platform. This one roared a thunderous blast of sound. Perhaps if it dove down, it would break the barrier. Jari could move below and get Kila!

The cat readied itself for the inevitable charge as the vast winged beast soared. Then it dropped a rock on the field. The cat softly yowled in dismay as the blasted beast flew away.

It hadn't even dropped the stone onto the terrible creature that was about to kill Kila. Jari leaped, or tried to, but her legs only twitched. Her body barely moved, all of her strength now sapped by the invisible wall.

Below she could see the significant dent the heavy stone left on the ground. The vibration of impact resonated through her platform. There was even a big puff of dry earth from the collision.

As the dust began to settle back to the field, a small brown wolf stepped forward. The poor thing had two badly crushed legs, but the fact that it wasn't dead on impact was insanity. Jari's breaths were coming rapidly as she eyed the dragon that needed only to step on this pathetic crippled creature.

Then it shook like a desert fox fresh out of the oasis. Its legs popped back into place, and the creature walked forward. It stood fearless between the prisoners and the dragon who wished them dead. Jari would have thought it comical if she weren't beside herself with fear and dread.

As the cat stood up, the hound sat down. Then it gave a single bark and a long gaze. It even tilted its head as it stared at the colossal wyrm. All was silent except for another loud pop. Jari was close to passing out from her most recent attempt to push through the barrier.

The dragon near the defenders roared and continued to tear apart the walking dead still attacking. The second dragon seemed to grin as it took a deep breath and sprayed the poor brown wolf with a cloud of yellow smoke. Jari wept, knowing she couldn't make another leap.

Her body felt so close to fading, and this creature had no hope against the dragon. The cloud flowed thick around the poor thing. From all around, Jari could hear the people 'awww,' but it wasn't the wolf she mourned. Her tall ebony ears caught an annoyed sneeze.

The wolf was still alive! Some people were laughing now. How could they laugh as the children were going to die? She struggled to move, but her body was done.

The dragon roared and charged, moving to end her world. Yet the little brown wolf charged as well, and as it moved, it grew. In only a few strides, it became massive. When the two huge forms collided, it almost shook her caracal body right back into the barrier.

Jari lay in shock as the now-massive jaws clamped down on the vast pale-green neck. There was a loud, wet snap. The now-huge wolf tore the head off the spore wyrm.

It was almost enough to make her forget the sister who was still in danger. But there was yet another dragon below.

The sight of the colossal brown wolf brought so many questions. The one she still needed answered was the fate of Kila. The sound of those jaws crushing the horned dragon head echoed around the stands.

It went quiet for a long moment, the scent of fear rising from those below. Then the crowd cheered once again. The cry of delight tapered off as the necromancer spoke, her creepy voice coming from everywhere and nowhere all at once.

"This has been quite a show, but it seems wasteful to lose dragons in a reenactment. Perhaps you should call off your troops?"

Jari couldn't believe it; this woman had interceded. She'd saved Kila and Ninazu and all the others! Perhaps this queen wasn't what the rumors claimed. Maybe she had a heart after all?

She could try to sneak into the dungeons again tonight. Her sister could be back in the camp before morning. Jari was already planning the jailbreak as the Alder King's voice flowed through the air.

"Yes, it has been quite a show. Let us take a short break and then proceed with the Contest. I will see to it that these prisoners receive their sentence later on."

A peal of laughter came in eerie tones, then that same otherworldly voice.

"Oh, you need not worry about the remaining prisoners. They belong to me now."

In the distance, Jari could see the Autumn Queen hold up one hand and snap her fingers. Her slitted eyes looked down just in time to see a glimmer of purple light from the ground. It gleamed just under the feet of Kila and the others. All disappeared without a trace. The ground ate them.

Jari's mind reeled as her world was stolen by this queen. Her sister was gone, dead or at the mercy of the terrible woman. Jari could only think one thing as she slowly began to pull herself up once more.

I'm going to kill the death witch!

CHAPTER 5

Jari was to compete this afternoon. Her first bout was against a tall girl from Summer, some sort of earth spirit. She'd forgone the competition; her match forfeited to a no show. The caracal had woven back and forth for almost two hours until it became clear there would be no way to get near the Autumn Queen.

She needed to know if Kila was still alive, and if so, where she could be found. What power could possibly allow someone to make two dozen people disappear? How could she begin to hope to fight such a person? When it became clear that she couldn't get close to the private boxes, the caracal decided it was time to eat.

Her last meal had been breakfast the previous day. She had used her abilities nearly continuously since the night before. Her mind might be focused on her sister, but her stomach told her that it was past time to fill it.

Part of her wanted to go back to camp. She had some money left as well as the provisions in her pack. Perhaps even some of the venison she'd brought back from her hunt, assuming someone cooked it. But the thought of facing Keffi and the others frightened her. Telling the story of how she'd utterly failed gave her a cold spot in her chest.

Kila and Ninazu had been dropped into the underworld. She couldn't face Keffi and the others. Another option was available to her, though.

Amaya had grown to the point that it had begun to acquire the usual pests that thrive in urban environments. If you'd shown Jari a dead mouse or bird, she would've been grossed out like most girls her age. But when the girl took the shape of a caracal, she could eat almost anything.

The flock of pigeons roosting near a fountain never saw the large toasted brown cat stalk up on their rooftop. As one flew by, she launched high into the air and used tooth and claw to snatch the creature from the sky.

The attack was so swift and silent not even the other birds saw what happened. Jari finished her snack. Now she had to fight the urge to try to battle her way through the crowds to attack the death witch outright.

It was common knowledge where the woman and her people were staying. A cat hunts best at night, so she would wait. The toasted brown feline curled up in the warm sunlight of a high rooftop and faded to sleep.

Dreaming of the ways a cat could kill a witch.

***

The caracal stretched her long legs as she roused from her rest. The sleep from that morning had been drugged and left her feeling foggy. Her rest in the Spring sun had recharged her powerful body, and her sense of purpose drove her forward.

The Beryl Gardens really were a breathtaking sight. But if Jari were able, she would've crushed the whole of this place. The city and its people were like a painted egg left in the warm sun. The beauty was shallow; inside was nothing but rot and decay. Jari found more beauty in a stooped old woman than in the whole of the Jewel of Spring.

Four towers surrounded the crystal peak of the domed garden, each rising high into the air. Walkways connected the higher levels, and the space inside held the royal apartments, servants' quarters, and guest suites. The royal guests of Autumn were said to be staying in the western tower.

As night took hold and darkness covered the outer walls, sharp claws dug into the white marble and slowly progressed toward the peak. It took nearly an hour for her strong legs to pull her to the edge of the balcony. There she witnessed another true beauty.

Sitting on a bench and looking out at the stars in the night sky sat a young and lovely woman, perhaps the prettiest Jari had ever seen. Long silver hair flowed over light brown skin; a flowing green silk dress hung from her like leaves swaying in the wind. The woman was humming a sad tune. The melody was a reminder of the little sister Jari wanted back so very much.

Her ebony nose sniffed the air. The woman's power was thick in the aura around her. Familiar, and yet she couldn't ever remember anything like it. Despite coming here to kill the witch, Jari was drawn to this woman. Nothing about this creature could be evil.

Then darkness made flesh walked out onto the overlook. The man was lean and walked much like she did, a stalking predator. He was tanned from the sun, with dark shaggy hair and eyes that scanned the darkness for threats. Jari had to hold herself back. She wanted to save this woman from the evil that even now stalked her.

He didn't slay the lovely woman or even attempt to harm her. He sat next to her and put a lean arm around her shoulders. His strong hand brushed long silver hair away as he leaned against her.

Jari sniffed again and almost yowled. There was nothing familiar about his power. She could sense it but not as she could others. It wasn't power in the air but an absence of it. As he drew near, she could feel the energy all around sucked into the void of his aura.

He wasn't ten feet tall, nor was he a walking effigy of flame, but the terror in her told her that this man could only be the Demon Prince of Autumn. The man who faced down armies and wiped out an entire race in one night.

There was no one more feared in all of the kingdoms of Spring and Summer, of the Wyld and free lands, than the one who was now five paces away. Jari was frozen in fear and despair. If she had any chance of killing the witch, it wasn't going to be in the presence of this man.

She twitched her large black ears as he began to speak, his words slow and awkward.

"I heard what happened, what you tried to do.... Are... are you ok?"

The woman shook her head. From her angle, Jari couldn't see the tears. She could smell the saltwater and knew, without doubt, the droplets were moving down those flawless cheeks.

"How could anyone do such a thing?" The woman sniffed. "In many ways, this is my home. This is the realm of my spirit. Why do I feel so out of place?"

There was a long pause, the man seeming to struggle to find words. He took her hand and traced slow spiraling lines on her smooth skin.

"There are monsters in this world. Not all live in caves and eat villagers. It needs people like you to show the path forward. People like me to clear it. I hear the children all survived?"

The last was a question, the answer to which Jari needed to know more than anything. The woman nodded and then pushed her form into his arms, leaning against him as she answered.

"Issabol was able to pull them through safely. They now belong to Autumn and will soon be at the school."

Jari almost shifted so she could scream at them. The children were alive! Kila was alive, and Ninazu and the others! They were at a prison in Autumn called 'Skool.' She almost jumped from the tower.

A new mission! Kila was alive, and all Jari needed to do was go to this kingdom across the world and break her out. She could still keep her oath to their father.

The cat lay motionless at the edge of the balcony as the two people spoke a while longer. Then the woman stood and flitted her wings, gliding up into the air. She hovered for a moment, savoring the sensation of the sky, and then landed. She took the man's hand and led him back toward the main room. He stopped and paused for a moment, then waved her on.

Jari's heart stopped. He turned and held out a hand, seeming to taste the power he was drawing from the air.

Aquamarine eyes met glowing orange as he looked over the rail. This is how it would end. She'd been arrogant and foolish to think she could get this close to the Demon and live. His tone sounded tired, and he shook his head as he spoke.

"I don't know what you think you were going to try to do...." He sighed and finished. "It would be best if she didn't have to know of any more killing today. Whoever hired you, they didn't pay you enough. Go now and I will let you live. If I ever see you again... I will end you."

The Demon gave her a slight smile. Jari could feel him drawing energy, bright orange flame gathering in his hand. He winked a dimly glowing eye at her.

She accepted his offer.

***

Before, she thought there was no chance. Part of her was sure the girls were dead and serving the necromancer. Jari couldn't bring herself back to the camp carrying that news.

Now she had news of hope and a long way to travel. She needed a map, and that would cost money. She was back at the tent in less than an hour after her brush with death. If she never laid eyes on that frightening man again, well, that was the goal.

Her belongings were untouched, and her clothes lay on the blankets where she'd left them. She shifted back to human and dressed. Keffi was sitting near the fire and looked up as she grew close. Her voice was still kind, but the removal of the only children had been a blow to the cheer of the camp.

"Thank the spirits, my kitten; I was so worried."

Jari leaned down, and both gave and received a hug. Until that moment, she didn't know how much she needed it. The cookpot smelled of rich venison, cooked slowly into a stew. They hadn't wasted her efforts.

She accepted the makeshift bowl and took a bite. It was a bit bland, but the flavor was much better than raw pigeon. She finished chewing and gave an altered account of events, the details held back that would needlessly worry the old woman and the people of the camp.

"Ninazu and Kila are both alive. They were taken to a place called 'Skool' in the Kingdom of Autumn. I will leave to find them shortly. I will bring them back. You have my word."

Keffi's battered face broke into a relieved smile. She pulled Jari in and kissed her cheek.

"You were a gift. So few with your strength would help those like us."

Jari felt her anger stir, not at the woman but at the way one so kind was treated.

"You gave us a place to stay when others wouldn't. You helped us stay safe. I only repay your favors."

Keffi squeezed her hand and gave a wry smile. Her words would remain with the girl for the rest of her days.

"Oh, child. It's not a favor when it's done for family."

Jari fought back her tears. The real Jewel of Spring was covered in dirt. Its shine was hidden from the world.

In the end, she didn't need the map. One of the men had been a trader and gave her detailed directions to the Autumn capital. After one final hug and a few quick goodbyes, she was gone.

Travel by wagons was slow. Having to buy and trade for food and shelter was a challenge Jari had faced because Kila needed both. Now she was alone.

A Fawnin in animal form could travel so much faster. She could hunt and eat on the move, drinking where she could find water. She could go days with short naps in trees or high in the cliffs.

Jari made the trip to the western outpost of Tuethna in just under two days. The sun hadn't even reached its peak before she crossed the border into the Mountain Wyld and headed south. The caracal moved at a swift run until she was past the mountain of caged flame. The trader had been clear; she must stay clear of the Wyld Hunt in the northwest of the realm of fire.

Then she moved swiftly through the canyons, living primarily on disgusting lizards. She got a bit off course and found herself in the Valley of Bones and had to move north some. Finally, she came to a swift river of cold water.

It was the Shinez River if she hadn't gotten lost. The trader had warned her not to try and swim the swift waters. They tended to pull you under, and many had drowned in the attempt.

Jari eyed the distance. It was maybe twenty paces across. She moved north until she found a large rock hanging over the water. It would give her elevation and cut the distance by a few paces. The caracal got a quick run and leaped high over the rushing water. The landing went badly. She'd been really close, but both back legs landed in the swift current.

She shimmered as she stretched human arms out and dug long claws into the soil of the bank. The cold water sapped her strength and pulled her hard toward the bottom. Seconds later, she hoisted herself up and shivered in the cold.

It can be strange having two natures. As a human girl, she loved the water. When she was a cat, she hated it. Neither form enjoyed this experience.

The cold was a danger to her wet body, and her clothes were in a tent two realms away. Power was hard to come by this far from Spring. She'd have to wait to shift back.

So Jari ran, moving fast across the grasses on the eastern border of Autumn. It took almost two hours, an interval she was disappointed in, before she could become a cat once more. The goal was to move west until she started seeing fruit trees. Then directions would be needed.

She'd already passed a couple of orchards: pears and then apples. Both were large and filled with people picking fruit. The cat would have to shift to speak to anyone, and naked girls attract more attention than she wanted.

It was just before twilight when she came upon a middle-aged woman alone and picking peaches from a small orchard just up from a little cottage. The cat crept closer and twitched large black ears, listening for other people.

There was a man chopping wood near a work shed. There were garments on the line. Clothes might come in handy if she wanted to speak to these people.

Jari moved down to the hanging laundry and looked at the garments. Two pairs of overalls, a couple of shifts, a nightshirt, and a sundress all hung dry in the cool air. She'd built up enough energy for another change. The air shimmered, and Jari shivered as she tried to pull the dress off the line.

"By the spirits, girl, that won't fit you at all."

Jari turned and lunged. She ran right up to the man. At his throat, she held the tips of her extended... fingers. Claws would've been much more intimidating. Her failed attempt just made the man shake his head.

"Kids these days. It always confuses me. Either way, it's chilly out here and about to get colder. Come on in, I think we got something that will fit better."

The man turned and walked away toward the cottage. He'd been careful to keep his eyes on hers, never once looking down. That more than his words made her follow him. Also, she was too low on energy to extend claws, much less change back to caracal. A human would freeze without clothes and shelter. He was holding a shawl as she walked in and turned so she could wrap it around her.

"The little room over here, there's a dresser full of clothes, you see. Our daughter was about your size...."

He paused, and his face darkened. The man pulled out a kerchief but only held it balled in his hand for a moment before he finished.

"The clothes should be a close fit. I need to finish the wood; you can rest a bit. If you don't feel like running off into the woods just yet, you might stay for supper. Chesa always makes more than she and I can eat."

Then the broad-shouldered man walked back out, leaving all his possessions with a girl he hadn't even heard speak. He didn't know how strong she was. Actually, as weak as her power was in this land, he might be able to defeat her with a shovel.

Even in this strange kingdom, Jari wasn't about to accept charity. She moved inside and picked out a simple blue dress and slipped it on. None of the shoes fit, but she found a pair of boots and used an extra pair of socks to make them serviceable. Then she grabbed a coat and moved back outside.

The man was splitting the logs with a worn bronze maul, an ax that was weighted with a sledge on one side. As one piece was split, he found another waiting, the smaller pieces being stacked for him.

Jari gave him a shy smile. "Mother always said to never show up empty-handed. I'm afraid I haven't much in the way of possessions. I'd like to work for my meal if that's ok."

The man smiled, but it didn't reach his eyes. There was a sadness there, a raw nerve Jari felt she might have scratched. His words were kind enough, though.

"You know, my mother said something similar. Then she also said that guests shouldn't be imposed on. I think maybe all mothers contradict themselves."

Jari didn't know why, but she liked this man. He dressed in worn trousers and a tunic that had started white and moved toward yellow. His boots were thick leather and carried some of his work with him. He swung the heavy maul repeatedly with no evidence of tiring. With the two working together, the wood was finished in short order.

He sat on the splitting log and motioned to another smaller one for her. She watched in amazement as he picked up a split chunk of the wood and began to channel his power. It was a slow process.

After a couple of minutes, he'd shaped the scrap into a perfect replica of a caracal. The legs and tail were well proportioned. Even the ears were large and tall with tiny splinters sticking up for the tufts of hair at the top. He handed it to her as he spoke.

"Just a little while ago, I saw a large cat sneaking around the side of the house there. It was heading toward the chicken coop. Or perhaps... it was the clothesline?"

Jari felt ashamed. She hadn't meant to steal anything, only to borrow some clothes so she could speak to them. Her head hung down low, but he chuckled softly.

"I haven't seen a cat like it since Chesa and I had to flee to the Wyld. There were a couple like it near the desert lands. Smaller, but the black ears and nose are pretty distinct."

Her face reddened. This man knew what she was and where she was from. He'd made no move to attack her, but claws started sliding out from her fingers. She had enough energy now to fight if needed. No wood shaper could defeat her. Her words came out with a hiss.

"What is it you think you can—"

"Ren! You didn't tell me we had company. My... aren't you a lovely girl. It's getting late, child. Are you lost?"

The woman was holding a large basket of peaches. Her hair was in a scarf, but though she'd spent decades in the sun, she was attractive and fit. The older woman's skin was nearly as brown as her own, and her eyes were almost the same dark shade as Kila's.

Jari was unsure whether to run or fight. Then again, no one had offered her violence. The man only explained he knew where she'd come from. She looked back at him.

"What is it you want?" Her words were a mix of anger and confusion.

The man only shrugged. "Well, for starters, I want to know if you like peaches. They're in season, and Chesa makes about the best cobbler ever. Also, would you like to stay the night? If you go out after dark, it will probably make us worry all night. Then we might oversleep from being tired. The chickens would starve."

Jari sat on her stump with her mouth hanging open. At one point, she thought he might remind her of her father. No, that wasn't even close. Wait, he said cobbler. What's a cobbler? Actually, she didn't care, just as long as it didn't contain lizard. After her long internal debate, Jari gave in.

"I suppose I could do it for the chickens...."

***

It took Chesa no time at all to have the stove ablaze. The way she moved the flames about made it clear what aspect she held. Jari was relieved when she was handed a knife and set to slicing and peeling the sweet juicy fruit in the basket.

Ren told her to try a bite. It was perhaps the sweetest thing she'd ever tasted. The desert had nothing to compare.

The couple moved through the small kitchen with the practiced efficiency of many years of working together. As they labored, they teased and bantered with one another, again with practiced ease. Soon the table was set for three, and the room was warmed from the cooking.

Chesa smiled at her. "Thank you for joining us...." The woman paused. "Why, I never got your name. What do you like to be called?"

"My name is Marjaria Marusthal, but please call me Jari. It's I who should thank you. I came to your home... empty-handed, shall we say."

Ren chuckled, and just then did Chesa look at the dress. Her face seemed to melt as if she saw the ghost of a long-lost loved one. Jari stood and moved to hug the woman.

"I'm sorry. I didn't know I'd upset you. You've been so kind; I can just go...."

The woman hugged her back. Almost too tightly. As if afraid Jari might run away. Ren cleared his throat and explained.

"About twelve autumns ago, we lived to the south in Summer. Our village had gotten behind on its taxes, and the magistrate needed to raise funds. They held a lottery among the children. Esha was one of those chosen. She was to be sold to pay down the tax debt."

The man's knuckles had gone white, his jaw clenched as he worked down the emotion enough to continue.

"Even had we been willing to accept the fate of our daughter, she, like her mother, was of the fire aspect. She would've been executed; fire isn't allowed in Summer. We fled north to the Mountain Wyld. When Queen Ornella made slavery illegal in Autumn, we came here."

Jari nodded for him to continue. His voice choked, and Chesa finished the story.

"Summer has laws about runaways. Since Esha couldn't be sold, they ordered her death. She was assassinated just down the hill near the well. The man who did it didn't know the power I hold. He didn't make it back to Summer."

She looked down at the dress and boots. The dresser and the little room all belonged to a girl about her age, killed for seeking a better life. Jari's own parents had fallen to that same greed. Most of her village had.

It was so confusing. This is where these people had sought safety? Here in the land of the evil necromancer, the kingdom of the Banshee of Autumn? She felt her own pain well up.

"My village was raided. My parents are dead or captured. Only my sister and I made it out. We fled to Spring, but my Kila was taken by the death witch. That Banshee! I'm here to kill her and take back my sister."

Ren and Chesa both froze. They looked at one another and then back to her. She could almost feel them thinking of a way to talk her out of it. It was Ren who spoke first.

"Jari, the news of the events in Spring was broadcast a couple of days ago. Spring attacked both the Autumn and Winter Queens. There was a call to arms throughout our land, and they overthrew the Alder King. I don't know what you saw...."

Chesa stepped in. "We love our queen. You wouldn't believe how much better life has gotten since—"

Her aquamarine eyes went to slits. Jari felt the rage burn hot in her core. As weak as she was, the yowl still found its way into her voice.

"They stole my Kila and put her in prison! Even now, she's held at skool!"

Jari felt pain start to push back the anger. How could they bathe in their own hurt and belittle hers? She would kill the witch and have Kila safe with her!

Chesa shook her head with a sigh before speaking in a soothing tone.

"Let's talk this over in the morning. It's clear you're upset, but I think there might be a misunderstanding. Can we enjoy a meal with you, let you get a good night of rest, and then talk more?"

Jari slowly let out the breath she didn't know she was holding. She looked down at the empty plate. A dinner of chicken and potatoes, well-seasoned and cooked to perfection, left her belly pleasantly full. They'd been so kind, and she was curious about cobbler.

Finally, she nodded and stood to clear the dishes. Chesa pulled an earthen dish from the oven and set it on the table. Ren grabbed some small clean plates and utensils.

Jari slid a spoonful of the thick fruit and crust into her mouth and almost died. Her eyes went wide, and she moaned softly. The fruit was sweet, and the crust added a hint of texture. The whole thing dissolved in her mouth.

It was by far the most delicious thing she'd ever tasted.

***

The dress was folded on the bed. The shift and the socks worn with it the night before were in a neat pile next to it. The bed itself was skillfully made. The door to the room closed silently.

As she slipped out of the cottage, Jari immediately shimmered into her caracal. Ren had told her the skool was near the capital. She'd already seen signs leading to the Blood Keep. She knew how to find Kila. The stop had been about information, and she'd gotten it. Her mission must continue.

As the large cat loped to the southwest, there was a slight pause as her aquamarine eyes stared back at the little house. They lingered for several long seconds.

Then the feline was swallowed by the darkness.

CHAPTER 6

T he winds shifted to blow in from the north, bringing a biting chill to the air. The trip to the Blood Keep took another two days of hard travel. The large cat was able to avoid anything that looked like a lizard, hunting for birds and rabbits.

Jari mostly ran and hunted at night. She slowed her pace as she moved deep into the realm of change. So far from Spring, her renewal aspect was weakened to a small fraction of her standard power.

It took hours to regain enough to change forms. Jari's spirit-infused body was still fast and strong, but a far cry from the vigor she felt in Spring.

The sun was just beginning to peek over the distant mountains to the east. The cat climbed the outer walls of the capital of Autumn and loped around the rooftops. It was a long way from the breathtaking views of Amaya and the Beryl Gardens.

Almost every building of any size was constructed of crimson stone. Even the roof tiles were shaped of the same material. Many were trimmed in various colors; some had even been painted. Still, the morning sun glinted on the stone and created a red haze throughout most of the city. Jari was starting to understand how the place got its name.

There was order to the streets. The Blood Keep didn't have the smell that large groups of people seemed to acquire. There were no windows open to empty chamber pots into the street. No gutters streamed with refuse.

This was surprising, but the thing that astonished the cat the most was the people's general cheerfulness. Almost all seemed content. They were busy and filled with purpose.

The carts were filled with fruit and bread instead of the bodies of the dead. There were a few meat carts selling mutton and pork, but no one was eating babies. As of yet, she hadn't seen anyone skinned alive.

Her aquamarine eyes narrowed as Jari's thoughts went dark.

Of course, these people are normal. Only the witch would do such things.

She need not shift her form to ask for directions at this point. The whole of the city was equipped with signs leading to the strange prison called School. Jari wasn't great at reading, but the characters were clear enough once she saw how the letters were wrong in her head.

Kila was the one Mother had worked so hard with on such things. Her own training was from her father and much more direct. As Jari finally made it to the place she'd traveled so far to reach, she noted the walls surrounding the buildings, courtyard, and large open circles.

The wall was no issue for her. Three jumps and sharp claws to gain traction on the smooth stone put her inside the perimeter. In moments she was in the branches of a large tree overlooking strange circles.

There was no safe way to scout the buildings, but only moments after she was secure in her perch, a group of children ran out and began playing in the open area. These were young, perhaps five or six at most. Maybe Kila would be in another group.

The cat watched silently as the little ones played.

***

Jari had no way of knowing that as she watched the events below, she was being watched as well. A plump older man inside the main office had gotten the ghost's report of a stranger near the training fields. He recorded the event in his ledger and sent word to the very woman Jari was hunting.

His instructions came only moments later. He gave further directives to other ghosts who moved in and out of his office at all times. Two girls were pulled from one of the newer classes and sent to the royal apartments.

A young troll was sent to watch over the younger children in addition to the usual security. The only change to the typical day on the training fields was a tall, lean man with short dark tusks. He strolled around the open areas and smiled at the children.

All the while carrying a long stone spear.

***

Jari had never seen a troll from this close before. The cat marveled at the fact that the smaller races were unafraid of the figure. They actually seemed to be quite fond of him.

The groups of young ones had young trolls and gnomes, humans and brownies, pixies and sprites. It was a stew pot of all shapes and sizes. One ogre seemed to get too rough at one point. He was given correction quickly and was soon playing again.

The sun began to move through the sky, and other groups cycled through the area. One even looked about the right age for Kila. This group had a comically hyper blonde girl who almost blew Jari out of the tree at one point. Her tall ears listened for any hint of a musical voice and sniffed for her sister's familiar scent. There was nothing.

The day grew long, and it was midafternoon before Jari's patience began to run out. An older group had come out to the open space she surveyed. Instead of playing or chasing one another, these were warriors.

Young, some would be a little older than her own fourteen springs. Or was it fifteen? She realized her birthday was likely spent running and eating lizards.

The group below was focused. They used the large circles much as Jari had in her qualifying rounds in Spring. Her mind fluttered at the fond memories when she and her sister were together. She remembered when there was a plan for a better future and the hope of reaching it.

The tall, lean troll no longer walked the area. Now he practiced his own skills against the others. Some fought battles; others practiced weaves of spirit casting. The display was distracting, and the voice below almost knocked her off a branch.

"May I speak to you for a moment?"

Jari was caught off-guard. She shifted her form while leaping from the tree. Her long claws lashed around as her other hand pushed the boy against the thick trunk. She held four razor-sharp points a finger's width from the pale flesh of his throat.

He was a bit taller than her. His blonde hair was just long enough to want to curl. His skin resented the sun by tending to freckle. There was a slight lean to his nose.

The young man wore a uniform that seemed to be common among this age group. He would have been handsome if he weren't of this evil place. Despite Jari's best efforts to threaten him, he seemed more preoccupied with not looking down at her own naked form than in convincing her not to kill him.

She hadn't changed as well to her hybrid form as intended, and her voice held more yowl than usual.

"You'll tell me where they took the girl Kila... or you will die."

He again seemed to be more afraid of what was below her claws than of the threat they held. His only look of concern came about the same time as the air went wrong. Jari felt the hair on her tail and ears begin to hum. Little sparks of energy started to crackle all around her. A voice from behind her held more threat than she could hope to gather.

"If yall don't step away... they gonna need a bucket to git all yall home."

Jari turned to see a girl, perhaps her own age. She had long auburn hair that was beginning to stand up and hum with power. Her form was slender but wiry as if she'd worked long days for most of her life. Her eyes held murder. Before Jari could respond, a hand was held up; the boy was speaking now.

"It's ok, Zef. She's just confused and afraid."

"I'm not caring if the girl's on fire. If she don't back on up, this girl's gonna need a green dragon right quick."

As the other girl finished her threat, he turned to the cat in front of him.

"Jari won't hurt me. I'm not her enemy. I have a message from the Autumn Queen. She had Kila and Nazu brought to the royal apartments. She would like—"

Perhaps it was the threatening girl behind her. Maybe the sister who'd slipped her grasp once more. Jari snapped forward, retracted her claws, and punched the boy in the face.

She leaped back as a wave of force crashed into the ground where she'd been standing. Jari's foot pulled in the claws just before it slammed into the side of the girl's head. She darted for the wall as a tall, dark-green form moved in front of her.

Jari slid low and moved through his legs, lunging for the wall. She couldn't change back to a cat. Her hybrid form was much better for fighting, but she was no match for this whole group, even in her own realm.

A tall girl was pulling rock around lean limbs as she moved to block her path. Jari leaped high into the air, guessing no one that heavy could jump well. A wave of heat passed so close to her head that her ear tufts were singed again. Her large ears caught the boy's voice screaming from behind her.

"Don't hurt her! Stand down!"

Her path was clear. Jari ran straight up the wall and disappeared into the shadows.

***

Jari hated this place. She despised the witch who took Kila, this horrible land where she was so weak, and the awful children who'd tried to hurt her. She just wanted to go home.

Oh, how she longed to curl up in the blankets in the hut next to the southern oasis. To eat a meal with her family and listen to mother's stories. To hear Kila sing. Even a musical snore.

Jari had to wait over two hours until she could shift back to her caracal. In her human form, she would've needed clothes to keep from drawing attention. Even then, she likely would have gotten caught. The witch would be well protected, but it's hard to make anything cat-proof.

It was well after dark now. There was enough energy saved up to shift to hybrid for the kill. Then she and Kila would run. Ninazu would come if she could make it work. Even one passenger was going to make this a close thing.

Her padded paws made no sound on the roof tiles. The taller buildings to the west allowed deep shadows to form. These were her paths. She moved like a whisper, large black ears twitching and listening. Her guidance came in the words people used carelessly.

A new kitchen boy was given instructions: the queen took her meals on the fifth floor. A guard with a message moved to the eastern wall. It took the caracal little time to locate the faint musical snores coming through a window. They were muffled, as there was a wall between them, but Kila was nearby.

It took several nimble jumps to reach the fifth floor. The window was open and looked into a large bedroom. A four-post bed stood in the center while a large dresser sat across from it. A wardrobe was across from the window.

All the furnishings were well made but old enough to have seen generations of use. The bed was empty and still neatly arranged. It hadn't been slept in this night.

The cat hopped inside and moved to the door, cracked slightly and letting faint light peek through. Through the opening, Jari could see a large sitting room, complete with sofas surrounding a low table. A wide desk was stacked with papers and books. The far walls were covered in more of the same.

Her aquamarine eyes were slitted as they scanned the room, dim in the lamplight. There on the far sofa sat the witch. The small room next to this one held Kila.

Jari wasn't a fool. This was clearly a trap. Why else bring her little sister here? Yet she was so tired, so weak in this realm. She'd never felt so alone. Part of her knew she would die this night. A small part of her wanted to.

Yet she had given an oath and was going to try and keep it. Jari began to shift to her hybrid form, having waited hours to have the energy to do so. She crouched low to gain speed once she pushed through the door. Who knew what the witch could do?

"I don't know how you take your tea. I just had everything set out."

The woman was looking right at her! It was surreal seeing her this close. If she hadn't used magic on her appearance, the witch would be only a few years older than the cat stalking her. Her hair was long, brown, and curled at the temples. Her eyes were a brown shade that reminded Jari of Autumn's trees and the crackle of dry leaves under her paws.

The necromancer wore thick hose and a deep brown nightshirt. She had slippers that looked like little black dragons. Small wings flapped on the sides of each. If they were supposed to look scary, they failed terribly.

Jari looked at this woman she hated. The person who'd robbed her of her family and future. She would have her revenge and escape with Kila! She pushed the door open and blurred into the room, her long claws fully extended and aimed right at the woman's throat.

The witch raised a hand and spoke.

"Maeve... Stay."

Jari turned at the last second. Horror and confusion swirled in her mind as she saw the strange wolf creature. The same one had faced a spore wyrm. The thing killed a dragon with little effort. Those jaws were aimed at her now.

The form had been curled up on a round cushion. It didn't have a scent. It made no sound, and to Jari's ears, that was some feat. She didn't know it was there until the woman spoke, freezing it mid-lunge.

Now Jari's claws hovered in the air, a half a pace from the throat she needed to tear out. Tears began to trickle down her face as she realized there was no way to defeat the beast.

Even if she defeated the witch, the wolf would kill her. Then Kila would die alone in this foul land. Her mind raced as she was torn; she needed to find a way!

The Banshee spoke again, calm and matter of fact.

"It would help if you pulled the claws in. My brother gives her commands. I'm afraid the rest of us make suggestions."

Jari looked out of the corner of her eye. The beast was even now creeping toward her. She closed her eyes and slid the long claws back, her hands becoming human. Jari shook her head slowly; she'd failed, and... something was wiggling against her leg.

The cat-girl looked to see the wolf leaning against her. The creature was now wagging its tail so hard that the whole back half of the thing was shaking. She was along for the ride. Jari looked back to the witch who was holding out a thick green robe.

"I'm not sure if you get cold. I know some who never do. Yet it's a bit odd to have this conversation with you naked."

Jari just stared at the offered garment. Then at the steady hand holding it out to her. Her voice still held a bit of the yowl of her caracal.

"Why... did you take... my sister?" Her emotions were halting her words. Her eyes still carried malice.

The woman nodded to the sofa and set the robe down on the table.

"Ok, well, it's not like there are any men about."

The witch reached down and poured two cups of tea, seemingly unafraid of the assassin in her quarters. Then she picked up one cup and gestured to the other. Only then did the woman answer the question.

"I think it important to point out that at the time, I didn't know who was down there and who they might have as a sister. Of those I took, eight have been reunited with their families. Four more have decided to make a home in Winter. The rest have accepted my offer to live here. Your sister isn't a captive." The witch took a long sip of her tea. "Kila has been adopted by the Keep."

Jari processed the statement. The clever words of the Banshee of Autumn were everyday talk in the streets. It was an easy claim to make, yet it might be a lie that could never be proven. She looked back at the witch. Her next question would be harder to speak lies to.

"You know I came to kill you?"

The woman now gave a tired smile. She looked exhausted, and her face spoke of long hours of sadness. Her answer again held no small amount of surprise.

"You, my dear girl, aren't the first. I like to consider motives when I decide punishments. You thought I stole your baby sister, and you fought to get her back. I've been looking for you for a while now. Kila has been beside herself with worry." The witch sighed and tilted her head before adding. "I think there's hope for you yet."

Jari felt her anger growing cold, more from exhaustion than from being convinced. She sighed and reached for the robe, pulling it over her shoulders and folding it in the front. She didn't tie it closed; she might need to move quickly. Her yowl softened as she spoke.

"Why didn't you protect yourself? I was an instant from killing you."

The queen shook her head slowly, blowing on the hot liquid in her cup.

"You almost tried." Another blow for the tea. "I had Maeve sleep in here because she's a clear threat, and she gave you pause. You're strong, Jari, but I'm a queen. If we both decided this was a fight to the death, then I'd have to break your sister's heart."

Jari snorted before she could stop herself. The woman was full of herself. Then without moving a finger, the queen began to radiate power. Her hair started wafting through the air as her eyes shifted to an otherworldly white. The room was alive with the dead. Ghosts of all ages and sizes filled the space. From all of them came the eerie words.

"Not all is as it appears!"

Then they were gone, the queen's eyes now back to that strange shade of brown. The witch looked up with a smile.

"Kila said I should kiss you on the nose when I said that." The woman shrugged. "But we just met."

Jari was so confused, though she was pretty sure that the woman was right. This power was well beyond her own. Questions swirled in her mind once more. She chose the one that would mean more than anything.

"You swear to me that Kila is well?"

The woman set the cup on the table and stood to stroll to the room behind one sofa. Her little dragon slippers flopped as she moved. When the witch reached the door, she waved Jari to come over.

There on a small bed were two little girls. One had skin so dark that even Jari's caracal eyes had to focus hard to see her in the shadows. Next to her head was a small brown foot. It ran up to the girl who looked so much like her. Looked just like their mother.

Jari felt her knees go weak. The stress and worry all collapsed around her. She wilted to the cool stone floor. She was so tired and confused; she just wanted....

A heavy brown wolf chose that very moment to sit on her.

It took the queen a few seconds to convince the creature that her cushion was a better spot to lie down. Then she helped Jari up and hugged her. For a long moment, the girl held back, having so long hated this woman.

Finally, she returned the embrace. The moment this woman took Kila, she'd saved her. It was Jari's oath to keep, and she thought herself robbed of the task. Now she began to see the terrible decisions the queen had to make.

Then Jari remembered what she'd done. She stiffened as she pushed back from the embrace.

"I'm a criminal! I tried to kill a queen.... I attacked that boy and his friends! I lied to the people who helped me.... I—"

The woman motioned her back to her spot.

"Fix up your tea. The biscuits are perfect. Norim made them for us. You'll meet her later."

The queen sighed, the breath leaving her slowly. "As for me, I decide how to punish those who try to kill me. I once had someone taken from me. Someday I might tell you how far I went to get them back."

Jari tilted her head. "Was it your brother? He frightens me."

It was the first time Jari heard the woman laugh. The sound was hearty and musical at the same time. Then the queen covered her mouth, remembering the sleeping girls.

"I needed that, I think. No, I assume if anyone took my brother, they'd give him back before I knew he was missing. Honestly, he scares me right now. I fear what he's going to do to get someone back."

Jari gave a strained chuckle. "Well, it's not like he is going to try and kill a queen."

She'd meant it as a jest, but the woman's face darkened. The Banshee shook her head.

"I'd be relieved if it was only a queen. My brother has declared war on Summer."

This also confused her. Jari was no ruler, but it seemed wrong that others could wield a queen's authority.

"I know he's a prince, but surely he cannot command your troops against your will."

The woman shrugged. "You said you feared him. Let me say you have no idea. My brother won't need my troops or anyone else. Jack might well destroy Summer entirely by himself. He has... anger issues."

Jari shuddered. "I met him in Spring. He spared my life."

This made the woman turn to her with her own look of surprise.

"Was he with the pretty girl with the wings?"

Jari nodded, thinking of the vision of beauty. "Yes."

"Be glad she was there. Jack tries harder when Joobel is around. She's not around right now. That's a story for another time. You attacked some of my children, I hear?"

Jari hung her head. It was such a short time ago that she wanted to kill this woman. Now she found she desperately wanted her approval.

"I'm sorry, your queenliness. I—"

The woman laughed, more restrained this time.

"Call me Claire. If others are around, then 'my queen' or 'your grace' is fine. Please go on."

"I thought Kila would be at the school. A boy found me and caught me off guard. I... I hurt him and a couple of others." After a short pause, Jari added, "Your grace."

Claire stuck her tongue out at the last words. Then she considered the information for a moment.

"I think they like you. You said you hurt some of them?"

Jari nodded. "I punched him, kicked a girl, and knocked a couple of others down."

Claire chuckled as Jari said this. "Yeah, I'd say they like you."

Jari lifted an eyebrow. "How could you possibly think that?"

"Well, the boy I sent to talk to you is my little Stormcloud. Few have ever slain a dragon. Maeve has killed a couple, and my own Harvest has done in a few. We even have a gnome with the title. But Bayu has killed several. With the exception of the prince, he might someday be the most powerful mortal in our world. If you hit him and didn't get turned into a crater full of paste, then he must like you."

Jari winced. "I also kicked the girl...."

Claire tilted her head. "What did she look like?"

"She had pretty long, red hair."

Claire froze. "Did she see you hit the boy?"

Jari nodded. "Yeah, she got crazy mad."

The queen sighed with a frown. "Ok... they don't all like you. By the spirits, you must be fast!" Claire thought for a moment. "I'll talk to Zef. We can't replace any more roofs right now."

Jari cocked an eyebrow. "Roofs?"

"It's a long story, just please don't hit the Tempests anymore."

Jari nodded. "I'll try not to. Wait... you act as if I will see them again."

The queen put down her teacup and reached for a stack of papers. She shuffled around for a moment and found the one she wanted. Claire smiled as she held it out. Jari took the parchment and frowned. While she could read a word she was familiar with, the wall of text was far beyond her.

"I... I'm sorry. I can read a little, but my sister is better. My path leads another way."

Claire gave her a grin. "Well, my dear Jari, how about I let you know what it says. I have a bargain for you."

Jari's eyes widened in fear. "I... I'm sorry, I don't want to lose my soul."

A third laugh came from the queen. She waved for a second before words were able to form.

"Ah, that one is new. It's my own fault, I suppose. I start half those rumors to help protect my people. No dear, I'm offering you a home and an education. You will, of course, be able to live with Kila, and by default, Ninazu. The two are inseparable, I'm afraid. In return, I ask that you help us build a better kingdom. You're unique in our land, as are your sisters."

The cat cocked one eyebrow. "Sisters?"

Claire smiled and nodded. "The two are *inseparable*."

Jari considered the offer. In the end, it was no different than what they'd have had to do in Spring. Kila would sign into military service to allow her security.

Yet there were concerns; both she and the younger girls would be weak here. This was far from the realm that nourished them. Also, it was an open-ended deal. Service could mean picking apples or killing those who opposed the queen. Jari might break an oath if she didn't get answers first.

"We'd be of little use here. My power is a shadow of what I could do in Spring. Why would you want those who can barely function?"

Claire reached in her pocket and pulled out a small disk. It was light purple and a little bigger than a coin. The queen placed it in her hand. Jari held it and blinked curiously; her bright aquamarine eyes flicked up to the queen.

"What's this?"

"That is a portal disk; inside is a pearl of heart-seed. It's the bedrock of your realm, the pure essence of renewal. Focus on the warmth inside, then pull energy through it."

Jari closed her eyes and tried to do so, failing for only a moment until she seemed to catch the stream of energy. It was pure and felt like cool water on a parched throat. In moments she could feel the power building inside her.

Looking back up, she realized the value of the thing. What some would do to have access to the fullness of their power anywhere!

"I cannot afford this. I could never afford this. This is a debt that could never be paid!"

The queen smiled and shrugged. "I got a few of those from someone who was motivated to make peace with my kingdom. I'm not asking you to buy it. I'm offering you a home; you can add to our society. You said you were too weak to stay, and I'm saying that isn't an issue."

Claire's smile faded. "That said, don't tell anyone you have it. Trust me when I say no one will find it on accident."

"What of Kila and Ninazu, would—"

Claire shrugged. "They had theirs put in a couple of days after they arrived."

Jari tilted her head. "Put in?"

Claire pulled the first button of her nightshirt loose and pressed the skin over her breastbone to reveal the faint outline of a similar disk. Jari's eyes went wide, and the queen shook her head.

"No cutting or pain. I can have it in place in two seconds, and you'll feel only pressure. Though we haven't finished negotiating. We can deal with the jewel if you decide to stay."

The girl nodded. If they chose to leave, it wouldn't be an issue. The offer was tempting; they would have food and a place to live. If they were trained like the others, they might also become much more powerful.

Yet, what if she was made into a weapon, her sister sent into battle? Jari wasn't very experienced, but she understood that bargains were governed by the old magics. Breaking one could be disastrous.

"Tell me what our obligations would be. How would we pay for our food and shelter? What would we have to do?"

"You're a smart one, Jari. Honestly, I'd ask you to apply yourself in your studies, learn, and grow. I expect the same of the younger girls, though they would have more time to play. When you have moved toward your potential, I expect you to pursue your passions and help Autumn thrive. That is all."

Without even thinking, Jari began to pull in her ears, her face becoming fully human. Teeth and claws receded away even as the long tail shortened until it disappeared.

The flow of power from the gem was already becoming second nature to her body. Her mind was focused on the offer. It sounded too good to be true. It probably would be just that. Yet, it's not as if others were knocking down her door to take them in. There was one more thing to discuss.

"My sister... do you know what she is?"

Claire sighed with a nod. "Kila's a Siren and is probably more valuable to certain people than I care to think about. Honestly, I'm more interested in Ninazu. Do you understand what she is?"

Jari started to nod, then hesitated. She knew the girl could soothe the hurt of painful memories. Honestly, she didn't know the name of the ability or its potential. Finally, she decided to season her answer with caution.

"I know she helped Kila deal with the loss of our parents. I don't understand fully."

The queen stood, finger tapping her lower lip as she began to pace. "Do you know of Bloom? Autumn's green healing dragon?"

Jari shook her head, though she remembered one of those at the training yards mentioning a green dragon. Claire answered for her.

"The irony of a realm of change holding a powerful healing dragon isn't lost on me. Yet we have several who can heal broken bodies; some can even reshape old wounds to return function. But there's little we can do for the scars on the mind."

The queen paused and smiled, brown eyes alight with excitement.

"I have seen some who can take away pain, and the woman who made these biscuits can calm a person with a touch. Ninazu's power is new to us, and we've labeled it Wellness for now. Think about how many could be helped if we could lift the wounds made to the heart and mind."

Jari realized that given a choice between power and peace, this woman was much more excited about the latter. A Siren could mold a battlefield, yet this queen was so enthusiastic over helping her people that she was pacing over a girl who couldn't even afford food in Spring. This, more than anything else, convinced Jari that she'd found a home, in a place she'd never have expected.

"I'll accept your offer. We will stay in Autumn as long as you'll allow it. I assume we will not continue to sleep in the queen's quarters."

Claire gave a sad smile. "I'm actually enjoying the company tonight, but honestly, it's not safe. I have a price on my head even now. They would fail, but some assassins still try for the amount of money offered. We have excellent security at the school. You'll all be safe in the dorms."

Jari almost laughed at the mention of security. She'd moved right into the walls of the place.

"I'm not sure the school is quite as safe as you think. I went right inside."

The queen sat down before leaning forward with a smile. "I know. I was aware you'd arrived the moment you entered the fence. It's why the girls were brought here. I wanted to have this conversation before you left. Did you happen to see a young troll moving around?"

Jari nodded and the queen continued. "Tedar was there to keep an eye on you. I also spoke to Bayu and had him let you know to come to see me. I'd hoped you would use the door, though."

Her aquamarine eyes went wide. "So you could've had me attacked at any time?"

"I don't like to see people hurt. Had you attacked innocents, I'd be oath-bound to protect them. These are my children, and I defend my people. I claimed your sister and the others the day I took them. You came here on your own. Even now, you aren't mine. Not until we make this official."

The queen leaned over and picked up a quill, tapping it twice to her lips while she moved the contract into place. The queen signed her name in a pretty flowing script and then handed the instrument to her.

Now human eyes looked down as Jari took a deep breath. She wasn't the best at reading, but she could write her name. As she finished the signature, she slid the paper back to the woman.

Claire shook her head. "That's for you; I don't need it. The contract is only for your peace of mind. Now may I place the jewel for you? We must keep some secrets, and I'd hate to see it get lost."

Jari nodded and gripped the sofa tightly. It took more time to adjust her robe than it did for the queen to shape the flesh around the jewel. The woman leaned back and inspected her work, then nodded and stood.

"I've enjoyed our talk, but I'd like to get what sleep I can. I have a bedroll you can place next to the girls if you like, or feel free to use one of the couches. Tomorrow we will set up your room in the dorms and get you settled."

Jari considered for a moment and then looked up. "I'll make sure we all attend school, but what of the children who live in the villages? How do they attend?"

Claire nodded. "We have a portal system all over the kingdom. They use them to shorten the distance."

Jari shrugged. "So... would we have to stay in the dorms?"

The queen once more tapped a finger to her lip.

"What did you have in mind?"

CHAPTER 7

The huge death drake circled the small peach orchard twice before choosing a landing site down the hill from the cottage. The sun was now well above the horizon, and both Ren and Chesa were deep into the bright-green trees laden with yellow-orange fruit.

Jari jumped before the dragon reached the ground, landing on her feet, if you can believe it. Despite her excitement, she waited for the dragon to settle and helped both Kila and Ninazu down. The woman riding with them needed no assistance.

It's hard to hide something the size of Harvest, and both of the farm's caretakers came walking out from the trees before the four ladies ever made it to the little house. Jari started to run to them but froze, remembering the way she'd left things.

As fearless as she was in a fight, she now found herself studying the ground near her feet with what would appear to be significant interest. The queen and the girls with her stood near the dragon. All were aware that words needed to be spoken.

Ren stepped forward and kneeled in front of the raven-haired girl, peering up into her aquamarine eyes. His words were like daggers.

"You lied to us! You said you would talk it over before you left. We were worried for you, Jari!"

Part of her had grown in the weeks since her parents were taken. Now she felt small. Streaks began to form on her cheeks as she took a deep breath and answered the man.

"I was mistaken... about more than a few things. I was blinded by my own anger, and I treated you poorly. It was wrong... and I'm sorry."

Chesa stepped forward and put a hand on the man's shoulder. He leaned over and hugged Jari tightly. The older woman joined him, squeezing firmly until they stood and walked over to the woman who'd arrived in the most conspicuous of ways.

Claire moved with purpose, though Jari could still see dark circles under her eyes. The queen spoke with a casual tone, despite the authority of her office.

"I suppose you can guess who I am. I've been told that these new Autumn residents may have an alternative to life in the dorms. Jari has asked that I approach you about hosting these girls while they are in school. Is that something you'd be interested in speaking about?"

Ren's eyes grew wide. He glanced over to Chesa, who'd stood silent. The couple seemed to be in shock. After only a moment, they asked Claire and Jari to come inside and discuss the matter further.

Ren started to worry after the smaller girls, then went pale as he looked to the death drake who moved to stand watch over them. The little ones seemed more interested in the chickens.

Jari waited for all to move inside before she addressed the couple.

"Ren and Chesa, you were kind to me when I was a stranger. As I told you, my sister and I lost our parents to a raid in the desert. The queen has offered us a home in the capital. I accepted her offer, but both Kila and Ninazu have been through a good deal."

Jari looked to Claire, the queen nodding for her to continue. Her hands clenched tightly as she asked these kind people for so much.

"I think they would do better in a home, a real home with a family. I know this is asking a lot, and all three of us are... different from the rest of the kingdom's children. I thought you might be ok with different."

Claire took over from there, already shaping the offer she'd explained to the older girl.

"The school would provide uniforms, classroom supplies, and rations. You'd take care of discipline, housing, and helping them to adjust. I realize your home is a bit small for five people, so we have stone shapers who could stop by and expand things a bit. The younger girls don't know what we are discussing. If this isn't something you want to take on, then I under—"

"We will take them."

Chesa's voice was a bit louder than was necessary. Even Ren looked shocked at his wife's words. He looked at her with cautious eyes.

"Are you sure, dear? Three children are a lot to take on, and as Jari said, they've been through a lot. It will take time and effort to help them adjust."

The woman looked to her husband and smiled. "I want them. If I said no, you'd never forgive me. This house has been empty for too long. I cannot have any more children of my own."

Chesa looked to the queen as she grabbed her husband's hand.

"We will take them. The help building up the house is appreciated but not needed. Ren can shape wood and will have no trouble getting them enough room. You can leave them with us now if you like."

Jari's heart was overwhelmed. It always feels good to be wanted. She hadn't only gotten Kila back, but had gained another sister and a family all at once. She still intended to find her mother and father, but she'd only get stronger in the next few years. That oath could wait.

Claire nodded and reached in her pouch, pulling out a small object of strange shimmering purple. It looked like five small balls clustered together. She set it on the table and spoke.

"The children are to be in school when it's in session. Should one of them get sick, send her anyway. We can fix that in short order. Otherwise, I like to see them involved in outside activities as much as possible. There is talk of games between our school and Winter's. I think Jari would give Autumn quite an edge. Also, I think—"

The sound flowed in through the open windows of the small house. It was like humming, only the tones were more precise, and the melody was a chorus of beautiful, otherworldly voices.

Jari felt her body fill with power. It wanted to move, to run and leap. Her feet wanted to flow in time with the song. She looked to the queen.

Claire smiled and looked to the door. "The details can wait; let's go out and make proper introductions."

With that, she turned and walked out the door. Jari watched as Ren shrugged and stood to take Chesa's hand. Both were almost dancing as they walked outside. Jari rolled her eyes as she walked out the door to see Kila singing a Siren song of power to a coop full of chickens.

Little bird feet were moving in time with the music. Beaks were swaying to the tune while Ninazu was clapping and laughing at the spectacle. Even the huge death drake seemed to enjoy the odd scene.

Both Ren and Chesa stood astonished at the girl whose joy seemed to flow through the sound. Kila turned to see everyone staring at her. Her brown cheeks reddened slightly as she shrugged.

"Nazu wanted to see the chickens dance."

The queen turned and grinned as she spoke to the couple.

"This is Kila; she's Autumn's only Siren. Her new sister is called Ninazu, and her power is called Wellness. You've met Jari, our Fawnin, who sometimes likes to be a cat."

"Caracal," Jari corrected with a smile.

"Yes, it's a fancy cat," the queen quipped back.

Ren still seemed to be in shock, but Chesa appeared to have recovered and moved to the small girls. She leaned down and whispered her question so only they could hear it.

"Would you like to try some of my peach cobbler?"

However faint the whisper, Jari's ears heard every word. She reached up to take the queen's hand in her own as she yelled over to the younger girls.

"Say yes, sisters! You won't be sorry!"

***

It was late afternoon in the squatter's camp outside the city of Amaya. It had been many days since the guards had taken the heart from the people there. The girl Ninazu had been a light of hope for many. Now she was assumed dead.

The other girls who came later were also gone. Only the stooped old woman held out hope. Keffi would scold anyone who spoke of the children as if they were no more.

It wasn't getting proven right that warmed Keffi's heart as a couple stepped out of the forest. The two men patrolling quickly intercepted them, but no words needed to be exchanged. Each of the woman's hands was linked with two wonderful girls Keffi loved dearly.

The man carried a large crate. Behind him, Jari held an even bigger one. The younger girls ran to hug her and made their way around to all the other people. They greeted them and showed off the new uniforms they wore.

Jari set her crate down next to the cold embers of the campfire. Inside were several vials of what appeared to be green smoke, several wrapped bundles of dried meat, and various fruits from the orchards of northern Autumn.

Ren set down his own crate, full of a smaller box of his own peaches as well as some sturdy bowls and plates. It also held two large trays of a now-legendary cobbler.

The older sister had negotiated a weekly visit to the camp through a portal. She was also able to have the Keep help with a care package of sorts to come with them on each visit. A gift from the kingdom she now called home. Few have bargained with Autumn's Queen and come out ahead. Jari felt she might be one of them.

The evening was spent in fellowship. The newly formed family now gained many aunts, uncles, and a dozen or so grandparents. As the sun found its way over the western horizon, the family took their leave.

The five of them moved into the woods, back through the portal that carried them home. Jari knew it was best not to stay too late.

Tomorrow was her first day of school.

END

Dear reader,

The novel you just read is part of a series. I'm already working hard to get more volumes out and I have over a dozen novels and short stories being revised and edited in this world.

I've decided to work independently of major publishers so I'm able to work toward the story I want to tell as opposed to following trends and taking the risk of stopping before the tale is complete.

When you're finished reading this, please loan it to someone you know who enjoys this type of story. Take a few minutes and leave a review on the vendor you bought it from. A good review on Amazon, Barnes & Noble, Kobo, Google Play, or Apple Books will help me build a reader base that will grow my ability to get more books to market.

Also, taking a moment to log on to a book website and leave a review would do wonders for our small publisher. Goodreads, Library Thing, Book Riot, Bookish, Booklist, Fantasy Book Review, LoveReading, Kirkus, and R/books all have a base of readers who might otherwise never hear about our work.

Finally, visit our publisher website that has previews of current and future books as well as full-color maps. We are working on fan art, character summaries, and accept reader suggestions for future works.

www.decharlathan.com

Thank you again for purchasing this book. Don't miss the next volume of short stories. We hope you enjoy reading our work as much as we enjoy creating it.

Jeremy Graves

www.ingramcontent.com/pod-product-compliance
Lightning Source LLC
Chambersburg PA
CBHW031941240626
47153CB00003B/821